LAWS
of the
Night

Credits

Development: Richard E. Dansky

Development Assistance: Cynthia Summers & Michael Rollins

Authors: All new material by Richard E. Dansky. Reprinted material from **Antagonists** by Jennifer Albright with Nicky Rea and Phil Brucato. Reprinted material from **The Apocalypse** by Geoffrey Fortier, William Spencer-Hale, Sam Chupp, Ian Lemke and Mike Tinney. Reprinted material from **The Masquerade Players' Kit** by Ian Lemke and Mike Tinney. Reprinted material from **The Masquerade 2nd Edition** by Geoffrey Fortier, Frank Branham, Mark Rein•Hagen, Ian Lemke and Mike Tinney. Reprinted material from **Vampire: The Masquerade 2nd Edition** by Mark Rein•Hagen, Graeme Davis, Tom Dowd, Lisa Stevens and Stewart Wieck.

Mind's Eye Theatre Design: Mark Rein•Hagen, Ian Lemke and Mike Tinney

World of Darkness Created by: Mark Rein•Hagen

Original Sabbat Concepts by: Steve Brown

Editing: Beth Fischi

Art Direction: Aileen Miles and Lawrence Snelly

Interior Photography: J. Lank Hancock

Cover Design: Katie McCaskill

Layout and Typesetting: Katie McCaskill

Models: Omar "Hair" Miller,Ian "Ian" Campbell, Paul "Diablo Blanco" Mercer, Kalina "Cats" Mercer, Pagan Megan Walters, Michelle "Legs" Kinsey, Dan Edmonds, Becky Markey, Charles "Gimp" Christianson, Tracy Armogan, Maureen "Mmmm" Kumpf, Seth Hancock, J.J. Hancock, Idaho Stokey, Ted Levine, Tom "Andersonville" Kerns, Rat Man, Adam "Ace" Eberle, Chris Nations, Michael "Party!" Rollins, William Wallace

Special Thanks to:

Andrew "Friday? Monday? At Some Point?" **Bates**, for getting his vampiric kid brother into all sorts of trouble.

Laura "I'm a Tzimisce? Eww." **Perkinson**, for making someone's arms go all flippy floppy.

Fred "I Hate New Haven" **Yelk**, for wiping the home of the Malfunction Junction off the face of the earth.

Greg "GAMA Madness" **Fountain**, for fobbing his nominating chores off on a defenseless developer.

Mike "Velvet Frog" **Chaney**, for his hard rockin' contribution to Dark Ages Day.

Very Special Thanks to:

Steven Herman, Adam Cristian Eberle, Allen Tower, Rene Hawthorne, the folks from the Coterie of the Pale Heart in Kansas City, Michael Rollins and Kyle Vogt for all of the input on what needed to be fixed.

Ray from the vending machine company, who keeps the office well stocked with caffeine. Without you, this book never would have happened.

Table of Contents

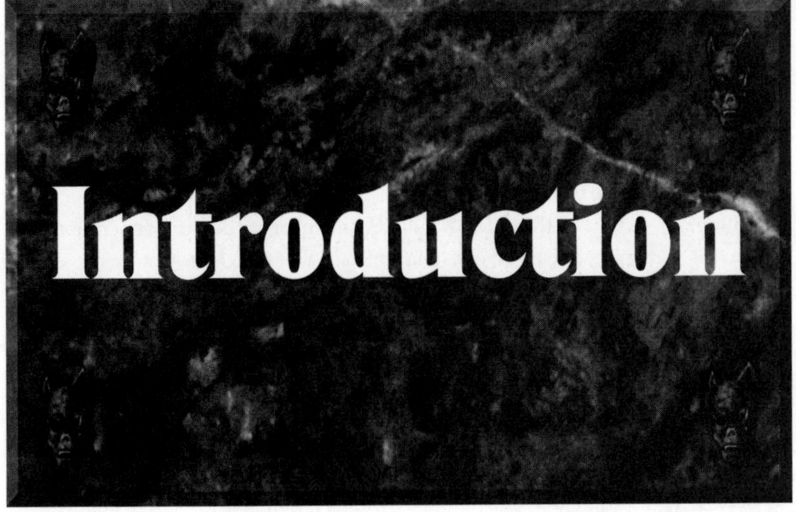

What This Book Is and Isn't

Laws of the Night is a pocket guide to the rules of **Mind's Eye Theatre**, specifically **The Masquerade**. It is intended to serve as a quick and easy reference to all of the extant rules for the system. In addition, **Laws of the Night** offers quick fixes for confusing rules descriptions and solutions to common complications that the original rules did not address (e.g., what happens when two Kindred with Majesty meet? Can a Garou spend Rage to counter Celerity? etc.). You'll also find information from **Masquerade 2nd Edition, The Masquerade Players' Guide** and **Antagonists**.

What this book is *not* is a third generation rules system, nor is it intended to replace **Masquerade 2nd Edition**. It is a compilation of rules on everything from Blood Bonds to Disciplines, and nothing more. You won't find setting information here, or any Storytelling hints. It's just the rules, all the rules, and nothing but the rules, provided in a format that you can use in-game so that you don't have to hunt down a Storyteller every time you have a question on interpretation.

The book is divided into three chapters, with an appendix. The first contains the basic rules of character creation for **Masquerade**. The second lists the clans and bloodlines available for play, as well as the Disciplines available to them. The third covers the basic rules system of Masquerade, as well as matters such as Blood Bonds, diablerie and the Sabbat. The appendix contains a recap of the basic rules for **Mind's Eye Theatre** and a FAQ.

Much of the material contained in this book has previously appeared in some form in **Vampire: The Masquerade 2nd Edition, The Masquerade 2nd Edition, The Masquerade Players' Kit, Apocalypse** and **Antagonists**. New material has been added, and some old material has been either corrected or superseded.

Lexicon:

Abilities — The measure of a Kindred's expertise in specific fields. Measured in Traits.

Aggravated Wounds — Wounds inflicted by a special source (fire, sunlight, Lupine claws, etc.) that are especially difficult to heal.

Ancilla — An "adolescent" vampire.

Anarch — A rebel among the Kindred, one with no respect for the elders. Most fledglings are automatically assumed to be anarchs by the elders.

Antediluvian — One of the eldest Kindred, a member of the third generation.

Archetypes — Basic personality types, from which Nature and Demeanor are chosen.

Archon — A powerful vampire who wanders from city to city serving a Justicar.

Attributes — The measure of a Cainite's basic Physical, Social and Mental statistics. Measured in Traits.

Book of Nod, The — The "sacred" book of the Kindred, never published in its entirety.

Beast, The — The urges which prompt a vampire to forsake all Humanity.

Beast Traits — A measure, in Traits, of how inhuman a vampire has become. Acquired as a result of Frenzy.

Bidding — The risking of Traits in order to win a Challenge.

Bloodline — A group of vampires with a distinct heritage outside of the 13 basic clans.

Blood Bond — A mystic servitude to another vampire as a result of drinking his or her blood three times.

Blood Pool — The maximum amount of blood any vampire can hold at any one time.

Boons — Favors owed.

Caitiff — A vampire with no clan.

Camarilla, The — A global sect of vampires in which all Kindred may hold membership.

Challenges — The method by which disputes are settled in Masquerade.

Childe — A derogatory term for a young, inexperienced, or foolish vampire.

Clan — A group of vampires who share certain mystic and physical characteristics.

Coterie — A group of Kindred who protect and support one another.

Damned, The — All vampires as a whole.

Derangements — Mental instabilities acquired by Kindred.

Diablerie — The cannibalistic behavior common among Kindred, involving the consumption of the blood of another vampire.

Disciplines — The supernatural powers all vampires possess according to their lineage.

Domain — The fiefdom claimed by a vampire, most often a prince.

Elder — A vampire who is 300 years of age or older.

Elysium — The name given for the places where the elders meet and gather, commonly operas, theaters or other public places of high culture.

Embrace, The — The act of transforming a mortal into a vampire by draining the mortal's blood and replacing it with a small amount of the vampire's own blood.

Experience — Points given to characters as they progress through multiple games. Used for increasing the character's statistics and powers.

Frenzy — When a vampire completely loses control and her Beast takes over.

Garou — A werewolf.

Generation — The number of steps between a vampire and the mythical Caine.

Gehenna — The impending Armageddon when the Antediluvians shall awaken.

Ghoul — A servant created by allowing a living mortal to drink Kindred blood.

Golconda — The state of being to which many vampires aspire, in which a balance is found between opposing urges and scruples.

Haven — The home of a vampire or the place where he sleeps during the day.

Healing — The process of using Blood Traits to restore Health.

Health — The measure of how much physical damage a vampire has taken.

Inconnu — A sect of vampires who have removed themselves from both mortal and Kindred affairs.

Influences — The measure of how much control a Cainite has on mortal institutions. Measured in Traits.

Jyhad, The — The secret war being waged between the few surviving vampires of the third generation, using younger vampires as pawns.

Kindred — A vampire.

Lupine — A werewolf.

Masquerade, The — The effort begun after the end of the great wars to hide Kindred society from the mortal world.

Methuselah — An elder who no longer lives among the other Kindred. Many Methuselahs belong to the Inconnu (qv).

Neonate — A young, newly created Kindred.

Numina — The special powers possessed by human hunters.

Pack — The basic social unit of the Sabbat.

Path Traits — The Sabbat equivalent of Beast Traits.

Prestation — The complicated system of owed favors among the Kindred.

Primogen — A city's ruling council of elders.

Prince — A vampire who has established a claim to rulership over a city and is able to support that claim. The feminine form is still prince.

Progeny — A collective term for all the vampires created by one sire.

Regnant — One who has a Blood Bond over another Kindred.

Retainers — Humans who serve a vampire master. They are generally either ghouls or mentally dominated by their vampire master.

Rites — Special Sabbat Rituals performed for religious or other reasons.

Sabbat, The — A sect of vampires controlling much of eastern North America. They are violent and bestial, reveling in needless cruelty.

Sect — General name for one of the three primary groups among the Kindred — the Camarilla, Sabbat or Inconnu.

Sire — The parent-creator of a vampire, used both as the female and male form.

Status — How well respected a Kindred is. Measured in Traits.

Thrall — A vampire who is Blood Bonded and thus controlled by another Kindred.

Trait — The unit by which statistics in Masquerade are measured.

Vaulderie — A communal Sabbat sharing of blood.

Viniculum — The communal Blood Bond within a pack, forged through Vaulderie.

Vessel — A potential or past source of blood, typically a human.

Vitæ — Blood.

Willpower — The measure of how strong a Kindred's will is. Measured in Traits.

Witch-hunter — A human who searches for vampires in order to kill them.

Chapter One: Character Creation

Character Creation Process

- **Step One: Inspiration** — Who are you?
  - — Choose your clan
  - — Choose a Nature and Demeanor
- **Step Two: Attributes** — What are your basic capabilities?
  - — Prioritize Attributes (seven primary, five secondary and three tertiary)
  - — Choose Traits
- **Step Three: Advantages** — What do you know?
  - — Choose five Abilities
  - — Choose three Disciplines
  - — Choose three Influences
- **Step Four: Last Touches** — Fill in the details.
  - — Assign Blood Traits
  - — Assign Willpower Traits
  - — Choose one Beast/Path Trait (Sabbat members must choose a Path)
  - — Assign one Status Trait ("Acknowledged")
  - — Choose Negative Traits (if any)
- **Step Five: Spark of Life** — Narrative descriptions.

The cornerstone of any roleplaying game is the character. This is especially true in live roleplaying, where dice, character sheets and other typical trappings of gaming vanish. Below are the basic rules for generating a character for **Masquerade**, including the variations necessary to create Sabbat characters.

Included in this chapter are: **Basic Character Creation — Negative Traits — Generation — Archetypes — Traits — Attributes — Abilities — Sabbat Abilities — Influence — Blood Traits — Willpower — Beast Traits — Sabbat Paths of Enlightenment — Path Traits — Derangements — Sabbat Derangements — Merits & Flaws — Experience.**

Step One: Inspiration

Before you write a single thing, you need to find inspiration for the type of character you want to play. Once you're inspired, you need to develop a rough idea of who your character is.

This development involves choosing a concept, a clan and a personality (defined by choosing a Nature and Demeanor — see below). The better you relate these three aspects of your character, the more intricate and complete the end result will be. A character's Demeanor is often completely different from his concept, and the stereotypical image of a clan can be contradicted by choosing a contrasting Nature or Demeanor.

Clan

Your choice of clan is arguably the most important element of your character. Your clan describes the essential lineage of your character. (Unless you are Caitiff, you are always of the same clan as your sire). The seven clans from which players may choose are all members of the vampire sect known as the Camarilla. There are other clans, but they exist either in their own sects or on the outskirts of Kindred society.

You do not necessarily need to choose a clan, for some younger Kindred are of such diluted blood that no single clan's characteristics are imprinted upon them. These Caitiff are increasingly common among the Kindred, but they are outcasts — accepted by none, scorned by all. If you wish to play such a character, simply list Caitiff as your clan. For a full description of all of the clans and bloodlines available for play in **Masquerade**, see Chapter 2.

Nature and Demeanor

At this point, you should choose personality archetypes that suit your concept of your character's disposition and image.

Your character's Nature is the most dominant aspect of her true personality. While Nature describes who your character really is on the inside, your chosen Nature is not necessarily the only archetype that applies — people aren't one-dimensional.

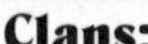

Clans:

• **Brujah** — Respecting no authority and acknowledging no leaders, the "rabble" consider themselves free.

Disciplines: Celerity, Potence, Presence

• **Gangrel** — Loners and rustics, the "outlanders" are the only Kindred who dare venture outside the city.

Disciplines: Animalism, Fortitude, Protean

• **Malkavian** — Commonly perceived to be insane, the "kooks" possess an uncanny vision and wisdom.

Disciplines: Auspex, Dominate, Obfuscate

• **Nosferatu** — Ostracized and misunderstood by others, the hideous "sewer rats" live out their sordid existence in hiding.

Disciplines: Animalism, Obfuscate, Potence

• **Toreador** — Known for their hedonistic ways, the "degenerates" prefer to think of themselves as artists.

Disciplines: Auspex, Celerity, Presence

• **Tremere** — Wizards of an ancient house, the "warlocks" work together to spread their influence and power.

Disciplines: Auspex, Dominate, Thaumaturgy (Path of Blood)

• **Ventrue** — Aristocrats of rarefied tastes and manners, the "blue bloods" are fiendishly cool and cunning.

Disciplines: Dominate, Fortitude, Presence

• **Caitiff** — Those with no clan: the outcasts and the dishonored.

Disciplines: Any (except Thaumaturgy)

• **Assamites** — Assassins and silent killers in the night, the childer of Hassam take payment for their services in blood.

Disciplines: Celerity, Obfuscate (Unseen Presence, Mask of 1000 Faces), Quietus

• **Followers of Set** — Dedicated to spreading corruption, the Sand Snakes prepare for the day when their forefather returns to lead them.

Disciplines: Obfuscate (Unseen Presence, Mask of 1000 Faces), Presence (Awe, Entrancement), Serpentis

• **Giovanni** — The closest-knit of the clans, the Giovanni seek to control the dead even as they manipulate the living.

Disciplines: Dominate (Command, Forgetful Mind), Necromancy, Potence

• **Lasombra** — Puppetmasters in the darkness, the Lasombra rule the Sabbat and control the shadows.

Disciplines: Dominate, Obtenebration, Potence

• **Panders** — The Caitiff of the Sabbat.

Disciplines: Any they have been taught (Dementation, Obtenebration and Vicissitude are restricted)

• **Ravnos** — Tricksters and thieves, the Ravnos are masters of deceit.

Disciplines: Animalism (Beast Within), Chimerstry, Fortitude

• **Tzimisce** — Called Fiends for good reason, the Tzimisce are noble yet cruelly inhuman.

Disciplines: Animalism, Auspex, Vicissitude

Note: Sabbat members of unaligned or Camarilla clans may have different disciplines than those who keep to their original political affiliation. See Chapter 2 for more details.

You should also choose a Demeanor to describe the personality you pretend to possess. This is the role you play in the world, the facade you present. It should probably be different from the archetype you have chosen as your Nature, but whatever you choose is only your typical pose; people can change outward behavior as quickly as they change their mood.

Step Two: Attributes

Attributes are everything a character naturally, intrinsically is. Are you strong? Are you brave? Are you persuasive? Questions such as these are answered by the Attributes, the Traits that describe the basic, innate potential of your character.

Choosing Attributes

The first step is to prioritize the different categories of Attributes, placing them in order of importance to your character. Are you more physical than you are social? Does your quick thinking surpass your physical strength?

Categories of Attributes:

• **Physical Attributes** describe the abilities of the body, such as power, quickness and endurance.

• **Social Attributes** describe your character's appearance and charisma — her ability to influence others.

• **Mental Attributes** represent your character's mental capacity and include such things as memory, perception, self-control and the ability to learn and think.

The concept and clan of your character may suggest what your Attribute priorities should be, but feel free to pick any way you please. For now, think in the broadest of perspectives — you can get more specific after you understand the big picture.

Choosing Traits

After you've chosen the order of the three Attribute categories, you need to choose specific Traits from each category. Traits are adjectives that describe your character's strengths and weaknesses, defining your character just as a character in a novel is defined. In your primary (strongest) Attribute category, you can choose seven Traits. In your secondary category, you can choose five. In your tertiary (weakest) category, you can choose only three. Thus, you receive a total of 15 Attribute Traits. You can take the same Trait more than once, if you wish, reflecting greater aptitude. Descriptions of the specific Physical, Social and Mental Attributes can be found on pages 18-23.

Step Three: Advantages

Advantages delineate what and whom your character knows, and are divided into three categories: Abilities, Disciplines and Influences.

Choosing Abilities

Abilities represent your training and knowledge beyond the outline provided by your Attributes. They are what you have learned and what you can do rather than what you are. Abilities let you perform specialized tasks that are only possible with training: picking locks, driving with skill or reading the Dead Sea Scrolls. Each character begins the game with five Abilities. A full listing of Abilities can be found on pages 23-29.

Choosing Disciplines

Disciplines are vampiric powers — the supernatural abilities available to a vampire. Each vampire begins the game with three Disciplines, but a vampire may only choose the Disciplines that his clan typically possesses (see the clan lists in Chapter 2). Each Discipline has two powers at the basic level. If your character has a Discipline, the first power listed must be chosen first. Your character cannot advance to intermediate level powers in a given Discipline until he learns all the beginning powers of that Discipline. You may opt to work your way up to the intermediate level of a Discipline rather than choosing the basic levels of three different Disciplines. However, you must have your Storyteller's permission before selecting the advanced levels of any Discipline. Full descriptions of each Discipline can be found in Chapter 2.

Choosing Influences

Influence reflects your character's control over mortal society. The source of most power and conflict in vampiric society, Influence is the primary means of waging wars of intrigue. For instance, if you own a nightclub, that is reflected by an Influence Trait. If you are a wealthy stock market investor, that is also a function of Influence.

You may choose three Influence Traits, each of which represents a contact or holding in the area. You can take a single Influence Trait (such as High Society) more than once, indicating a greater degree of dominance. The only limitations on your Influence selection are those imposed by the background and identity of your character (but even seemingly weird Influences can be justified). Descriptions of most common Influences can be found on page 31-37.

Step Four: Last Touches

At this point, you fill in the details of your character, including various positive and negative Traits, Status, generation and Health.

Blood Traits

Blood Traits work like other Traits, but they can only be used to heighten your physical power or heal yourself, and they can only be regained by feeding. Your Blood Pool indicates your maximum Blood Trait capacity, not necessarily the amount of blood you currently have in your system. Blood Traits are not assigned adjectives; each simply represents a volume of blood (about a vial's worth).

You start the game with three Blood Traits (unless you have lowered your generation by using Negative Traits). These Traits are either used as sustenance or as desperate situations arise.

Willpower

Willpower reflects your basic drive, self-confidence and tenacity. It is essential for controlling the actions and behavior of your character, especially in times of stress when predatory instincts emerge. You may choose only one Willpower Trait at this point in the game, although you can gain more by lowering your generation (see below).

Humanity

Beast Traits represent how close your character is to the Beast. The more Beast Traits you have, the more likely you will periodically lose control and enter into a state the Kindred call "frenzy." The more Beast Traits you possess, the less human you become. When your character accumulates five Beast Traits, she is completely overwhelmed by the Beast and becomes a mindless raving monster. At that point, you must create a new character; your last one is now an uncontrollable monster.

Kindred must also start the game with a single Beast Trait. If you wish, you may take a second Beast Trait, which is worth the equivalent of two Negative Traits. However, remember that your character goes into a permanent frenzy upon receiving the fifth Beast Trait, so you would need only three more to lose your character.

Status

One of the main aspects of your background is Status — an indication of where your character stands in vampiric society, particularly within your city. You start with a single Status Trait, which represents the fact that you have been presented to and recognized by the prince. If you are Caitiff, or choose to be an anarch, you have no initial Status Trait. This could be because you have never been presented to the prince, or you may have such a terrible reputation that any former Status has been lost. (You *can* acquire more than one Status Trait by taking on Negative Traits, but anarchs and Caitiff cannot gain Status this way.)

Your initial Status Trait is always the word "Acknowledged," representing the prince's acknowledgment of your existence. You can also choose or earn other Traits as the story progresses.

Negative Traits

At this point, you may increase your character's power by selecting counterbalancing flaws. By taking a Negative Trait, you can, for example, add a new Trait to your Attributes or take another Ability. Negative Traits are Attributes that have a negative effect upon your character. They can be used against you in a challenge (a contest staged between you and other characters). Each Negative Trait is equal to one positive Trait; for each Negative Trait you take, you receive a positive Trait of your choice. You can take no more than five Negative Traits unless you have the Storyteller's permission. You can take whatever Negative Traits seem to fit your character; you need not take the full five, or any at all.

Each Negative Trait you take allows you to choose one of the following options:

• Take one additional positive Trait in any category of Attribute: Physical, Social or Mental. (The maximum number of Traits you can possess in a given category is listed in the Generation Chart in Chapter Three.)

• Take one extra Ability or Influence.

Generation

Unless a player buys down his generation with Negative Traits, his character will start at 13th generation. For every two Negative Traits spent in this fashion, the character can lower his generation by one. A character can *never* buy his generation lower than 8th, unless he has the express permission of the Storyteller. More information on generation can be found in Chapter Three.

Health

Characters are considered to be at full health at the beginning of each story unless the Storyteller states otherwise. Of course, characters can be hurt or even destroyed during a story. There are three levels of health beneath Healthy: Wounded, Incapacitated, and Torpor. See Chapter Three for details.

Generation Table

Generation	Blood Traits	Willpower Traits Starting	Willpower Traits Max	Maximum Traits
13th	3	1	3	10
12th	4	1	3	10
11th	5	2	4	11
10th	6	2	4	11
9th	8	3	5	13
8th	9	3	6	14
7th	11	4	7	16
6th	13	4	8	18
5th	16	5	9	20
4th	20	6	10	25
3rd	?	?	?	30

Step Five: Spark of Life

Characters do not consist of Traits alone. Other aspects, such as motivations and secrets — while not necessarily important in terms of game mechanics — are vital to roleplaying. In many cases, the Storyteller provides, or at least suggests, these "sparks of life" for you. Your character needs to be woven into the story, and these flourishes allow the Storyteller to do just that.

Other Aspects

• **Background Story** — You need to create a background narrative for your character, describing her life before the Embrace: what she did, how she lived and what was unique about her. This background may describe what your character did for a living, how she saw herself and what others thought of her. It will probably influence who she is now — indeed, many Kindred cling to the trappings of their former lives because they find it difficult to abandon their concepts of themselves as humans. Their pasts remain with them forever.

Regardless of when you were Embraced, whether in the days of Ancient Rome or in the modern age, you have spent 50 waking years or less as a vampire. All other years of undead existence are assumed to have been spent in torpor.

• **Motivations** — What is your purpose? What motivates you on a night-to-night basis? Is it hate, fear, lust, greed, jealousy or revenge? Describe your motivations in as much detail as possible; ask the Storyteller for help if you can't think of anything. Unless you are an experienced player, it's likely that the Storyteller will provide you with a motivation or two at the start of the chronicle.

• **Appearance** — Find props and a costume that will help others understand or at least recognize your character at a glance. You need to not only act like your character, but look like him as well. Your character's appearance makes his Physical (and many Social) Traits visible to other characters.

• **Equipment** — Your character likely begins the game with equipment of one sort or another. Ask a Narrator for more details on your personal possessions and assets. If you want to spend money on equipment right away, feel free. You may buy weapons, clothing, homes, condos, cars... anything. Use an appropriate catalog for prices. (Be sure to get your Storyteller's approval if you wish to buy anything unusual or dangerous.)

• **Quirks** — By giving your character quirks (interesting personal details), you add a great deal of depth and interest to her. Write a few sentences on the back of your character sheet about the strange and interesting things that define your character. Examples of quirks include a twisted sense of humor, a gentleness toward animals or a habit of grunting when answering yes to a question.

Nature and Demeanor

Characters do not fit into neat and tidy categories. Molds — basic patterns or templates — for an infinite number of different personalities, archetypes should not be seen as absolute standards of personality. Each individual varies from her original archetype in many ways. The archetypes listed below provide examples of the variety of human personalities, and are intended to guide, not to restrict.

Archetypes have a practical impact on the game, for characters can be manipulated according to their personalities. A character's Nature may be strong enough to pull him out of a frenzy if he is about to do something that contradicts it. For example, a Bravo would be allowed a chance to stave off his frenzy if confronted by a lighter held by an anarch he had bullied in the past.

Nature also works like a Negative Trait: If you know someone's Nature, you may use it as a Negative Trait in any type of challenge, or confrontation between characters. The Nature should have something to do with the challenge, so you could bid a Martyr Nature when trying to talk someone to going into a burning building to rescue a wounded Kindred. However, you could not use a Child Nature when trying to look at an aura.

Archetypes

• **Architect** — You seek to create something of lasting value, a legacy.

• **Bravo** — You are something of a bully; you like to be feared.

• **Caregiver** — You seek to nurture others.

• **Child** — You never really grew up, and you want someone to take care of you.

• **Conformist** — A follower at heart, you find it easy to adapt, adjust and comply.

• **Conniver** — There's always an easier way, one that usually involves someone else doing your work.

• **Deviant** — You're just not like everyone else.

• **Director** — You're accustomed to taking charge of a situation.

• **Fanatic** — You have a cause and it gives your life meaning.

• **Gallant** — You are as flamboyant as you are amoral.

• **Hedonist** — Life is meaningless, so enjoy it as long as it lasts.

• **Jester** — Always the clown, you can't take life, or death, seriously.

• **Judge** — You seek justice and reconciliation.

• **Loner** — You are forever alone, even in a crowd.

• **Martyr** — You need to be needed, and enjoy being morally superior.

• **Rebel** — No need for a cause; you rebel out of habit and passion.

• **Survivor** — You struggle to survive, no matter what the odds.

• **Traditionalist** — You prefer the orthodox and conservative ways.

• **Visionary** — Wisdom is your quest, insight your key.

Sabbat Archetypes

These Archetypes are only available to Sabbat characters. Members of the Camarilla or of unaligned clans and bloodlines may not choose these Archetypes during character creation.

- **Daredevil** — You love taking risks and will seize any opportunity to do so.
- **Dark Pioneer** — You can't change the traditions of the past, but you'll do everything you can to create the traditions of the future.
- **Dark Poet** — You want to share the beauty of darkness with the rest of the world.
- **Drunk Uncle** — When things are going well, you're everyone's best friend. When things are going poorly, you're their worst nightmare.
- **Interrogator** — It's not the answers that matter; it's the pleasure you get asking the questions.
- **Recruiter** — It makes sense to build your side up before trying to tear theirs down.
- **Shamanist** — You see your killer's role as part of the supernatural order.
- **Stalker** — The chase is all; the capture and feeding almost anticlimactic.
- **Sorority Sister** — You do whatever the in-crowd does, and do it better.
- **Torturer** — Pain isn't a profession for you, it's a calling.

Traits

Traits have two primary purposes. The first and most important purpose is to enable you to describe your character concretely and thereby empower your roleplaying. The second is to enable you to interact with other characters in terms of the game system. The mechanics of **The Masquerade** revolve around the Trait system; every challenge is resolved using them.

The premise of this system is that a character who is described by a specific Trait tends to be pretty good at things that involve that Trait, and is certainly better than someone who doesn't have the Trait at all. For example, someone who is Brawny is a better arm wrestler than someone who isn't. Likewise, a marathon runner needs to be Tireless in order to finish a race still standing, and a child who is Persuasive has a good chance of convincing his mom that he didn't break a vase on the living room floor.

Attributes (Bidding Traits)

Creative players can think of ways to use nearly any Trait in nearly any challenge. Though this is most praiseworthy, players can sometimes go too far. To avoid this, the general rule on bidding Traits is very strict: You can only bid Traits from the category that best suits the nature of the challenge (i.e., Traits bid are from the same category — Physical, Mental or Social). Even then, however, not all Physical Traits (or Mental, or Social) are appropriate to all "Physical" (or "Mental," or "Social") challenges.

For example, beginners might think they can use all their Physical Traits in combat. This is incorrect. If your character is trying to kick someone, Resilient is not an appropriate Trait to bid as part of the attack. Likewise, if your character is trying to read an opponent's aura, Creative might not be an appropriate Trait.

For such an "inappropriate" Trait to be allowed, both parties must agree. When an opponent bids a Trait that you feel is extremely inappropriate, politely tell her that you're not going to allow its use. If she is insistent, reevaluate your grievance. If you still can't agree, appeal to any witnesses of the contest. Then, if there is still deadlock and no one is willing to compromise, seek out a Narrator to make a ruling. Appeals to a Narrator in these situations, however, should occur very, very rarely. Learn to handle confrontations on your own, quickly and socially.

To keep things simple, you can ignore the subtleties of Traits and, say, use any Physical Trait in any Physical Challenge. This approach is particularly useful when you have a number of novice players. Eventually you will go beyond this boring convention and only allow players to use Traits appropriate to the situation at hand. This method is more complicated, but it can be a lot more fun. Try it out.

Physical Traits

Athletic: You have conditioned your body to respond well in full-body movements, especially in competitive events.

Uses: Sports, duels, running, acrobatics, grappling and Celerity.

Brawny: Bulky muscular strength.

Uses: Punching, kicking or grappling in combat when your goal is to inflict damage. Power lifting. All feats of strength.

Brutal: You are capable of taking nearly any action in order to survive.

Uses: Fighting an obviously superior enemy.

Dexterous: General adroitness and skill involving the use of one's hands.

Uses: Weapon-oriented combat (Melee or Firearms). Pickpocketing. Punching.

Enduring: A persistent sturdiness against physical opposition.

Uses: When your survival is at stake, this is a good Trait to risk as a second, or successive, bid.

Energetic: A powerful force of spirit. A strong internal drive propels you and, in physical situations, you can draw on a deep reservoir of enthusiasm and zeal.

Uses: Combat. Celerity.

Ferocious: Possession of brutal intensity and extreme physical determination.

Uses: Any time that you intend to do serious harm. When in frenzy.

Graceful: Control and balance in the motion and use of the entire body.

Uses: Combat defense. Whenever you might lose your balance (stepping on a banana peel, fighting on four-inch-thick rafters).

Lithe: Characterized by flexibility and suppleness.

Uses: Acrobatics, gymnastics, dodging, dancing and Celerity.

Nimble: Light and skillful; able to make agile movements.

Uses: Dodging, jumping, rolling, acrobatics. Hand-to-hand combat.

Quick: Speedy, with fast reaction time.

Uses: Defending against a surprise attack. Running, dodging, attacking. Celerity.

Resilient: Characterized by strength of health; able to recover quickly from bodily harm.

Uses: Resisting adverse environments. Defending against damage in an attack.

Robust: Resistant to physical harm and damage.

Uses: Defending against damage in an attack. Endurance related actions that could take place over a period of time.

Rugged: Hardy, rough and brutally healthy. Able to shrug off wounds and pain to continue struggling.

Uses: When resisting damage, any challenge that you enter while injured. Earth Melding.

Stalwart: Physically strong and uncompromising against opposition.

Uses: Resisting damage, or when standing your ground against overwhelming odds or a superior foe.

Steady: More than simply physically dependable: controlled, unfaltering and balanced. You have firm mastery over your efforts.

Uses: Weapon attacks. Fighting in exotic locations. Piloting oil tankers.

Tenacious: Physically determined through force of will. You often prolong physical confrontations, even when it might not be wise to do so.

Uses: Second or subsequent Physical Challenge.

Tireless: You have a runner's stamina — you are less taxed by physical efforts than ordinary people.

Uses: Any endurance related challenge, second or subsequent Physical Challenge with the same foe or foes. Celerity.

Tough: A harsh, aggressive attitude and a reluctance ever to submit.

Uses: Whenever you're wounded or winded.

Vigorous: A combination of energy, power, intensity and resistance to harm.

Uses: Combat and athletic challenges when you're on the defensive.

Wiry: Tight, streamlined, muscular strength.

Uses: Punching, kicking or grappling in combat. Acrobatic movements. Endurance lifting.

Negative Physical Traits

Clumsy: Lacking physical coordination, balance and grace. You are prone to stumbling and dropping objects.

Cowardly: In threatening situations, saving your own neck is all that is important. You might even flee when you have the upper hand, just out of habit.

Decrepit: You move and act as if you are old and infirm. You recover from physical damage slowly, are unable to apply full muscular strength, and tire easily.

Delicate: Frail and weak in structure; you are easily damaged by physical harm.

Docile: The opposite of the Ferocious and Tenacious Traits; you lack physical persistence and tend to submit rather than fight long battles.

Flabby: Your muscles are underdeveloped. You cannot apply your strength well against resistance.

Lame: You are disabled in one or more limbs. The handicap can be as obvious as a missing leg or as subtle as a dysfunctional arm.

Lethargic: Slow and drowsy. You suffer from a serious lack of energy or motivation.

Puny: You are weak and inferior in strength. This could mean diminutive size.

Sickly: Weak and feeble. Your body responds to physical stress as if it were in the throes of a debilitating illness.

Social Traits

Alluring: An attractive and appealing presence that inspires desire in others.

Uses: Seduction. Convincing others.

Beguiling: The skill of deception and illusion. You can twist the perceptions of others and lead them to believe what suits you.

Uses: Tricking others. Lying under duress.

Charismatic: The talent of inspiration and motivation, the sign of a strong leader.

Uses: In a situation involving leadership or the achievement of leadership. Awe contests.

Charming: Your speech and actions make you appear attractive and appealing to others.

Uses: Convincing. Persuading. Entrancement Challenges.

Commanding: Impressive delivery of orders and suggestions. This implies skill in the control and direction of others.

Uses: When you are seen as a leader. Presence Challenges.

Compassionate: Deep feelings of care or pity for others.

Uses: Defending the weak or downtrodden. Defeating major obstacles while pursuing an altruistic end.

Dignified: Something about your posture and body carriage appears honorable and aesthetically pleasing. You carry yourself well.

Uses: Presence Challenges. Defending against Social Disciplines.

Diplomatic: Tactful, careful and thoughtful in speech and deed. Few are displeased with what you say or do.

Uses: Very important in intrigue. Leadership situations.

Elegant: Refined tastefulness. Even though you don't need money to be elegant, you exude an air of richness and high society.

Uses: High society or Toreador parties. Might be important in some clans for advancement. Defending against Social Disciplines.

Eloquent: The ability to speak in an interesting and convincing manner.

Uses: Convincing others. Swaying emotions. Public speaking.

Empathetic: Able to identify and understand the emotions and moods of people with whom you come in contact.

Uses: Gauging the feelings of others. Beast Within contests. Not useful in defense against Social Disciplines (might actually make it easier to use them on you).

Expressive: Able to articulate thoughts in interesting, significant, meaningful ways.

Uses: Producing art, acting, performing. Any social situation in which you want someone to understand your meaning.

Friendly: Able to fit in with everyone you meet. Even after a short conversation, most find it difficult to dislike you.

Uses: Entrancement Challenges. Convincing others.

Genial: Cordial, kindly, warm and pleasant. You are pleasing to be around.

Uses: Mingling at parties. Starting an Entrancement Challenge. Generally used in a second or later Social Challenge with someone.

Gorgeous: Beautiful or handsome. You were born with a face and body that is good-looking to most people you meet.

Uses: Modeling, posing. Beast Within Challenges. Entrancement Challenges.

Ingratiating: Able to gain the favor of people who know you.

Uses: Dealing with elders in a social situation. Entrancement Challenges. Defending against Social Disciplines.

Intimidating: A frightening or awesome presence that causes others to feel timid. This Trait is particularly useful when attempting to cow opponents.

Uses: Dread Gaze and Majesty Challenges. Inspiring common fear. Ordering others.

Magnetic: People feel drawn to you; those around you are interested in your speech and actions.

Uses: Presence Challenges. Beast Within Challenges. Seduction.

Persuasive: Able to propose believable, convincing and correct arguments and requests. Very useful when someone else is undecided on an issue.

Uses: Persuading or convincing others.

Seductive: Able to entice and tempt. You can use your good looks and your body to get what you want from others.

Uses: Subterfuge, Entrancement, Summoning and Seduction.

Witty: Cleverly humorous. Jokes and jests come easily to you, and you are perceived as a funny person when you want to be.

Uses: At parties. Entertaining someone. Goading or insulting someone.

Negative Social Traits

Bestial: You have started to resemble the Beast of your vampiric nature. Maybe you have clawlike fingernails, heavy body hair or a feral glint in your eyes; however your Beast manifests, you definitely seem inhuman.

Callous: You are unfeeling, uncaring and insensitive to the suffering of others.

Condescending: You just can't help it; your contempt for others is impossible to hide.

Dull: Those with whom you speak usually find you boring and uninteresting. Conversing with you is a chore. You do not present yourself well to others.

Naive: You lack the air of worldliness, sophistication or maturity that most carry.

Obnoxious: You are annoying or unappealing in speech, action or appearance.

Repugnant: Your appearance disgusts everyone around you. Needless to say, you make a terrible first impression with strangers.

Shy: You are timid, bashful, reserved and socially hesitant.

Tactless: You are unable to do or say things that others find appropriate to the social situation.

Untrustworthy: You are rumored or perceived to be untrustworthy and unreliable (whether you are or not).

Mental Traits

Alert: Mentally prepared for danger and able to react quickly when it occurs.

Uses: Preventing surprise attacks. Defending against Dominate Challenges.

Attentive: You pay attention to everyday occurrences around you. When something extraordinary happens, you are usually ready for it.

Uses: Preventing surprise attacks. Seeing through Obfuscate when you don't expect it. Preventing Dominate.

Calm: Able to withstand an extraordinary level of disturbance without becoming agitated or upset. A wellspring of self-control.

Uses: Resisting frenzy or commands that provoke violence. Whenever a mental attack might upset you. Primarily for defense.

Clever: Quick-witted resourcefulness. You think well on your feet.

Uses: Using a Mental Discipline against another.

Creative: Your ideas are original and imaginative. This implies an ability to produce unusual solutions to your difficulties. You can create artistic pieces. A requirement for any true artist.

Uses: Defending against aura readings. Creating anything.

Cunning: Crafty and sly, possessing a great deal of ingenuity.

Uses: Tricking others. Command Challenges.

Dedicated: You give yourself over totally to your beliefs. When one of your causes is at stake, you stop at nothing to succeed.

Uses: Useful in any Mental Challenge when your beliefs are at stake. Defense against Forgetful Mind.

Determined: When it comes to mental endeavors, you are fully committed. Nothing can divert your intentions to succeed once you have made up your mind.

Uses: Facedowns. Useful in a normal Mental Challenge.

Discerning: Discriminating, able to pick out details, subtleties and idiosyncrasies. You have clarity of vision.

Uses: Auspex-related challenges.

Disciplined: Your mind is structured and controlled. This rigidity gives you an edge in battles of will.

Uses: Thaumaturgy contests. Facedowns. Useful in a Mental Discipline contest.

Insightful: The power of looking at a situation and gaining an understanding of it.

Uses: Investigation (but not defense against it). Reading Auras. Using Heightened Senses. Seeing through Obfuscate when you expect it.

Intuitive: Knowledge and understanding somehow come to you without conscious reasoning, as if by instinct.

Uses: Reading auras. Seeing through Obfuscate.

Knowledgeable: You know copious and detailed information about a wide variety of topics. This represents "book-learning."

Uses: Forgetful Mind contests. Remembering information your character might know. Employing Thaumaturgy.

Observant: Depth of vision, the power to look at something and notice the important aspects of it.

Uses: Heightened Senses. Picking up on subtitles that others might overlook.

Patient: Tolerant, persevering and steadfast. You can wait out extended delays with composure.

Uses: Facedowns or other mental battles after another Trait has been bid.

Rational: You believe in logic, reason, sanity and sobriety. Your ability to reduce concepts to a mathematical level helps you analyze the world.

Uses: Defending against emotion oriented mental attacks. Defending against an aura reading. Not used as an initial bid.

Reflective: Meditative self-recollection and deep thought. The Trait of the serious thinker, Reflective enables you to consider all aspects of a conundrum.

Uses: Meditation. Remembering information. Defending against most Mental attacks.

Shrewd: Astute and artful, able to keep your wits about you and accomplish mental feats with efficiency and finesse.

Uses: Defending against a Mental Discipline.

Vigilant: Alertly watchful. You have the disposition of a guard dog; your attention misses little.

Uses: Defending against investigation, Forgetful Mind and Command. Seeing through Obfuscate. More appropriate for mental defense than for attack.

Wily: Sly and full of guile. Because you are wily, you can trick and deceive easily.

Uses: Tricking others. Lying under duress. Confusing mental situations.

Wise: An overall understanding of the workings of the world.

Uses: Giving advice. Dispensing snippets of Zen. Defending against Dominate Challenges.

Negative Mental Traits

Forgetful: You have trouble remembering even important things.

Gullible: Easily deceived, duped or fooled.

Ignorant: Uneducated or misinformed, never seeming to know anything.

Impatient: Restless, anxious and generally intolerant of delays. You want everything to go your way— immediately.

Oblivious: Unaware and unmindful. You'd be lucky if you noticed an airplane flying through your living room.

Predictable: Because you lack originality or intelligence, even strangers can easily figure out what you intend to do next. Not a very good Trait for chess players.

Shortsighted: Lacking foresight. You rarely look beyond the superficial; details of perception are usually lost on you.

Submissive: No backbone; you relent and surrender at any cost rather than stand up for yourself.

Violent: An extreme lack of self-control. You fly into rages at the slightest provocation, and frenzy is always close to the surface. This is a Mental Trait because it represents mental instability.

Witless: Lacking the ability to process information quickly. Foolish and slow to act when threatened.

Abilities

While you can easily and quickly execute many complex actions in **Mind's Eye Theatre** with simple challenges, this is not always the case. Sometimes Abilities — the skills, talents and knowledges that characters use — are necessary.

An Ability allows your character to engage in, if not excel at, a particular type of activity that she would not normally be able to attempt. Performing such a task often involves risking Traits: if the character is defeated in the challenge, she may choose to temporarily sacrifice a level in the appropriate Ability to call for a retest. While any Traits risked are lost regardless, it is possible to still win the challenge. An Ability lost in this manner is recovered at the beginning of the next session. If your character loses all her levels in an Ability in this manner, she may not use that Ability again until she recovers at least one level.

Often, a challenge of one sort or another accompanies the use of Abilities. The Narrator choreographs some of these challenges, not only assigning the relative difficulty of the challenge in Traits, but also actually performing the test with you. The Narrator also sets a difficulty against which the Static Challenge is performed; interprets the amount of time required to attempt the skill; and may even ask you to pretend that you're performing the skill or to drop out of play for the duration of the task.

Also, you can use other Abilities, such as Subterfuge or Melee, directly against another player. These rarely require the assistance of a Narrator. Note that you may choose Abilities multiple times to represent a high degree of expertise in that skill or in a broad number of fields, as is the case with Performance, Science and Linguistics.

Animal Ken

Vampires are among the most efficient predators in the world. For humans, this is not always apparent, but animals seem instinctively aware of this and actively avoid the undead. A character who possesses Animal Ken, however, has practiced long and hard to regain (or simply never lost) the ability to interact and cooperate with natural animals. Given time and access to an animal, she may train it to perform simple tasks (i.e. fetch, guard, attack, etc.). When the command is given, the animal must make a Mental Challenge to successfully understand and carry out the order. The difficulty of the test will be based on the level of domestication of the animal as well as on the complexity of the task required. The character may also attempt to calm an injured, attacking or frightened animal by defeating it in a Social Challenge.

Brawl

You are adept at using your body as a weapon. This includes any form of unarmed combat, from dirty in-fighting to highly stylized martial arts. The Brawl Ability may be used in coordination with claws, teeth and other types of natural weaponry. In this manner, even a character who is stripped bare can still represent a formidable foe.

Bureaucracy

Each day, the world becomes increasingly burdened with a staggering amount of complexity, paperwork and red tape. A Kindred knowledgeable in the ways of bureaucracy has the power to navigate this system and use it to her benefit. Bureaucracy can allow the character to appropriate licenses, use contractual agreements to her advantage and recover, alter or destroy files from organizations (using aliases or other red herrings, of course). Such actions may ruin a rival or cover up an embarrassing breach of the Masquerade. Bureaucracy often requires a Mental or Social Challenge, depending on the type of roleplaying the character performs or as a Storyteller sees fit. Difficulty depends on such factors as security, accessibility of the information or the cooperation of the target.

Computer

An information superhighway is being built, with electron asphalt, silicon off-ramps and fiber-optic expressways. It's enough to make an elder Kindred's head spin. Some younger and more energetic members of the Damned have learned the secrets of this other world and can use them to their advantage. Kindred with this Ability can infiltrate systems, swap data, steal business and scientific secrets, and access records. A Mental Challenge is required to accomplish these and other similar acts, with the difficulty based on system security and accessibility, equipment, time and rarity of information as assigned by a Storyteller. Failure can lead to investigation by natural and sometimes supernatural agencies that operate in the computer sphere.

Drive

Most adults have at least some familiarity with modern vehicles; this Ability goes beyond these basics. A character with this skill is an adept driver capable of tailing and avoiding tails, avoiding collisions and using her vehicle as a weapon. These actions often require a Physical or Mental Challenge. Factors influencing difficulty could include vehicle type, road conditions and the sort of stunt desired. Furthermore, because the Drive Ability allows a character to move quickly from one game scene to another, the Storyteller can reduce any "out of game" travel time usually assigned for moving from scene to scene if a character has this Ability and access to a vehicle.

Finance

Money talks, and you are fluent in its language. You can follow money trails, perform and verify accounting tasks and understand such concepts as investment, buyouts and the like. The difficulty for this Mental Challenge depends on the precautions that the subject takes, the amount of money in question and the availability of information. In most chronicles, the level of Finance Ability a character has determines his income. In general, $250 per level is a good rule of thumb, but this may vary widely from game to game. The final ruing is, of course, up to the Storyteller.

Firearms

Sometime during your existence, you spent the time to familiarize yourself with a range of guns and similar projectile weapons. The most common use of this Ability is in combat, but a Storyteller can also allow you to attempt a Mental Challenge to perform other functions. You not only to understand how to operate firearms, but you can also care for them, repair them and possibly make minor alterations. A character without this Ability may still use a firearm, but cannot benefit from any other Ability-based advantages. Those without the Firearms Ability may also choose to use Mental Traits instead of Physical Traits during a challenge in which a firearm is involved.

Investigation

You possess the learned skills of a diligent investigator. You can often pick out or uncover details and clues that less attentive individuals would overlook or ignore. With a Mental Challenge, you can tell if a person is carrying a concealed weapon or the like. When dealing with plots, you may also request a Mental Challenge with a Storyteller to see if any clues have been overlooked, to piece together clues, or to uncover information through formal investigation. Hunters often employ this Ability to track down their Kindred prey. This sort of attention to detail is most often found among former private investigators, police officers, government agents and insurance claims personnel.

Law

Any judicial system, whether legal, civil or criminal, is based on layer after layer of confusing tradition, precedence and procedure. Your experiences with it, however, allow you to make the system work for you. You can use the Law Ability to write up binding contracts, defend clients, and know your rights and those of others. The difficulty of the Mental Challenges necessary to accomplish these tasks depends on factors like precedence, the severity of the crime, the legal complexity of the subject or the legal action desired.

Leadership

You have the gift of influencing and inspiring others — a function of confidence, bearing and a profound understanding of what motivates others. After defeating a subject in a Social Challenge, you may use this Ability to cause him to perform a reasonable task for you. Subjects must first be under your command or serving as your subordinates. Examples include: an elder and her clan, an officer and his soldiers, a CEO and his employees or a crime lord and her henchmen. These requests may not endanger the subject or violate the subject's Nature or Demeanor.

Linguistics

You have received tutelage in one or more languages other than your native tongue. In their long lifetimes, some Kindred pick up a multitude of languages, some long dead. These can be anything from ancient hieroglyphics to common national languages or complex dialects. You must specify the language when you choose the Linguistics Ability, and you may not change it. Each level can represent an individual language, or, assigned to the same language more than once, a particular fluency with that single language. This skill allows you and anyone who also knows the language to speak privately. Furthermore, you can translate written text in one of the languages you know. This may or may not require a Mental Challenge, depending upon the clarity of the text.

Medicine

This Ability represents an adeptness at treating the injuries, diseases and various ailments of living creatures. You can help a living creature to recover a single Health Level per night with rest and a Mental Challenge. Collecting and properly storing blood requires this skill as well as the appropriate equipment. The severity and nature of the damage, equipment at your disposal and any assistance or distractions influence the difficulty of a challenge. Other uses of this Ability include forensic information, diagnosis, pharmaceutical knowledge and determining the health and blood content of living creatures.

Melee

You possess a degree of training or experience in armed combat. Whether you acquired this experience on a medieval battlefield, in an urban slum or from formal training does not matter. You can use any weapon, from beer bottles and battleaxes to katanas and crossbows. A character without this Ability may not use any of the advantages of Abilities in armed combat, including retests.

Occult

On the fringe of mundane society, a wealth of arcane and alternative knowledge exists. Most of this knowledge offers enlightening insight into the nature of our mysterious universe. This Ability allows you to tap and use this esoteric information. Examples of these uses include, but are not limited to: identifying the use and nature of visible magicks, rites and rituals; understanding basic fundaments of the occult; or having knowledge of cults, tomes and artifacts. Most uses of the Occult Ability require a Mental Challenge. The difficulty of this challenge is subject to many factors, such as obscurity, amount of existing data and the character's individual scope of understanding (vampires know more about their own Disciplines, and so on). For a Tremere not to have least one level in Occult is unheard of.

Performance

You have the gift to make your own original creations and/or express those creations to your peers. A Social Challenge determines the genius of your creativity or the power with which you convey it. With a successful Social Challenge, you can even entrance particularly sensitive types of Kindred. When you take the skill, you should declare your specialty, some examples of which include painting, poetry, composing music or playing a single type of instrument. While not all Toreador actually create art, those who do tend to be truly gifted in their field.

Repair

You possess a working understanding of what makes things tick. With time, tools and parts, you can fix or slightly alter most of the trappings of modern society. This knowledge also allows you to excel at sabotage. The Repair Ability is widespread among inventors, mechanics and handymen. Using this Ability usually calls for a Mental Challenge, the difficulty of which depends on such factors as the item's complexity, tools and parts available, extent of damage and time spent on the repairs.

Science

You have a degree of factual and practical expertise in a single field of the hard sciences. This knowledge allows you to identify properties of your field, perform experiments, fabricate items, bring about results or access information a player could not normally use. A Mental Challenge is necessary for all but the most trivial uses of this skill, difficulty depending on resources (equipment, data, etc.) available, complexity of the task and time. You must choose a field of study when you take the Science Ability. A few examples are Physics, Biology, Electronics and Chemistry. Other fields can be allowed at the Storyteller's discretion.

Scrounge

Scrounge enables you to produce items through connections, wits and ingenuity. Many individuals who lack the wealth to purchase the things they desire or need (Nosferatu and poorer Brujah among them) develop this Ability instead. Materials acquired with Scrounge aren't always brand new, are rarely exactly right and often require some time to acquire, but this Ability can sometimes work where finance or outright theft fail. A Mental or Social Challenge is necessary to use Scrounge. Some factors that influence the difficulty of the challenge include the rarity and value of an item and local supply and demand.

Security

You have a degree of experienced knowledge of the variety of ways people defend and protect things. Not only can you counter existing security, such as locks, alarms and guards, but you can also determine the best way to secure items and areas. Other uses include breaking and entering, infiltration, safecracking and hot-wiring. Almost all applications of the Security Ability require a Mental Challenge determined by the complexity of the task, the thoroughness of the defenses, your equipment and the length of time required.

Streetwise

You have a feel for the street, know its secrets, how to survive out there and how to use its network of personalities. You can get information on events, deal with gangs and the homeless and survive (if somewhat squalidly) without an apparent income. Some uses of Streetwise require a Social Challenge that is influenced by such things as the composition of the local street community and the current environment on the street. A Nosferatu without at least a level of this Ability is an unusual creature indeed.

Subterfuge

Subterfuge is an art of deception and intrigue that relies on a social backdrop to work. When participating in a social setting or conversation with a subject, you can attempt to draw information out of him through trickery and careful probing. The Kindred, whose taste for intrigue and politics is practically unequaled, favor this Ability.

A successful use of Subterfuge can reveal information such as one's name, nationality, Negative Traits, friends and enemies. The first requirement is that you get the target to say something dealing with the desired knowledge, perhaps by entering a conversation about foreign culture to find out a character's nationality. If you can accomplish this, then you may propose your true question and initiate a Social Challenge. If you win, your target must forfeit the information. To use the Ability again, you must once again lure him into a conversation. Furthermore, Subterfuge may not reveal more than one Negative Trait per session, and it may be used to defend from others with Subterfuge. You could even slip false information that they would believe to be true if you defeat your opponent in the Social Challenge.

Conversely, you may also use the Subterfuge Ability to conceal information or lie without detection. You may not, however, use it to lie while under the influence of Command or other such Disciplines.

Survival

You have the knowledge and training to find food, water and shelter in a variety of wilderness settings. Each Mental or Physical Challenge allows you to provide yourself or another living creature with basic necessities for one day. You can also use this Ability to track beings in a wilderness setting; the Storyteller usually sets the nature and difficulty of this challenge. Important factors in a Survival challenge are abundance or scarcity of resources, time of the year, equipment and the type of wilderness. Many Gangrel possessed this Ability in their days as mortals and find it useful even now when "living" off the land.

Sabbat Abilities

In addition to all of the Abilities listed above, Sabbat characters may also choose from among the following:

Black Hand Knowledge

You have access to much information about this secretive group within the Sabbat. You can find out about current members, rituals and philosophy, as well as (perhaps) some plans. A Mental (or in some cases Social) Challenge will be in order to acquire information you do not already possess.

Blind Fighting

Many Sabbat games and Monomacy ritual fights require use of this Ability. Blind fighting means you are practiced at fighting without the aid of your eyes. Many packs blindfold new initiates and teach them to fight that way. Your pack has trained you to use your instincts, hearing and innate hunter nature without relying on the use of your vision. You may use this Ability to retest whenever you are fighting in the dark or blindfolded. This Ability also enables you to initiate challenges in the dark.

Camarilla Lore

This Ability allows a member of the Sabbat to acquire information about who's who in the Camarilla. It may only be possessed by converts, Nosferatu or Malkavian *antitribu*, infiltrators of any clan or those with a really good reason to have it. A Mental Challenge will be required for the character to attempt to gain new knowledge.

Fire Walking

You may enter a trancelike state which relieves you from Rötschreck and allows you to cross burning coals during some Sabbat rituals. You do not get nervous around fire if you can sit apart and meditate for five minutes before encountering the flames. You may use this Ability to retest any Rötschreck tests regarding fire. If you are able to meditate, you may use this Ability without a test to resist fear during rituals.

Fortune Telling

You may or may not have the psychic chutzpah to really do this, but with a Social Challenge, you can make people believe you do. This Ability allows you to try your hand at any common fortune telling art such as palmistry, tea leaves, Tarot cards, the I Ching, dice or runecasting. You may engage in a Social Challenge to convince your client that you are telling the truth or are a real psychic.

History

You know your history. With a successful Mental Challenge, this Ability allows you to research history quickly and efficiently, enabling you to acquire information on just about any period if it's not already in your head. You may have had no interest in history in your mortal life, but now you find it fascinating. The Sabbat has taught you much through its rituals and Path teachings. Like you, many Sabbat possess this Ability because of their education and strict indoctrination within the sect.

Panhandling

You beg with skill and ease…people just end up giving you money. You may engage in a Social Challenge at any time to encourage passers-by to share the wealth. Your Demeanor may vary from a crying child to an aggressive old drunk.

Ritual Knowledge

Because the Sabbat translates so many of its practices into ritual form, most members can figure out how to make a ritual to accomplish a given objective. This Ability allows you to create, construct and enact a ritual for common practice. This does not include Thaumaturgy, but might include a hex or a curse that could rob the target temporarily of one to three Traits. Specific ritual requirements, like how many Traits the pack must spend to extract Traits from their target, etc., are up to the discretion of the Storyteller. This Ability also allows you to recognize that a ritual is in use should you witness it. Unless you are also a Thaumaturgist and have witnessed or studied the ritual before, you will not be able to identify the exact ritual.

Sabbat Lore

You are privy to much information, including the activities of the sect in cities other than your own. You know many rituals and enjoy gathering as much knowledge as you can about different goings on within the sect. A Mental Challenge is required to gather knowledge you don't already have.

Sewer Lore

You know the sewers of your city like the back of your hand. The more abilities you possess in Sewer Lore, the better you know the happenings in the passages, the escape routes of other vampires, etc. You must engage in a Mental Challenge to use this Ability.

Snake Charming

You can mesmerize snakes and enjoy handling them. This Ability will allow you to retake a Social Challenge when you are sure you are engaged with a Setite or Serpent of the Light. It will also allow you to charm snakes for show or for certain Sabbat rituals.

Torture

You know how to inflict pain, and you are efficient at doing so. This Ability will allow you to retake any Physical Challenge when you are in a torture situation (i.e. when you are the torturer). Regular combat is not an appropriate use for this Ability.

Influence

Influence is the mechanism by which Kindred control the daily affairs of the innumerable hordes of kine for their often inscrutable reasons. It may take the form of contacts, allies or direct control of a mortal agency. In a practical sense, Influence can make almost any Kindred's life easier. It can be used to protect one's haven, hunting habits or illegal activities, not to mention the power it can levy against one's foes — or fellow Kindred.

Characters may expend Influence Traits to accomplish goals relating to a specific aspect of mortal society. Many Influences, such as Street and Underworld, perform similar functions, but generally one will be more efficient at performing the task in question. Set by the Storyteller, the difficulty of a task equals the number of Traits that must be expended to accomplish the task, and can be subject to sudden change depending upon circumstance. The suggested guideline listed along with each area of Influence can change dramatically between chronicles or even between sessions. After all, you may not be the only Kindred attempting to Influence something.

Sometimes a Narrator will require a challenge of some sort to represent the uncertainty or added difficulty involved when exercising Influence. Some uses of Influence may not actually cost Influence to use, but rather require that the Kindred simply possess a certain level of the Influence in question.

To use Influence actively, you should explain to the Narrator what sort effect you wish to create. The Narrator then decides the Trait cost, the time involved (both real and in-game) and any tests required to achieve the Influence effect. Influence Traits used this way are *temporarily* considered to have been expended and are not recovered until the next session. The effects of using Influence can be instantaneous and brief, or slow to manifest and permanent, depending on the nature of the manipulation and the degree of power the character wields.

Sometimes players will want to perform actions that do not seem to fall under any single Influence group, or which may require the use of multiple Influences. Say a Toreador ancilla wants to open the premier nightclub in her city. Obviously, she will need Finance, but High Society and Media might be useful to stimulate interest and promote the club as something really spectacular. Furthermore, what if the area targeted for her venture is not zoned for clubs? Bureaucracy could be useful in changing zoning, not to mention in acquiring the proper licenses and permits. Therefore, in certain cases, a Storyteller may decide that two or more types of Influence are necessary to accomplish a goal. Not only is this more realistic, but it also encourages characters to interact more widely than they might have otherwise in order to obtain the Influence they need.

Kindred can trade Influences with each other much like children trade baseball cards. These trades may be permanent or temporary. In the case of permanent trades, the old owner erases the Trait from his sheet and turns over the appropriate Influence Card (if your chronicle uses these) to the new owner. The new owner then records her newly acquired Influence Trait on her character sheet. Temporary trades of Influence occur when a Kindred is merely doing a favor or loaning her Influence to someone else. In this case, the owner does not erase the Trait, but instead makes a note that it is no longer in her possession. The holder of the Influence Trait may use it immediately or hold onto to it until she feels she needs it. However, the original owner of the Influence Trait may *not* regain the Trait until the current holder expends or voluntarily returns it.

Sometimes characters may wish to try to counteract the Influence of other characters. In such cases, it generally costs one Trait per Trait being countered. The Kindred willing to expend the most Influence Traits (assuming she has them to spend) achieves her goal; all Traits used in this sort of conflict are considered expended. An example would be if one Kindred was trying to get a story published in the newspaper as another was trying to squelch it.

In practice, the use of Influence is never instantaneous and rarely expedient. While a character may be able to, say, condemn any building in the city, it will not be torn down that night. For sake of game flow, a Storyteller may allow trivial uses of Influence to only take half an hour. Major manipulations, on the other hand, can become the center of ongoing plots requiring several sessions to bring to fruition.

The guidelines below by no means limit the number of Influence Traits that can be spent at one time or the degree of change a character may bring about. They are merely an advisory measure to help Storytellers adjudicate the costs of certain actions.

Actions followed by an asterisk (*) below indicate that their effects can generally be accomplished without expending an Influence Trait.

Time Limits

Obviously, an unwise Kindred can find his Influences tied up in the hands of others for a long time if he is not careful. For this reason, some chronicles dictate that the Trait reverts to its original owner after a certain time. A good rule of thumb for this is that one month is the maximum duration of any loan of Influence. If your chronicle's sessions are scheduled less frequently than once a month, the Storyteller(s) should probably expand this window of opportunity. Any exchange of Influence Traits requires the presence and assistance of a Narrator.

Bureaucracy

The organizational aspects of local, state or even federal government fall within the character's sphere of control. She can bend and twist the tangle of rules and regulations that seem necessary to run our society as she sees fit. The character may have contacts or allies among government clerks, supervisors, utility workers, road crews, surveyors and numerous other civil servants.

Cost	Desired Effect
1	Trace utility bills*
2	Fake a birth certificate or driver's license
	Disconnect a small residence's utilities
	Close a small road or park; Get public aid ($250)
3	Fake a death certificate, passport or green card
	Close a public school for a single day
	Turn a single utility on a block on or off
	Shut down a minor business on a violation
4	Initiate a phone tap; Fake land deeds
	Initiate a department-wide investigation
5	Start, stop or alter a city-wide program or policy
	Shut down a big business on a violation; Rezone areas
	Obliterate records of a person on a city and county level
6	Arrange a fixed audit of a person or business

Church

Even churches are not without politics and intrigue upon which an opportunistic Kindred may capitalize. Church Influence usually only applies to mainstream faiths, such as Christianity, Judaism, Buddhism and the Islamic faith. Sometimes other practices fall under the Occult Influence. Contacts and allies affected by Church Influence include: ministers, bishops, priests, activists, evangelists, witch-hunters, nuns and various church attendees and assistants.

Cost	Desired Effect
1	Identify most secular members of a given faith in the local area
	Pass as a member of the clergy *
	Peruse general church records (baptism, marriage, burial, etc.)
2	Identify higher church members
	Track regular congregation members; Suspend lay members
3	Open or close a single church; Dip into the collection ($250)
	Find the average church-associated hunter
	Access to private information and archives of church
4	Discredit or suspend higher-level members
	Manipulate regional branches
5	Organize major protests; Access ancient church lore
6	Borrow or access church relics or sacred items
7	Use the resources of a Diocese

Finance

The world teems with the trappings of affluence and the stories of the rich and famous. Kindred with the Finance Influence speak this language of money and know where to find capital. They have a degree of access to banks, megacorporations and the truly wealthy citizens of the world. Such characters also have a wide variety of servants to draw upon, such as CEOs, bankers, corporate yes-men, financiers, bank tellers, stock brokers and loan agents.

Cost	Desired Effect
1	Earn money; learn about major transactions and financial events
	Raise capital ($1,000); Learn about general economic trends*
	Learn real motivations for many financial actions of others
2	Trace an unsecured small account
	Raise capital to purchase a small business
3	Purchase a large business
4	Manipulate local banking (delay deposits, credit alterations)
	Ruin a small business
5	Control an aspect of citywide banking (shut off ATMs)
	Ruin a large business; Purchase a major company
6	Spark an economic trend

Health

In our modern world, a myriad of organizations and resources exists to deal with every mortal ache and ill, at least in theory. The network of health agencies, hospitals, asylums and medical groups is subject to exploitation by a Kindred with Health Influence. Nurses, doctors, specialists, lab workers, therapists, counselors and pharmacists are just a few of the workers within the health field.

Cost	Desired Effect
1	Access a person's health records*
	Use public functions of health centers at your leisure
	Fake vaccination records and the like; Get a Blood Trait
2	Access to some medical research records
	Have minor lab work done; Get a copy of coroner's report
3	Instigate minor quarantines
	Corrupt results of tests or inspections; Alter medical records
4	Acquire a body; Completely rewrite medical records
	Abuse grants for personal use ($250)
	Institute large scale quarantines
	Shut down businesses for "health code violations"
5	Have special research projects performed
	Have people institutionalized or released

High Society

An elite clique of mortals exists that, by virtue of birth, possessions, talent or quirks of fate, hold themselves above the great unwashed masses. High Society allows the character to direct and use the energies and actions of this exceptional mass of mortals. Among their ranks, one can find dilettantes, the old rich, movie and rock stars, artists of all sorts, wannabes, fashion models and trendsetters.

Cost	Desired Effect
1	Learn what is trendy *
	Learn about concerts, shows or plays well before the public *
	Obtain hard-to-get tickets for shows
2	Track most celebrities and luminaries
	Be a local voice in the entertainment field
	"Borrow" $1,000 as idle cash from rich friends
3	Crush promising careers
	Hobnob well above your station *
4	Minor celebrity status
5	Appear on a talk show that's not about to be canceled
	Ruin a new club, gallery, festival or other high society gathering

Industry

The dark world of the Gothic-Punk milieu is built by pumping and grinding machinery and the toil of endless laborers. A character with the Industry Influence has her ashen fingers in this pie. Industry is composed of union workers, foremen, engineers, contractors, construction workers and manual laborers.

Cost	Desired Effect
1	Learn about industrial projects and movements *
2	Have minor projects performed; Arrange small "accidents"
	Dip into union funds or embezzle petty cash ($500)
3	Organize minor strikes; Appropriate machinery for a short time
4	Close down a small plant; Revitalize a small plant
5	Manipulate large local industry
6	Cut off production of a single resource in a small region

Legal

The Kindred presence is even present in the hallowed halls of justice and the courts, law schools, law firms and justice bureaus within them. Inhabiting these halls are lawyers, judges, bailiffs, clerks, DAs and attorneys.

Cost	Desired Effect
1	Get free representation for small cases
2	Avoid bail for some charges; Have minor charges dropped
3	Manipulate legal procedures (small wills, minor contracts, court dates)
	Access public or court funds ($250); Get good representation
4	Issue subpoenas; Tie up court cases
	Have most legal charges dropped; Cancel or arrange parole
5	Close down all but the most serious investigations
	Have deportation proceedings held against someone

Media

The media serves as the eyes and ears of the world. While few in this day and age doubt that the news is not corrupted, many would be surprised at who closes these eyes and covers these ears from time to time. The media entity is composed of station directions, editors, reporters, anchors, camerapeople, photographers and radio personalities.

Cost	Desired Effect
1	Learn about breaking stories early *
	Submit small articles (within reason)
2	Suppress (but not stop) small articles or reports
	Get hold of investigative reporting information
3	Initiate news investigations and reports
	Get project funding and waste it ($250)
	Access media production resources; Ground stories and projects
4	Broadcast fake stories (local only)

Occult

Most people are curious about the supernatural world and the various groups and beliefs that make up the occult world, but few consider it anything but a hoax, a diversion or a curiosity. They could not be farther from the truth. This Influence more than any other hits the Kindred close to home and could very well bring humanity to its senses about just who and what shares this world with them. Among the occult community are cult leaders, alternative religious groups, charlatans, would-be occultists and New Agers.

Cost	Desired Effect
1	Contact and use common occult groups, practices
	Know some of the more visible occult figures *
2	Know and contact some of the more obscure occult figures *
	Access resources for most rituals and rites
3	Know the general vicinity of certain supernatural entities and possibly contact them
	Can access vital or very rare material components
	Milk impressionable wannabes for bucks ($250)
	Access occult tomes and writings (part of an alleged *Book of Nod*)
	Research a Basic Ritual
4	Research an Intermediate Ritual
5	Access minor magic items; Unearth an Advanced Ritual
6	Research a new or unheard of ritual or rite from tomes or mentors

Police

"To protect and serve" is a popular motto among the chosen enforcers of the law. But these days, even those ignorant of Kindred have reason to doubt the law's ability to enact justice. Perhaps they should wonder whom the law defends, whom it serves and why. The Police Influence encompasses the likes of beat cops, desk jockeys, prison guards, special divisions (such as SWAT and homicide), detectives and various clerical positions.

Cost	Desired Effect
1	Learn police procedures *
	Police information and rumors; Avoid traffic tickets
2	Have license plates checked; Avoid minor violations
	Get "inside information"
3	Find bureau secrets;Get copies of an investigation report
	Have police hassle, detain or harass someone

4	Access confiscated weapons or contraband
	Start an investigation
	Get money, either from evidence room or as an appropriation ($1,000)
	Have some serious charges dropped
5	Institute major investigations; Arrange setups
	Instigate bureau investigations; Have officers fired
6	Paralyze departments for a time; Close down an investigation

Politics

It is said that imitation is the sincerest form of flattery. If this is so, the movers and shakers among the Kindred should be quite taken by the artful and cut-throat antics of their mortal counterparts in the field of politics. Some of these individuals include statesmen, pollsters, activists, party members, lobbyists, candidates and the politicians themselves.

Cost	Desired Effect
1	Minor lobbying
	Identify real platforms of politicians and parties *
	Be in the know *
2	Meet small time politicians; Have a forewarning of processes, and laws
	Use a slush fund or fund raiser ($1,000)
3	Sway or alter political projects (local parks, renovations)
4	Enact minor legislation; Dash careers of minor politicians
5	Get your candidate in a minor office
	Enact more encompassing legislature
6	Block the passage of major bills; Suspend major laws temporarily
	Use state bureaus or subcommittees
7	Usurp countywide politics
	Subvert, to a moderate degree, statewide powers
8	Call out a local division of the National Guard
	Declare a state of emergency in a region

Street

Disenchanted, disenfranchised and ignored by their "betters," an undercurrent of humanity has made its own culture and lifestyle to deal with the harsh lot life has dealt them. In the dark alleys and slums reside gang members, the homeless, street performers, petty criminals, prostitutes and the forgotten.

Cost	Desired Effect
1	Has an ear open for the word on the street
	Identify most gangs and know their turfs and habits
2	Live mostly without fear on the underside of society
	Keep a contact or two in most aspects of street life
	Access small time contraband
3	Often gets insight on other areas of influence
	Arrange some services from street people or gangs
	Get pistols or uncommon melee weapons

4	Mobilize groups of homeless; Panhandle $250
	Can have a word in almost all aspects of gang operations
	Get hold of a shotgun, rifle or SMG
5	Control a single medium-sized gang

Transportation

The world is in constant motion, its prosperity relying heavily on the fact that people and productions fly, float or roll to and from every corner of the planet. Without the means to perform this monumental task, our "small" world quickly returns to a daunting orb with large, isolated stretches. The forces that keep this circulation in motion include: cab and bus drivers, pilots, air traffic controllers, travel firms, sea captains, conductors, border guards and untold others.

Cost	Desired Effect
1	A wizard at what goes where, when and why
	Can travel locally quickly and freely *
2	Can track an unwary target if they use public transportation
	Arrange passage safe from mundane threats (sunlight, etc.)
3	Seriously hamper an individual's ability to travel
	Avoid most supernatural dangers when traveling
4	Temporarily shut down one form of mass transit.
	Route money your way ($500)
5	Reroute major modes of travel; Smuggle with impunity
6	Extend control to nearby areas
7	Isolate small or remote regions for a short period

Underworld

Even in the most cosmopolitan of ages, society has found certain needs and services too questionable to accept, and in every age, some organized effort has stepped in to provide for this demand regardless of the risks. Among this often ruthless and dangerous crowd are the likes of hitmen, Mafia, Yakuza, bookies, fencers and launderers.

Cost	Desired Effect
1	Locate minor contraband (knives, small-time drugs, etc.)
2	Obtain pistols, serious drugs, stolen cars, etc.
	Hire muscle to rough someone up
	Fence minor loot; Prove that crime pays (and score $1,000)
3	Obtain rifle, shotgun or SMG; Arrange a minor "boost"
4	White-collar crime connections
5	Arrange gangland assassinations; Hire a hitman or firebug
	Supply local drug needs

University

In an age where the quest for learning and knowledge begins in schools, colleges and universities, information becomes currency. University Influence represents a certain degree of control and perhaps involvement in these institutions. Within this sphere of Influence, one will find the teachers, professors, deans, students of all ages and levels, Greek orders and many young and impressionable minds.

Cost	Desired Effect
1	Know layout and policy of local schools *
	Access to low level university resources
	Get records up to the high school level
2	Know a contact or two with useful knowledge or skills
	Minor access to facilities; Fake high school records
	Obtain college records
3	Faculty favors; Cancel a class; Fix grades
	Discredit a student
4	Organize student protests and rallies
	Discredit faculty members
	Acquire money through a grant ($1,000)
5	Falsify an undergraduate degree
6	Arrange major projects
	Alter curriculum institution-wide
	Free run of facilities

Blood

Blood Traits aren't assigned adjectives as other Traits are; each Blood Trait simply represents a volume of blood. A breakdown of the ways Blood Traits can be used follows:

• Upon awakening from sleep each night, you expend one Blood Trait. This represents the basic nourishment your character requires to survive.

• Blood Traits can be used to heal Health Levels on a one-for-one basis. The wounds are healed instantly. Note, however, that injuries inflicted by fire and sunlight (aggravated wounds) require three Blood Traits and a Willpower Trait to heal. You may also let other vampires drink your blood, thereby healing them. However, if a vampire is in torpor, only the blood of a vampire three generations or more lower than she is can revive her.

• Vampires often use blood to fuel Disciplines, such as Celerity or the Path of Blood.

• You may use blood to boost your Physical Traits during a Physical Challenge. Each Blood Trait spent adds one to your total Physical Traits for the duration of a single conflict. Employed in this manner, you can use Blood Traits just as if they were Physical Traits, including the ones used to bid. This lasts for the duration of the conflict, not the challenge. The difference is that a conflict may actually involve several challenges. You may hold onto used Traits up to five minutes after the last challenge in the conflict is completed, at which time all marked Traits are gone. Each used Trait must be marked in some manner (eg., crossed with an X).

The most common way a character can regain Blood Traits is by feeding, but a Kindred can never imbibe more Traits than she has in her permanent Blood Pool. Vampires of lower generation have much larger pools than those of higher generation, which is one of the greatest advantages of generation.

Willpower

Willpower gives a character the extra strength to overcome obstacles and to succeed where others would surrender and fail. Each character begins the game with a number of Willpower Traits. For vampires, the number of Traits depends on the character's generation. These Willpower Traits can be used for almost anything that the player deems important. For example:

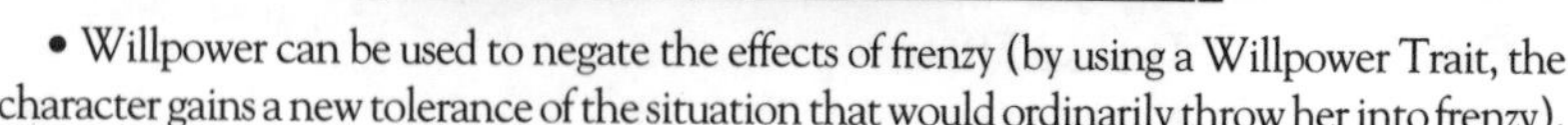

• Willpower can be used to negate the effects of frenzy (by using a Willpower Trait, the character gains a new tolerance of the situation that would ordinarily throw her into frenzy).

• Willpower allows a character to replenish all lost Traits in any one category: Physical, Social or Mental.

• Willpower allows a character to ignore the effects of wounds, up to and including Incapacitation, for one challenge.

• A Willpower Trait can be expended to negate the effects of any one Mental or Social Challenge.

Once a Willpower Trait has been used, it is gone until the end of the story. At this time, the character regains all Willpower used during the course of the story.

Beast Traits

While the existence of most vampires consists of a rollercoaster ride of psychological drawbacks and recoveries, some Kindred live in a consistently primitive, regressed world. These Kindred have succumbed to the bestial side of vampiric nature and often cannot control what they do. Beast Traits are a measure of how much a Kindred has given in to her dark side, the Beast. Beast Traits affect several things:

• **How often the Kindred goes into frenzy**

Each Beast Trait has a description of a type of event that will send that character into a state of frenzy. Unless the character resists by spending a Willpower Trait, the character will automatically frenzy if that situation comes up. (See the section on "Frenzy" for more details on the effect this has on a character.)

• **Waking up early**

In games that begin at sunset, a player with Beast Traits may not join play for 15 minutes for each Beast Trait her character has. A character with three Beast Traits will have to start play at least 45 minutes after sunset.

Upon receiving the fifth Beast Trait, the vampire goes into a state of permanent frenzy. The player has no control over the character and must surrender it to the Storyteller and start anew.

Beast Traits are categorized as either Rage, Control or Terror Beast Traits, in order to define the type of frenzy that each Trait causes. There are also two levels of Beast Traits: Subhuman and Monstrous. Subhuman Traits cause frenzies based on fairly uncommon events. Having a Subhuman Trait will tend to make you frenzy occasionally, unless of course an enemy discovers and exploits it.

Monstrous Traits are far deadlier. Most vampires with Monstrous Traits tend to spiral out of control very quickly, either being destroyed or staked and stored away as a result. No prince likes a loose cannon, particularly not an irrational one, in his domain.

Receiving Beast Traits

Kindred acquire Beast Traits when performing an act of violence or cruelty. It is up to a Narrator or the Storyteller to decide what warrants penalizing the player with a Beast Trait.

Generally a Narrator will have the player perform a Simple Test. If the player wins, she will not gain a Beast Trait. If she draws, she will gain a Subhuman Beast Trait. If the player loses the Simple Test, she will gain a Monstrous Beast Trait.

It also bears mentioning that a Kindred who performs a heinous action while under the effects of a frenzy is by no means exempt from gaining additional Beast Traits as a result of her actions — thus the downward spiral begins.

Rage

Subhuman Beast Traits

• **Vigilante** — Frenzy whenever you encounter the death of a person (be it Kindred or kine). You are tormented by all the killing that vampires do, so much so that a death will send you into an uncontrollable rage. You will seek out and try to destroy the murderer. If you do not know the murderer, you will blame the nearest person and go after him.

• **Frustrated** — Frenzy whenever beaten in a Mental Challenge. You will kill the next person who messes with your mind. If you lost a Static Challenge against a lock or alarm system, that object is history. That person over there looking at you funny is obviously trying to take control of your mind. Get him.

• **Item** — Frenzy when encountering a particular item, like a stake. The stake wielder is asking for it. You may end up with some other item besides a stake, which the Storyteller must choose. Were you attacked by a psychotic with a pair of scissors when you were young? Or were you once shot 137 times with an Uzi?

Monstrous Beast Traits

• **Furious** — Frenzy whenever someone crosses you in some way. Someone is not following your orders. Perhaps he has been telling the Harpies all about your little plan and now the word has spread all over town. Or maybe your rival has Blood Bonded your favorite ghoul to herself. That makes you *really* angry.

• **Violent** — Frenzy whenever witnessing an act of violence. This is what happens to vigilantes who go overboard. If you see two Kindred fighting, you might beat up the one who is attacking (because he's just too violent). Beat up the other one (after all, he let himself be attacked). Attack the spectators (just because you're in the mood). Often this frenzy will continue until someone helps you stop, as you are only causing more violence (although it's really their fault!).

• **Bullied** — Frenzy whenever beaten in a Social Challenge. Whoever won the Social Challenge deserves to get beaten up. The worst problem with this frenzy is that you cannot be talked down from a frenzy. (A Kindred will have to beat you in a Social Challenge to talk you down.)

Control

Subhuman Beast Traits

• **Blood** — Frenzy whenever encountering a quantity of spilled blood. The smell of about a pint of blood when it is out in the open drives you wild. Start by lapping up the blood in front of everyone. Once the taste gets into your body, you need more blood until you are full. Even then, you may not stop.

• **Hunger** — Frenzy whenever you are down to only a single Blood Trait. The Hunger starts to drive you, and you need the blood. Drink your first victim dry, then leave the dry husk as you pursue more blood. Feeding is all that matters. Covering up your killing is not part of being a "real" vampire.

• **Lust** — Frenzy whenever encountering a willing victim to feed from. Feeding is like sex. When you find someone to feed from who is just as enthusiastic as you are, the drinking is more than just taking blood. You tend to get carried away and drink too much. Then you need to find more and more blood to help atone for your sins.

Monstrous Beast Traits

• **Blood Smell** — Frenzy whenever encountering a crowd of people, animals or Kindred. This is similar to the Subhuman Beast Trait: Blood, but far more crippling. The smell of

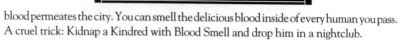

blood permeates the city. You can smell the delicious blood inside of every human you pass. A cruel trick: Kidnap a Kindred with Blood Smell and drop him in a nightclub.

• **Desire** — Frenzy whenever encountering whatever you most want. You want to be prince? He's standing right over there. Take him out and the position is yours. Infatuated with the beautiful Toreador? Her "guardian" is approaching you now. This is a particularly nasty Trait to have.

• **Diablerie** — Frenzy when encountering an incapacitated Kindred. This is not a very common situation, unlike most Monstrous Beast Traits. However, whenever you find a helpless Kindred, you have trouble resisting the easy way to lower your generation. Drink his blood, then his soul. Stock up on Willpower, or the Sheriff will be after you in no time.

Courage

Subhuman Beast Traits

• **Phobia** — Frenzy when affected by a phobia. Perhaps you suffered from some phobia in your mortal life that grew into a terrible fear in your immortal life. Flee until you find some protection from whatever ails you. The Storyteller may wish to choose from the following phobias or assign you a new one:

• **Sunlight** — Frenzy whenever exposed to sunlight, a sun lamp or UV radiation. Sunlight kills vampires, and so this is one of the few useful Beast Traits. However, sun lamps and black lights (which normally cause only a mild tingling to the skin) send you into a flight of terror. Avoid tanning salons and scope out your nightclubs carefully.

• **Fire** — Frenzy whenever exposed to flame. This is another potentially useful Trait, as fire is a great danger to vampires. Most vampires, however, will not freak out when they see a campfire, or when someone lights a cigarette. You will.

Monstrous Beast Traits

• **Pain** — Frenzy whenever you take damage. Pain sends you running away screaming from whatever hurt you. The pain is so intense that you will forget to heal the wound with blood until you are calmed down. However, you will calm down five to 10 minutes after you get away from whatever hurt you.

• **Shame** — Frenzy whenever beaten in a Physical Challenge. You are so unsure of yourself that any loss in a Physical Challenge will break your will. You will try to get away from the person who won the Physical Challenge. See what the Harpies say after you have a mental breakdown when failing to knock down a door.

• **Religion** — Frenzy when confronted by a religious symbol. You've probably confronted someone with True Faith at some point. He messed with you so well that even a cross (or another appropriate religious artifact) will send you racing away. You can actually stand being around the object, but must enter a frenzy if you touch one or have it presented before you.

The Paths of Enlightenment

Vampires who possess humanity are constantly waging a battle between self-control and bestiality. Most do not want to frenzy, become violent and potentially murderous. The Sabbat, however, enjoy goading the Beast within and are often encouraged to frenzy. Consequently, without humanity, it would seem that they would all become crazed monsters and killing machines. However, each member of the Sabbat follows a Path of Enlightenment, chosen at character creation time. This Path provides a code of ethics that both prevents the vampire from constantly frenzying and establishes a sense of morality within a creature whose innate sense of right and wrong has long since perished. Path Traits assume the position of Beast Traits for Sabbat vampires by determining what kind of situation or circumstance will cause them to frenzy.

The Path of Caine

Most followers of this Path, primarily Assamite *antitribu*, are fairly reserved in character and knowledgeable in demeanor. They study philosophy, ancient languages and other subjects that will guide them along the path of wisdom; practice diablerie in order to grow closer to Caine; seek knowledge of Caine, and will pursue it at almost any cost, including their own unlives. They often desire hours alone to spend in meditation and actively fight against frenzy. They are generally respectful of their elders and aloof toward humans, believing that vampires were created by God and therefore should act according to their natures: predators don't usually get chummy with their food.

Path Traits

• **Diabolist** — Frenzy whenever you are prevented from committing diablerie. The victim must be present. If others are getting in your way, remove them; they are preventing you from becoming closer to Caine.

• **Abelite** — Frenzy whenever two or more of your packmates have succumbed to the Beast. You believe frenzy is for the weak and uncontrolled, not for you. Frenzy is the crime that caused Caine to murder Abel. Pack morale dropping so low makes you furious and forces you into unwilling frenzy.

• **Self-controlled** — Frenzy whenever anyone accuses you of having frenzied: you possess far too much self-control and have never in your unlife stooped so low.

• **Separatist** — Frenzy whenever you witness a vampire revealing himself to a mortal. Vampires are not meant to live alongside juicebags. You are the superior species and should hold yourselves aloof.

• **Scholar** — Frenzy whenever someone directly prevents you from acquiring knowledge of Caine. In other words, if a Nosferatu dangles a page of *The Book of Nod* in front of your face and refuses to let you see it, frenzy.

The Path of Cathari

Followers of this Path believe in the religious dualism of two creators: one good, who made the spiritual world, and the other the evil creator of the material world. As vampires, they are part of the material, or evil, world. They accept their inherent evil, seeking wealth and pleasure, avoiding Final Death, Embracing others without restraint and preying on mortals without qualms, because they also believe in reincarnation (specifically, that slain mortals will return, as will slain vampires). They avoid Final Death because they believe they will return as mortals, without their powers and pleasures, and they court temptation, succumbing to the Beast whenever they feel like it.

Path Traits

• **Pack Fiend** — Follow another vampire into frenzy whenever possible. What could be more fun? You should probably attack his or her target, but the next closest person will do if the other is entirely out of reach or already decimated.

• **Creator** — Frenzy whenever anyone in your pack hesitates to create new vampires. A victim of some sort must be present.

• **Final Death** — Frenzy whenever directly threatened with Final Death.

• **Materialist** — Frenzy whenever someone damages your possessions. Catharists believe in living comfortably and making their eternal life as enjoyable as possible. Destruction of your property is a blatant insult to your person and your code of ethics. Defend your stuff!

• **Hedonist** — Frenzy whenever you are restrained from seeking pleasure. This can include feeding, acquiring new property or engaging in activities you find enjoyable. You ought to enjoy your immortal gifts, and no one can prevent you from doing so.

The Path of Death and the Soul

This Path claims followers who neither fear Final Death nor seek it out. It is the oldest Path still practiced by the Sabbat today, having been founded as a Tzimisce death cult which transformed into a legitimate school of thought during the Age of Enlightenment. To this day, followers of the Path seek to study death in all its forms. They are fascinated by the occult and wish to discover all they can about its uses and theory.

Path Traits

• **Excavator** — Frenzy whenever anyone prevents you from occult discovery. Either they must be withholding information they have told you they possess or they have destroyed some puzzle-piece you desired.

• **Debater** — Frenzy whenever anyone blows you off during a philosophical discussion. You are attempting to discern the keys to the universe, and all they can do is snidely say, "Uh-hunh, whatever."

• **Discoverer** — Frenzy whenever you are prevented from killing for the sake of knowledge. You do not fear death; you wish to communicate with it. Allow no one to interfere with your experiments.

• **Passion** — Frenzy whenever three or more of your packmates begin talking in raised tones at once, battle-cries and the like excepted. You abhor the ruling of emotion over logic and refuse to tolerate it in those close to you. You must force them all to regain their composure, even if they are in little pieces by the time you do it!

• **Persona** — Frenzy whenever you are accused of emotional behavior or cowardice with regard to death. You do not fear Final Death. You will prove it right now.

The Path of Harmony

The Path of Harmony is the gentlest of the Paths currently practiced by the Sabbat. Its principles involve finding a balance between one's vampiric nature and remaining humanity. All life is precious, and though vampires must prey upon humans to live, they are not to be wasted or treated as valueless. This is a Path which calls for its followers to have strong morals, humane ideals and emotional stability. In some ways it is akin to the Path of Golconda. Harmonists oppose the needless taking of life, though they have no qualms about the taking of blood. They are often highly attuned to nature and seem the least evil members of the Sabbat.

Path Traits

• **Protector** — Frenzy whenever your pack needlessly kills a mortal. All life is to be respected, and if you kill all the mortal food, you also destroy yourselves.

• **Naturalist** — Frenzy whenever your pack needlessly destroys the environment. Dumping cans of gasoline or motor oil into a body of water, burning a forest or nature preserve or blowing up a building full of mortals are a few such events that set you off.

• **Drinker** — Frenzy whenever your feeding is interrupted. It is the natural order of things for you to engage in this behavior. Someone or something is disrupting your contact with your harmonious inner nature. Get 'em!

• **Dedication** — Frenzy whenever anyone for whom you have a Vinculum rating is destroyed. You abhor waste and will risk your own life for those to whom you are Bonded.

• **Failure** — Frenzy whenever you fail to achieve a goal. This goal can be as small as feeding before 10 P.M. or as large as capturing a renegade sect member. Any time you fail at something important to you, you are disrupting the natural order of things. You hate that!

Path of Honorable Accord

Followers of the Path of Honorable Accord believe in honor as a path to inner discipline. In order for the sect to operate at maximum potential, members must behave with honor and bravery. Devotees are fair to those they believe act justly and courageously and are harsh with the weak and cowardly. Personal honor requires followers of the Path to act generously, uphold the Sabbat, defend it and their comrades with their lives, and observe the rites and rituals faithfully. They place the goals and well-being of the sect above their own.

Path Traits

• **Ritualist** — Frenzy whenever anyone refuses to participate in the Vaulderie or any other Sabbat ritual. They are obviously untrustworthy and disloyal to the sect. They are the unquestionable target of your wrath.

• **Deception** — Frenzy whenever you discover a fellow Sabbat lying to you (or whenever you discover that one has done so in the past). You expect lies from the infidels, but one of your own? You must teach them to be honorable if it's the last thing you do!

• **Promise** — Frenzy whenever anyone breaks a promise to you, regardless of sect or species. You value honor above all else and violation of it makes you want to destroy.

• **Obedience** — Frenzy whenever someone disobeys your leader or, if you are the leader, disobeys you. The Sabbat must act in accordance with itself in order to successfully win the Jyhad. Disorder is not to be tolerated.

• **Insult** — Frenzy whenever you hear anyone, including sect members, slight, insult or blatantly show disrespect for the Sabbat. In order to be strong, you must all stand together. Those who tolerate insults or slights of any kind are cowards unwilling to defend their honor. Your first target is the person responsible for the insult; your second target is the person who allowed it to be said!

The Path of Power and the Inner Voice

The original followers of this Path, devotees of Lord Marcus of the Lasombra, are among the strongest leaders the sect has ever seen. Current followers of this path are passionately devoted to the success of the sect — and of themselves. They reflect the sect's need for power as well as its desire to create a world free of the Antediluvian threat. Followers of this Path are driven by instinct and take their own advice over anyone else's. They treat their underlings fairly and have a healthy sense of competition for positions of authority. Most believe they are the best leaders the sect has ever seen, even if they are not yet in a position of power. Devoted to ambition and strength, these vampires cannot bear humiliation and will not accept defeat. They will not back down in a fight if they believe they are right or physically stronger. Rarely do they offer anyone help without obtaining something in exchange, nor do they easily accept in positions of power those whom they believe to be weaker or less capable than themselves. However, if devotees of this Path find a leader whom they can respect, their loyalty will be unfailing.

Path Traits

• **Underling** — Frenzy whenever someone fails at a task you set them. To fail is to be weak, and only those who are strong will survive. You must punish those who are weak to teach them to be strong.

• **Humiliation** — Frenzy whenever you lose face in front of a crowd. This can be either publicly or within your pack. The loss of a Status Trait will invoke this frenzy.

• **Follower** — Frenzy whenever you are forced to follow someone you believe to be weak or unworthy. If you are a pack leader and a bishop you believe to be incompetent gives you a direct, obligatory task, the next person who even suggests a plan deserves to suffer. You can't take it out on your superior, but behind closed doors, look out!

• **Interruption** — Frenzy whenever anyone interrupts your private contemplation. You are trying to listen to your Inner Voice, and they are disrupting you. This is one of the primary foundations of your ethical beliefs. Teach them not to interrupt you again!

• **Respect** — Frenzy whenever you see a leader mistreating a successful underling. Those who complete their missions should be rewarded well. This Trait will also invoke frenzy if you see an underling disobey a leader whom you believe to be brave and worthy of her power. They must learn from the power of their superiors, not disrespect it.

Rules for Using Path Traits

The Sabbat are known to frenzy more than other vampires and have therefore learned more about how to ride the wave. Whenever a situation occurs where a Path Trait is invoked, the player must win or tie a Simple Test to see if she can resist tearing apart the individual or group in question. If the player loses, a second test may be performed to determine whether or not the character has enough control over her frenzy to focus on destroying property instead of people. If the second test is won, the player may attack an object of her choice instead of a person, group, etc. If the initial test is lost and the second test is also lost, the character must frenzy on the offending target. All tests involved with Path Traits are optional (Sabbat vampires *can* frenzy if they want to). Sabbat vampires may use two Willpower Traits to resist frenzy.

Acquisition of Path Traits

Vampires may only acquire Path Traits which belong to the particular Path they follow. Each Sabbat vampire Embraced more than a year before the start of gameplay possesses at least one Path Trait, acquired when she failed to follow her Path. For example, if a Tzimisce following the Path of Honorable Accord runs from a fair fight, he should receive a Path Trait as punishment. Narrators and Storytellers dispense Path Traits at their discretion. A character with five Path Traits can no longer control himself. His obsession with his Path drives him completely mad, and he can no longer distinguish between frenzy and normal conduct. The player must hand over the character to the Narrator or Storyteller.

Derangements

All Kindred possess some sort of neurotic need or even psychosis that guides their behavior. When you are under stress or find a situation offensive, a Derangement can "activate," controlling your actions. This curse is a form of frenzy. Other vampires who sense weakness in you can also activate your Derangements and cause you to frenzy.

Derangements are characterized by the situations that provoke their onset and by the behaviors that are exhibited when they are provoked. An activated Derangement always rules the mind of the character. Derangements are engaged only when a Narrator decrees, or when provoked by another character who knows you possess the Derangement. The other player must name the correct Derangement, the circumstances must be appropriate (you must be under some stress related to your Derangement) and your opponent must win a Social Challenge. Derangement frenzies last varying amounts of time, but 10 minutes is standard. They always end as soon as the circumstances of their onset are eliminated.

Sample Derangements include:

Amnesia

In highly traumatic situations, you sometimes forget who and even what you are. This typically occurs when you come face to face with your vampiric condition. You may simply forget the memory of a single situation, or you may forget everything about your identity, including your true nature. When events and situations that might remind you of your lost memories present themselves, those memories may return, sometimes doing so violently and sending you into a frenzy.

Crimson Rage

You have a tremendous capacity for rage and violence. When you are provoked, angered, bullied or threatened, you sometimes erupt into a frenzied rage during which you passionately attack the one who offended you. This frenzy may end as quickly as it began, but often only after you have vanquished your foe or have yourself been defeated.

Hunger

You suffer from a constant lust for blood. You crave it even when your Blood Pool is not yet depleted. When exposed to blood, you do whatever is necessary to get it. You'll attack for it if need be and drink it in reward. When you do feed, you seek to drink all you can until the source is depleted.

Immortal Terror

In the presence of sunlight and fire, you sometimes experience such extreme terror that you become completely unable to take any sort of action except to flee in fear. Even the sight of a lighter flame might instill you with a wave of fear. Your reaction is considered a frenzy, but it is a frenzy of fear rather than anger.

Intellectualization

You have recoiled from the horror of your situation and protect yourself by feeling nothing. You insulate yourself in a world of logic and intellectual vigor where emotions have no place. By isolating your incompatible needs and thoughts into separate compartments, you avoid losing control. However, the pressure inevitably mounts, and the dam eventually bursts. If your passion and emotion are thrust upon you during a stressful situation, you may frenzy. This frenzy may last for some time depending on how long it's been since you last "let off steam" (talk to a Narrator).

Manic-Depression

You suffer mood swings that take you from euphoric bliss to utter despair. You begin each game in either a manic or a depressive phase (Storyteller's call, or flip a coin). In your manic phase, you are wildly happy and excited — to the point that anyone or anything that tries to "bring you down" (i.e., make you listen to reason or frustrate you) may trigger a frenzy. You will readily spend Blood Traits for the most trivial of reasons. In your depressive phase, you act as per Undying Remorse (see below). You may switch from manic to depressive at the whim of the Storyteller.

Multiple Personalities

You possess a number of different personalities and may change Nature and Demeanor in times of great personal stress. Thus you behave in radically different ways at different times. Naturally this causes others to distrust and be wary of you. Your current personality persists until either you change personality again during a stressful situation or you expend Willpower to return to your "basic" personality.

Obsession

When a new person enters your life, or you are faced with a dramatic situation, you can sometimes become obsessed with that person or some fetish associated with the situation. This obsession is some sort of perverse ambition toward which you direct all your energy. If you are directly thwarted in your obsession, you may enter into a frenzy.

Paranoia

When someone threatens or stubbornly opposes you, you become convinced that the person is after you. You become obsessed with those you believe to be your enemies and make all kinds of insane preparations to protect yourself. During bouts of this Derangement, you trust no one and hold even your closest friends under suspicion. If you are pushed too far while in a paranoid state of mind, you may enter into a frenzy.

Perfection

When nothing seems to be going right, you can become obsessed with perfection. Everything must be perfect, and you use all your energy to prevent anything from going wrong. You focus all your attention on keeping everything about you in perfect, unaltered condition. When things become hopelessly confused, fault-ridden or messy, you may enter into a frenzy.

Power Madness

You can become so obsessed with control, power and dominance that you lose all control of yourself. When your ambitions are thwarted, you sometimes become enraged and attack those who oppose you. In general, you seek total and absolute control over everything and everyone around you.

Regression

In times of stress, when much is being demanded of you, you can become childlike, retreating to a less mature aspect of yourself. At such times you find it difficult to do anything for yourself, and without the aid of others, you are quite helpless. If, after you have become childlike, you are physically threatened, you may enter into a frenzy.

Undying Remorse

When reminded of some great evil or vile deed that you once committed, you sometimes enter into a state of such complete remorse and self-pity that you are incapable of taking any action except defending yourself. The pain can become so great that you enter into a frenzy.

Vengeful

When you have been wronged in any way, you can become so obsessed with vengeance that you direct all your energy toward it. You will not rest until your foes have been punished for their sins. If you are thwarted in this goal, you may enter into a frenzy. Once activated, this obsession persists until you have won your vengeance (or spent Willpower).

Sabbat Derangements

Only Sabbat characters may take the following Derangements:

Blood Addict

You are addicted to the blood of your pack. It gives you a physical and emotional high that can't be beat. For every period of six hours you go without consuming pack vitae, you lose one Physical Trait until you get your fix. When you wake, you are down one Physical Trait until you get pack blood.

Blood Taste

You hate the taste of blood. Your body craves it, but you think it tastes disgusting. You go out of your way to feed on drunks (the alcohol helps kill the taste), even going to such extremes as hanging out in mortal bars to get your dinners sloshed. You have tried everything to make it taste better, but nothing seems to help. The Vaulderie is torture; one person's blood is bad enough by itself, but the blood of a whole pack let out to go stale in the air like that is really vile. You must win or tie a Static Test each time you participate in the Vaulderie to see if you spit out the blood. If you fail the test, you must burn a Willpower Trait if you wish to keep the noxious fluid in your mouth.

Confusion

When you emerged from the grave during your Creation Rites, you had no idea what was going on. While you may have been nearly incapacitated by your intense confusion then, your befuddlement still lingers. Every time you see a Storyteller, or an individual you and she select, you become horribly confused about your Nature, identity and current events. This lasts for three to five minutes. You and the Storyteller might also choose to invoke your Derangement whenever you hear a prespecified word.

Creation Memory

High stress, especially violence, usually triggers plaguing memories of your Creation Rites. You may also choose a random factor and invoke the memories whenever you see a Storyteller or hear a specific word. Your thoughts will immediately return to the time of your creation, and you feel a pressing need to share these memories with whoever is around. This Derangement can be played as anything from a near frenzy to the burning desire to tell anecdotes. You are down one Mental Trait whenever you lapse into memory.

Handler

Guns are for pansies. If you can't do it with your hands, you don't deserve to do it. It is your philosophy that vampires are a superior species and should use their Disciplines as their war tools. Force the bravery out of those you fight. Ropes, stakes and weapons of nature are acceptable in a pinch, but firearms are a no-no.

Hangover Helper

You like to kill, but not if it's really hard work. You prefer to feed on those who have incapacitated themselves. You have cured many hangovers by feeding fully on those who have been in need of a remedy. Death is a wonderful cure for a hangover, and you feel so lovely afterwards.

Ideology Fanatic

You believe in Sabbat ideology so deeply that you are willing to do anything to spread the word. You believe in converting before killing, although those who are weak and stupid are not worth proselytizing. You are driven to convert from within the ranks of the enemy and will sacrifice your unlife to do so. Your personal mission is to win a willing Camarilla to the Sabbat. You may engage in one retest per night when

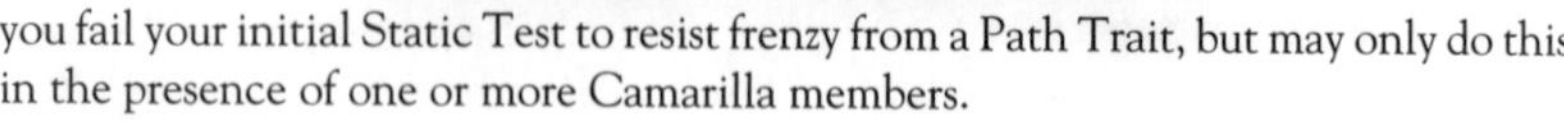

you fail your initial Static Test to resist frenzy from a Path Trait, but may only do this in the presence of one or more Camarilla members.

Mercenary

Killing is a gift. You are a great and powerful hunter and may, if you so choose, bestow the gift of death. However, it is not remotely worth your while if there is not an exchange, a gift for a gift. You happily kill for money, valuables or elder blood, but you refuse to bestow your gift without receiving one in exchange — the satisfaction of doing the sect or a friend a favor is not enough. You rarely kill those you feed from (a complete waste of time) and will not kill or feed from animals unless they have something you need, like a pelt, bones for some ritual you need performed or something else of value.

Obsession

You are obsessed with someone in your pack. You have a Vinculum of 10 for her and can't shake the desire to be constantly in her business and affections. You try to suck up as much of her attention and blood as you can and prevent others from getting what you crave.

Pack Feeding

You believe you can no longer feed on mortals or vampires other than those in your pack and become ill when vitae from other sources passes into your system. You have very high Vinculum ratings because all of your food comes from your pack. No one is sure if this is a psychological condition or a physical addiction, but it is reality for you. This Derangement makes diablerie almost impossible, and it is up to the Storyteller whether or not the character may spend Willpower Traits to attempt diablerie or to feed from another source.

Paranoid of Ancients

Everyone, everything that is not expressly Sabbat is a tool of the Antediluvians dedicated to your personal destruction. All of your loyal comrades are doomed along with you. You are suspicious and wary of anything outside the sect and will not infiltrate the Camarilla for fear of being taken over subliminally by their ancient masters. You feel the need to purify those who have made contact outside the sect to be sure they have not been overcome by the influence of the Ancients themselves.

Passion Player

While you strongly dislike and refuse to take part in torture, you believe that killing is your divine duty. Camarilla vampires avoid killing because they disrespect their Creator's wishes. They hide behind the Masquerade even when they do kill, though it is God's will for them to reveal themselves as the angels of death that they are. Each time you kill, you make sure your victim knows exactly what you are first.

Path Lust

You are obsessed with your code of ethics, following your Path to the letter and not backing down when some point regarding your Path philosophy is debated. Thanks to your overwhelming dedication to your Path, you enjoy the frenzy your Path Traits invoke. You may only engage in one Test per night to determine if you can control your frenzy.

Progenitor

You feel personally responsible for the procreation of your race. The world must be peopled with vampires, and the Sabbat (hopefully your pack) will sire them. You dream of breeding juicebags for food and having a universe run by the Sabbat, the superior species. All vampires who are not Sabbat are among the weak and are nothing more than prey.

Promise

You force people to promise you things in order to help them learn to keep their word. Honor is the only thing that will strengthen the sect, and it is your personal quest to be sure the sect is strong. You run the risk of frenzy if you discover that someone has lied to you.

Ritual Freak

The more rituals your pack performs, the happier you are. You insist on Vaulderie at least twice a night, once at rising and once before sleep. You encourage others to participate in rituals before every anticipated combat and after every unanticipated one. You believe everyone who ventures into the realm of infiltration should be blessed by a Sabbat priest before they go and upon each return.

Sect Fanatic

You love and are unwaveringly loyal to the Sabbat, for the Sabbat made you what you are today, a powerful hunter long past your miserable life as a juicebag. If it were not for your packmates or those who Embraced you, you would still be one of the small, weak and disgusting. Moreover, the ideology of the sect enchants you: You unquestioningly believe every word and will do anything to see that the Sabbat is victorious in the coming Jyhad with the Ancients. Consequently, killing the Camarilla infidels is a pleasure and a treat.

Strangler

You cannot bear the sight of blood. You shut your eyes during the Vaulderie and clean up as soon as possible afterwards. You enjoy killing and love the taste of blood, but must find ways to kill without bloodshed because the visuals are too much. If someone handed you a glass of blood outside of the Vaulderie, it would almost be too much for your stomach to handle.

Wrist Slitter

You love to bleed. You encourage others to drink from you at every opportunity and are willing to drink from them as well. You cannot live without that rush of your brothers' and sisters' blood in your veins. Even when you aren't hungry, you have been known to find a member of your pack and snatch their wrist, but you will not drain or harm them. The blood of immortals tastes delicious and full of truth, far richer than anything mortals could offer. To be denied pack blood is the worst punishment you could think of. You will, however, happily drain a mortal and then return to your pack to spread the wealth.

Merits and Flaws

Merits and Flaws allow you to describe your character in more detail than that provided by the basic character creation process. These new rules are optional: If you do not take Merits and Flaws for your character, you will not suffer a disadvantage in gameplay.

Merits may only be bought with Negative Traits. Flaws give you extra Negative Traits to spend on Merits or anything else. You can purchase as many Merits as you wish, up to the full amount of your Negative Traits (though that leaves you weak in other areas). Each Merit has a different cost, which is described in terms of Traits — if you wish to take it you must have already taken that number of Negative Traits (this includes Derangements or Flaws).

Each Flaw you purchase gives you additional Negative Traits that allow you to buy Merits. The amount of Negative Traits gained is listed with the Flaw. For instance, the Flaw: Light-Sensitive gives you three additional Negative Traits which you could use to buy the Merit: Unbondable, which costs three Traits.

Keep in mind that you can only take up to five Negative Traits' worth of Flaws (which makes it impossible for any character to have or spend more than 10 Negative Traits). Additionally, Merits and Flaws can only be bought when the character is first generated (unless the Storyteller makes an exception for someone who missed the opportunity earlier).

The Storyteller has the final say on all Merits and Flaws for each character, and may not choose to allow any in her game.

Psychological

Code of Honor (1 Trait Merit)

You have a personal code of ethics to which you strictly adhere. Even when you are frenzying, you will attempt to obey it. You can automatically resist most temptations that would bring you into conflict with your code. When battling supernatural persuasion that would make you violate your code, you gain two free bids to resist. You must construct your own personal code of honor in as much detail as you can, outlining the general rules of conduct by which you abide.

Higher Purpose (1 Trait Merit)

You have a goal that drives and directs you in everything. You do not concern yourself with petty matters and casual concerns because your higher purpose is everything. Though this purpose may sometimes force you to behave contrary to your survival instinct, it can also grant you great personal strength. You gain two extra bids on all rolls that have anything to do with this higher purpose. Be sure to discuss your idea for a higher purpose with the Storyteller.

If you have the Flaw: Driving Goal (see below), you cannot take this Merit.

Berserker (2 Trait Merit)

The Beast is in you, but you know how to direct and make use of it. You have the capacity to frenzy at will and are thus able to ignore your wound penalties until you've reached Torpor. However, you must pay the consequences of your actions while in frenzy, just as you normally would. Your chance of entering an unwilling frenzy is also unaffected.

Compulsion (1 Trait Flaw)

You have a psychological compulsion that causes you a number of different problems. Your compulsion may be for cleanliness, perfection, bragging, stealing, gaming, exaggeration or just talking. You may temporarily avoid your compulsion by spending a Willpower Trait, but it is in effect at all other times.

Dark Secret (1 Trait Flaw)

You have some sort of secret that, if uncovered, would embarrass you immensely and make you a pariah in the Kindred community. While it weighs on your mind at all times, it will only surface occasionally in stories — otherwise, it will begin to lose impact.

Intolerance (1 Trait Flaw)

You have an unreasoning dislike of a certain thing. It may be an animal, a class of person, a color, a situation, or just about anything at all. Some dislikes may be too trivial to be reflected here — a dislike of pomegranates or tissue paper, for instance, will have little effect on play in most chronicles. The Storyteller is the final arbiter on what you can pick to dislike.

Nightmares (1 Trait Flaw)

You experience horrendous nightmares every time you sleep, and memories of them haunt you during your waking hours. Sometimes the nightmares are so bad that you are one bid down on all your challenges for the next night (Narrator's discretion). Some of the nightmares may be so intense that you mistake them for reality.

Phobia — Mild (1 pt Flaw)

An overpowering fear of something causes you to instinctively and illogically avoid it. You must expend a Mental Trait if you wish to remain in the vicinity of the object of your fear.

Prey Exclusion (1 Trait Flaw)

You refuse to hunt a certain class of prey. For instance, an animal-lover might decide to hunt only humans, or a character might decide to spare a class of person she particularly admires: police, teachers, medical professionals, clergy, peace activists and so on. You are disturbed and occasionally frenzy when others feed from this type of prey (Narrator's discretion). If you accidentally feed upon this class of prey yourself, you will automatically frenzy and will risk gaining additional Derangements.

Ventrue cannot take this Flaw.

Overconfident (1 Trait Flaw)

You have an exaggerated and unshakable opinion of your own worth and capabilities — you never hesitate to trust your abilities, even in situations where you risk defeat. Because your abilities may not be enough, such overconfidence can be very dangerous. When you do fail, you quickly find someone or something else to blame. If you are convincing enough, you can infect others with your overconfidence.

Shy (1 Trait Flaw)

You are distinctly ill at ease when dealing with people and try to avoid social situations whenever possible. You are one bid down on all challenges concerned with social dealings. You are two bids down on any challenge in which you are the center of attention for a large group of people (over 10).

Soft Hearted (1 Trait Flaw)

You cannot stand to watch others suffer — not necessarily because you care about what happens to them, but simply because you dislike the intensity of emotion. If you are the direct cause of suffering and you witness it, you will experience nights of nausea and days of sleepless grief. You avoid situations where you might have to witness suffering and will do anything you can to protect others from it. Whenever you must witness suffering, you are one bid down on all challenges for the next hour.

Speech Impediment (1 Trait Flaw)

You have a stammer or some other speech impediment which hampers verbal communication. You should roleplay this impediment most of the time.

Low Self-Image (2 Trait Flaw)

You lack self-confidence and don't believe in yourself. You are two bids down in situations where you don't expect to succeed (at the Narrator's discretion, though the penalty might be limited to one bid if you help the Narrator by pointing out times when this Flaw might affect you). At the Narrator's option, you may be required to use a Willpower Trait to do things that require self-confidence, in situations that others would not be obliged to do so.

Short Fuse (2 Trait Flaw)

You are easily angered. You are two bids down when trying to avoid frenzy, no matter how you were provoked.

Vengeance (2 Trait Flaw)

You have a score to settle. This score may be from either your mortal or vampiric days. Either way, you are obsessed with wreaking vengeance on an individual (or perhaps an entire group), and make revenge your first priority in all situations. The need for vengeance can only be overcome by spending Willpower Traits, and even then it only temporarily subsides.

Driving Goal (3 Trait Flaw)

You have a personal goal, which sometimes compels and directs you in startling ways. The goal is always limitless in depth, and you can never truly achieve it. It could be to eradicate the Sabbat or achieve Golconda. Because you must work toward your goal throughout the chronicle (though you can avoid it for short periods by spending Willpower), it will get you into trouble and may jeopardize other actions.

Hatred (3 Trait Flaw)

You have an unreasoning hatred of a certain thing. This hate is total and largely uncontrollable. You may hate a species of animal, a class of person, a color, a situation — anything. You constantly pursue opportunities to harm the hated object or to gain power over it.

Mental

Light Sleeper (2 Trait Merit)

You can awaken instantly at any sign of trouble or danger, and do so without any sleepiness or hesitation.

Calm Heart (3 Trait Merit)

You are naturally calm and well-composed, and don't fly off the handle. You are always two bids up on all your tests to resist frenzy, no matter how you are provoked.

Iron Will (3 Trait Merit)

When you are determined and your mind is set, nothing can thwart you from your goals. You cannot be Dominated, nor can your mind be affected in any way by spells or rituals. However, the Storyteller may require you to spend Willpower points when extremely potent powers are directed at you.

Deep Sleeper (1 Trait Flaw)

When you sleep, it is very difficult for you to awaken. If you are awakened unexpectedly, you will be two bids down for all challenges during the following hour.

Confused (2 Trait Flaw)

You are often confused, and the world seems to be a very distorted and twisted place. Sometimes you are simply unable to make sense of things. You need to roleplay this behavior all the time to a small degree, but your confusion becomes especially strong whenever stimuli surround you (such as when a number of different people talk all at once, or you enter a nightclub with loud, pounding music). You may spend Willpower to override the effects of your confusion, but only temporarily.

Weak-Willed (3 Trait Flaw)

You are highly susceptible to Dominate and intimidation by others; you are, in fact, two bids down on all related challenges. Furthermore, you can employ your Willpower only when survival is at stake or it is appropriate to your Nature.

Absent-Minded (3 Trait Flaw)

Though you do not forget such things as Knowledges or Skills, you do forget names, addresses and when you last ate. In order to remember anything more than your own name and the location of your haven, you need to spend a Willpower Trait.

Awareness

Acute Hearing (1 Trait Merit)

You have exceptionally sharp hearing, even for a vampire. You automatically have two free bids on all challenges related to your hearing perception.

Acute Sense of Smell (1 Trait Merit)

You have an exceptionally keen sense of smell. You are automatically two bids up on all challenges relating to your sense of smell.

Acute Sense of Taste (1 Trait Merit)

You have an exceptionally keen sense of taste. You are automatically two bids up on any challenges relating directly to your sense of taste. You are able to make precise distinctions in taste.

Acute Vision (1 Trait Merit)

You have exceptionally keen eyesight. You are automatically one bid up on all challenges that involve sight perception.

Hard of Hearing (1 Trait Flaw)

Your hearing is defective. You are automatically two bids down on hearing perception tests. You may not take Acute Hearing if you take this Flaw.

Bad Sight (2 Trait Flaw)

Your sight is defective. You are automatically two bids down on all sight perception tests. This Flaw is neither nearsightedness nor farsightedness; it is a minor form of blindness and is not correctable. You may not take Acute Vision if you take this Flaw.

One Eye (2 Trait Flaw)

You have one eye — choose which, or determine randomly during character creation. You have no peripheral vision on your blind side, and are two bids down on any test requiring depth perception. This includes missile combat. Also, you may choose to cover one eye while you're playing.

Deaf (3 Trait Flaw)

You cannot hear sound. If you are not truly deaf this can be difficult to roleplay and you should get your Storyteller's approval before selecting this flaw.

Aptitudes

Computer Aptitude (1 Trait Merit)

You have a natural affinity with computers, automatically putting you two bids up on all tests to repair, construct or operate them.

Eat Food (1 Trait Merit)

You have the capacity to eat food. It's an ability you developed at an early point in your undead existence, or perhaps it has been a latent ability all along. This is considered disgusting by other Kindred, but can be of great assistance in maintaining the Masquerade.

Pitiable (1 Trait Merit)

There is something about you that others pity. This causes them to care for you as if you were a child (see the Archetypes section). Some Natures will not be affected by this Merit (e.g., Deviant and Fanatic), and some Demeanors may pretend they are not. You need to decide what it is about you that attracts such pity, and how much (or how little) you like it. When someone has challenged you with intent to do you harm, you may use this Merit as one free bid in your defense. You can never lose this bid as a result of a test, and you can use it only once in every challenge situation of this nature.

Daredevil (3 Trait Merit)

You are good at taking risks, and are even better at surviving them. You are one bid up on any challenge in which you try something particularly dangerous. This does not always apply to combat only when you are obviously outmatched.

Jack-of-All-Trades (5 Trait Merit)

You have a large pool of miscellaneous skills and knowledges obtained through your extensive travels, the jobs you've held, or just all-around know-how. You may automatically attempt any action even though you do not have the appropriate skill, and you need not spend Willpower to do so. However, if you lose this challenge, the Traits you bid are also gone. You can, of course, spend a Willpower Trait to avoid losing the Traits you just bid.

Illiterate (1 Trait Flaw)

You are unable to read or write.

Supernatural

Inoffensive to Animals (1 Trait Merit)

Animals do not fear or distrust you the way they do most Kindred. They treat you as they would any mortal and do not shy from your touch.

True Love (1 Trait Merit)

You have discovered, but may have lost (at least temporarily), a true love. Nonetheless, this love provides joy in a torrid existence usually devoid of such enlightened emotions. Whenever you are suffering, in danger or dejected, the thought of your true love is enough to give you the strength to persevere. In game terms, this love allows you two extra bids in a challenge, but only when you are actively striving to protect or come closer to your true love. Also, the power of your love may be powerful enough to protect you from other supernatural forces (Storyteller's discretion). However, your true love may also be a hindrance and require aid (or even rescue) from time to time.

Medium (2 Trait Merit)

You possess the natural affinity to sense and hear spirits. Though you cannot see them, you feel their presence and are able to speak with them when they are in the vicinity. It is even possible for you to summon them (through pleading and cajoling) to your presence. Spirits will not simply aid you or give you advice *gratis* — they will always want something in return.

Danger Sense (2 Trait Merit)

You have a sixth sense that warns you of danger. When you are in a perilous situation that would potentially surprise you, you have four seconds in which to react instead of the normal two seconds.

Faerie Affinity (2 Trait Merit)

Your presence does not frighten faeries; indeed, it attracts them, and you are naturally attuned to their ways.

Magic Resistance (2 Trait Merit)

You have an inherent resistance to the rituals of the Tremere and the spells of the mages of other creeds and orders. Although you may never learn the Discipline of Thaumaturgy, all such spells and rituals are two bids down when directed at you. Note: this includes all spells, beneficial and malign alike!

Occult Library (2 Trait Merit)

You possess a library of occult materials, which may include at least one version of *The Book of Nod*. You are not necessarily familiar with the contents of these volumes of knowledge (that is a function of your Abilities), but in time of need your library can be an invaluable source for research.

Spirit Mentor (3 Trait Merit)

You have a ghostly companion and guide. This spirit is able to employ a number of minor powers when it really struggles to exert itself (see "Haunted", below), but for the most part its benefit to you is through the advice it can give. This advice generally takes place between games, although at the Storyteller's discretion (and availability) this advice can occur during games as well. Be careful not to overtax your spirit mentor, as they can be taxed easily and thus be made unavailable for the remainder of the evening.

Unbondable (3 Trait Merit)

You are immune to being Blood Bound. No matter how much blood you drink from other vampires, you will never be Bound to them.

Luck (4 Trait Merit)

You were born lucky — or else the Devil looks after his own. Either way, you can repeat three failed tests per story. Only one repeat attempt may be made on any single test.

Destiny (4 Trait Merit)

You have a great destiny, though you may well not realize it. Your destiny will become more and more apparent as the chronicle continues. Prophecies and dreams guide your way, and grant you clues to your ultimate goal. The sense of direction and security that this feeling of destiny grants you helps you to overcome fear, depression and discouragement caused by anything not relevant to your destiny. Until your destiny is fulfilled, you may suffer setbacks, but nothing will thwart you permanently. How this is played is up to the Storyteller.

Guardian Angel (6 Trait Merit)

Someone or something watches over you and protects you from harm. You have no idea who or what it is, but you're sure it's there. You may be supernaturally protected, but you should never count upon your guardian angel. The Storyteller must decide why you are being watched over, and by what (not necessarily an angel).

True Faith (7 Trait Merit)

You have a deep-seated faith in and love for God, or whatever name you choose to call the Almighty. Perhaps your faith came to you before your Embrace and was strong enough to survive even this test; or, incredibly enough, the adversity you have experienced in your current condition has brought out what is best in you. You begin the game with one Trait of Faith. Your Faith provides you with an inner strength and comfort that continues to support you when all else betrays you. It can be used just like Willpower Traits to avoid frenzy and to retain your lost Traits in a challenge. The exact supernatural effects of Faith, if any, are completely up to the Storyteller (though it will typically have the effect of repelling Kindred). It will certainly vary from person to person and will almost never be obvious — some of the most saintly people have never performed a miracle greater than managing to touch an injured soul. The nature of any miracles you do perform will usually be tied to your own Nature, and you may never realize that you have been aided by a force beyond yourself.

You must not have any Derangements in order to choose this Merit, and if you ever get a permanent Derangement, you lose all Faith points and may only recover them through extensive penitence and work (and only when your Derangement is gone). No one may start the game with more than one Faith Trait. Additional Traits are only awarded at the Storyteller's discretion.

Cursed (1-5 Trait Flaw)

You have been cursed by someone or something with supernatural or magical powers. This curse is specific and detailed, it cannot be dispelled without extreme effort, and it can be life-threatening. Some examples follow:

- If you pass on a secret, your betrayal will later harm you in some way. (1 Trait)
- You stutter uncontrollably . (2 Traits)
- Tools often break or malfunction when you attempt to use them. (3 Traits)
- You are doomed to make enemies of those whom you love. (4 Traits)
- All of your accomplishments will inevitably, become somehow tainted. (5 Traits)

Repulsed by Garlic (1 Trait Flaw)

You cannot abide the smell of garlic, and the smallest taint of its scent will drive you from a room. The full force of its pungent odor will bring bloody tears to your face and render you nearly blind, while its touch can cause boils and even open wounds. You are always one bid down on any challenges when the smell of garlic is in the air.

Magic Susceptibility (2 Trait Flaw)

You are susceptible to the magical rituals of the Tremere, as well as to spells of mages of other creeds and orders. You are two bids down on all spells cast upon you, and all spells cast have twice normal effect on you.

Can't Cross Running Water (2 Trait Flaw)

You cannot cross running water unless you are at least 50 feet above it. "Running water" is any non-stagnant body of water more than two feet wide in any direction.

Repelled by Crosses (3 Trait Flaw)

You are repelled by the sight of ordinary crosses (just as if they were holy). Kindred who were of the Church prior to their Embrace are most likely to possess this Flaw; they perceive that their new form is a judgment from God.

Haunted (3 Trait Flaw)

A wraith that only you (and Mediums) can see and hear haunts you. It actively dislikes you and enjoys making your life miserable by insulting, berating and distracting you — especially when you need to keep your cool. It also has a number of minor powers it can use against you (once per story for each power): hide small objects; bring a "chill" over others, making them very ill at ease with you; cause a loud buzzing in your ear or the ears of others; move a small object such as a knife or pen; break a fragile item such as a bottle or mirror; trip you; or make eerie noises such as chains rattling. Yelling at the wraith can sometimes drive it away, but it will confuse those around you.

Dark Fate (5 Trait Flaw)

You are doomed to experience a most horrible demise or, worse, suffer eternal agony. No matter what you do, someday you will be out of the picture. In the end, all your efforts, your struggles and your dreams will come to naught. Your fate is certain and there is nothing you can do about it. Even more ghastly, you have partial knowledge of this, for you occasionally have visions of your fate — and they are most disturbing. The malaise these visions inspire in you can only be overcome through the use of Willpower and will return after each vision. At some point in the chronicle, you will indeed face your fate, but when and how is completely up to the Storyteller. Though you can't do anything about your fate, you can still attempt to reach some goal before it occurs, or at least try to make sure that your friends are not destroyed as well.

Light-Sensitive (5 Trait Flaw)

You are even more sensitive to sunlight than are other vampires. Sunlight causes twice the normal damage, and even moonlight (which is, after all, the reflected light of the sun) harms you. Indeed, even bright lights can be painful, but that pain can be mitigated by wearing sunglasses. When the moon is shining, the light it casts will cause wounds in the same way sunlight does for normal individuals. However, the wounds caused by the moon are not aggravated and can be healed normally.

Kindred Ties

Boon (1-3 Trait Merit)

An elder owes you a favor because of something either you or your sire once did for him. The extent of the boon owed to you depends on how many Traits you spend. One Trait would indicate a relatively minor boon, while three Traits would indicate that the elder probably owes you his unlife. See the rules on Prestation (Page 127) for more information. Generally, this elder should be a Narrator character. However, if both players are willing, this elder can be another player.

Prestigious Sire (1 Trait Merit)

Your Sire had or has great Status in the Camarilla, and this has accorded you a peculiar honor. Most treat you respectfully as a result, while some have only contempt for you, believing you to be nothing compared to them. This prestige could greatly aid you when dealing with elders acquainted with your sire. Indeed, your sire's contacts may actually approach you at some point offering aid. Though your sire may no longer have contact with you, the simple fact of your ancestry has marked you forever.

Special Gift (1-3 Trait Merit)

Your sire gave you a valuable gift after the Embrace. The Storyteller should create something suitable, and will decide how much a particular item is worth.

Reputation (2 Trait Merit)

You have a good reputation among the Kindred of your chosen city. This may be your own reputation, or it may be derived from your sire. You are able to interact with other Kindred as if you were one Status Trait higher than you actually are. You won't actually have an additional Status Trait to bid or spend, however, because you don't actually have this status (you are merely *perceived* as having it). A character with this Merit may not take the Flaw: Notoriety.

Clan Friendship (3 Trait Merit)

For any number of different reasons — appearance, bearing, background or demeanor — something about you appeals to members of a clan other than your own (your choice). You are one bid up on all challenges related to social dealings with members of this clan. This can be a two-edged sword; you are also marked by others as a sympathizer with that clan, whether you like it (or deny it!) or not.

Pawn (3 Trait Merit)

You can manipulate and have some control over another vampire — one of weaker generation than yourself. Your hold was likely formed through Blood Bond, but can also come from a variety of other sources, such as blackmail, bribes or threats — you decide. The pawn does not necessarily know that it is being controlled. Because this Merit does not always lend itself well to a **Mind's Eye Theatre** setting, be certain to consult your Storyteller before selecting it.

Enemy (1-5 Trait Flaw)

You have an enemy, or perhaps a group of enemies, who seek to harm you. The value of the Flaw determines how powerful these enemies are. The most powerful enemies (Methuselahs or archmages) would be five-Trait Flaws, while someone nearer to your own power would be worth only one Trait. You must decide who your enemy is and how you became enemies in the first place.

Infamous Sire (1 Trait Flaw)

Your sire was, and perhaps still is, distrusted and disliked by many Kindred in the city. As a result, you are distrusted and disliked as well. This is a heavy load, and one not easily shed.

Insane Sire (1 Trait Flaw)

Your sire has completely lost his grip on reality and has become dangerously insane. Any wrong he commits may affect your standing, and some of your sire's dangerous schemes may somehow involve you. Because their sires are already assumed to be insane, Malkavians cannot take this Flaw.

Mistaken Identity (1 Trait Flaw)

You look similar to another Kindred and are often mistaken for her, much to your chagrin. This individual's allies will approach you and tell you things you do not want to hear, her enemies will attempt to do away with you, and others will treat you in odd ways. Ultimately, you might be able to sort out things, but it will take tremendous effort.

Sire's Resentment (1 Trait Flaw)

Your sire dislikes you and wishes you ill. Given the smallest opportunity, your sire will seek to do you harm and may even attack you if provoked. Your sire's friends will also work against you, and many elders will thus resent you.

Twisted Upbringing (1 Trait Flaw)

Your sire was quite malevolent and taught you all the wrong things about Kindred society. All your beliefs about how vampires interact are wrong, and your faulty beliefs are likely to get you into a great deal of trouble. Over time, after many hard lessons, you can overcome this bad start (the Storyteller will tell you when). But until then, you will continue to believe what you were first told, no matter how others try to "trick" you into thinking otherwise.

Clan Enmity (2 Trait Flaw)

For some reason, something about you inspires contempt or hatred in members of a clan other than your own. You are two bids down on all tests for social dealings with members of this other clan. You can select the enemy clan randomly or choose it.

Diabolic Sire (2 Trait Flaw)

Your sire is engaged in acts that could cause a tremendous uproar in the Camarilla. She could be wantonly breaking the Masquerade, or hunting down the elders of the city and feasting on their blood. Archons are likely to come to you in order to discover your sire's whereabouts, and they may not believe you if you tell them you do not know.

Notoriety (3 Trait Flaw)

You have a bad reputation among the Kindred of your chosen city. This may be your own reputation, or it may be derived from your sire. Other Kindred treat you as if you have one Status Trait less than you actually do. Although you will still have this Trait to spend and bid, other Kindred will not immediately recognize it, unless they're forced to. A character with this Flaw may not take the Merit: Reputation.

Physical

These Merits and Flaws deal with your health and physical makeup.

Baby Face (1 Trait Merit)

You look more human than other vampires, enabling you to fit in the human world much more easily. Your skin is pink, you never really stopped breathing (even though you don't need to) and even sneezing comes naturally. You can make your heart beat as long as you have at least one Blood Trait. Nosferatu cannot take this Merit.

Double-jointed (1 Trait Merit)

You are unusually supple. You are one bid up on all Physical Challenges requiring body flexibility. Squeezing through a tiny space is one example of a use for this Merit.

Misplaced Heart (2 Trait Merit)

Your heart has actually moved within your body, though no more than two feet from its original position near the middle of your chest. Those who attempt to stake you find it very difficult to find the right location (which should be your most tightly guarded secret).

Efficient Digestion (3 Trait Merit)

You are able to draw more than the usual amount of nourishment from blood. Each two Blood Traits ingested increases your Blood Pool by three. Round down so leftover 'halves' are ignored. For instance, taking four Blood Traits raises the Blood Pool by six, and so does taking five Blood Traits.

Huge Size (4 Trait Merit)

You are abnormally large in size, possibly over seven feet tall and 400 pounds in weight. You therefore have one additional Health Level and are able to suffer more harm before you are incapacitated. Treat this extra level as one extra Healthy Level, with no penalties to rolls. When acting this part, players should dress appropriately with bulky clothes, unless they already have a stature that approximates this Merit.

Allergic (1-3 Trait Flaw)

You are allergic to some substance in a manner not unlike mortal allergies. While you do not get hives or sneeze, you are incapacitated by your reaction. If the substance was in the blood you drank, the reaction will be very strong, though touch alone is enough to disturb you. If it was in the blood, you will be three bids down on all challenges for 20 minutes. If you just touched it, the penalty is reduced to one bid. Choose from the list below or make up the substance to which you are allergic.

- Plastic: 1 Trait
- Illegal Drugs: 2 Traits
- Alcohol: 2 Traits
- Metal: 3 Traits

Disfigured (2 Trait Flaw)

A hideous disfigurement makes you easy to notice as well as to remember. You cannot take any Social Traits that would compliment your Appearance, much like the Nosferatu (who cannot take this Flaw). Furthermore, you are two bids down on any Social Challenge (except Intimidation) when your true appearance is visible.

Selective Digestion (2 Trait Flaw)

You can digest only certain types of blood. You can choose whether you can drink only cold blood (the blood of a dead person), blood with the taste of fear (found in blood only in moments of terror), blood with the taste of joy, or perhaps only certain blood types (A+, 0-, etc.). Ventrue characters may not take this Flaw, since they already have something like it through their clan weakness.

Child (3 Trait Flaw)

You were a small child at the time of the Embrace. Although time and experience may have changed your outlook, you are stuck with a child's body. You find it difficult to be taken seriously by others (two bid penalty to all relevant tests). Because you have never before experienced any sort of transformation change (never having undergone the experience of puberty), you are ill suited to withstanding the demands of the Hunger. Additionally, certain clubs may not admit you, because you are "underage."

Deformity (3 Trait Flaw)

You have some kind of deformity — a misshapen limb, a hunchback or whatever — which affects your interactions with others and may inconvenience you physically. You are one bid down on all tests of a physical nature. Furthermore, all challenges related to physical appearance are two bids down.

Lame (3 Trait Flaw)

Your legs are injured or otherwise prevented from working effectively. You suffer a three bid penalty to all tests related to movement.

Monstrous (3 Trait Flaw)

There is something wholly monstrous about you, something that makes you even more hideous than a Nosferatu. You scarcely look human, but the manner in which you differ is up to you. Perhaps you have grown scales or warts all over your body, or perhaps the scream you issued when you died has been permanently frozen on your face. You cannot win a Social Challenge (other than Intimidation) when your true visage is apparent. Nosferatu cannot take this Flaw.

One Arm (3 Trait Flaw)

You have only one arm — choose which, or determine randomly at character creation. You lost your arm before the Embrace and thus are accustomed to using your remaining hand, so you suffer no offhand penalty. However, you do suffer a two bid penalty to any test where two hands would normally be needed to perform a task. If you have two arms, when acting this part, one should hang limp at your side or be tied behind your back.

Permanent Wound (3 Trait Flaw)

You suffered injuries during the Embrace, which your sire did nothing to repair. You start each night at the Wounded Health Level. This can be healed like normal damage, but each evening, after sleep, your wounds always return.

Mute (4 Trait Flaw)

Your vocal apparatus does not function, and you cannot speak at all. You can communicate through other means — typically writing or signing.

Thin-Blooded (4 Trait Flaw)

You have weak blood and are unable to use it for anything but sustaining yourself from night to night and healing your wounds. Blood cannot be used to add to your Physical Traits, to fuel blood Disciplines or to create a Blood Bond. Moreover, you will not always be able to create a vampire. Half the time the Embrace will simply not work.

Paraplegic (5 Trait Flaw)

You can hardly move without assistance, such as a pair of crutches or a wheelchair. Even then it can be painful and cumbersome to do so. The Storyteller and you should take care to roleplay this Flaw correctly, no matter how difficult it makes things. A character may not take this Flaw along with the Merit: Double-jointed.

Experience

By doing, we learn how to improve what we've done. Thus, characters can take experience points (awarded for superior roleplaying, expert leadership or even simple survival) and convert them into improved statistics. Only one Ability, Trait or Discipline should be gained per session.

Using Experience

After experience points have been awarded, they may be spent to purchase new Abilities, Traits and Disciplines, improving upon the character and giving the player a sense of satisfaction as he watches his character grow and improve. The following lists the cost of improving Traits, Abilities and Disciplines:

• **New Attribute Trait** — One experience point per Trait.

• **New Ability** — One experience point per Ability Trait.

• **New Discipline** — Three experience points for Basic Disciplines, six for Intermediate Disciplines and nine for Advanced Disciplines. It costs an additional point to learn a Discipline outside of your clan.

• **New Willpower** — Three experience per Trait.

• **Buy off Negative Trait** — Two experience points per Trait.

• **New Influence** — One point per Influence Trait, with Storyteller approval.

• **New Merit** — The cost of the Merit, with Storyteller approval.

• **Buy off Existing Flaw** — The point cost of the Flaw, with Storyteller approval. This should not happen instantaneously, and it is recommended that Storytellers find a way to integrate the removal of a character's Flaw into an ongoing plotline.

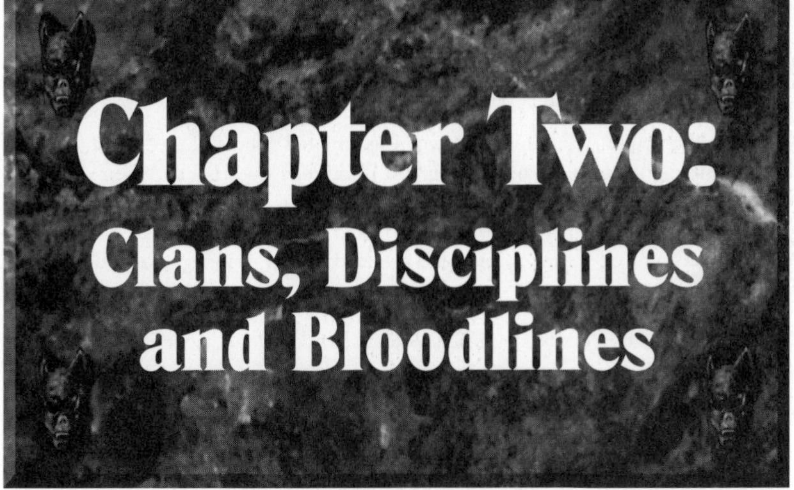

Chapter Two: Clans, Disciplines and Bloodlines

Included in this chapter are all of the clans and bloodlines available to players of **The Masquerade**. Also listed are the Disciplines that characters can learn.

Clans

Every vampire is a member of a clan (or bloodline, in rare instances). Each clan has its unique signature, perspective and powers. Below is a brief summary of the 13 clans, as well as several of the more commonly encountered bloodlines.

Assamite

Vampires are the killers in the night, and none more so than the Assamites, slayers of both Kindred and kine. Called in regularly by the world's Justicars as Archons and by princes as assassins, no clan is more feared by the Kindred. Secretive and taciturn, Assamites will travel anywhere in search of their targets, accepting as payment the blood of their employers. Assamites have gained a fearsome reputation as assassins of most remarkable skill.

Any Assamite hoping to reduce her generation must gather 200 Blood Traits from non-Assamite vampires of equal or lower generation for the potion to be effective — it usually takes decades to gather that much blood. The blood is generally stored in vials and canisters and is an Assamite's most prized possession. Each Assamite gives her sire a 10th of the blood she gathers.

Clan Disciplines: Celerity, Obfuscate (Obfuscate, Mask of 1000 Faces), Quietus

Advantage: Assamites are closely bound and extremely supportive of one another; many Kindred fear the retribution of their clan. Because of this, few Assamites are ever challenged outside of a contract. Additionally, Assamites have a special means of lowering their generation, as detailed above.

Disadvantage: Assamites have two blood-related disadvantages. The first is the clan requirement that all its members give a 10 percent blood tithe to their sires. The second is that they are unable to imbibe the blood of other Kindred, and if it is forced into them it acts as a toxin. Each Blood Point from another Kindred that somehow enters an Assamite's system inflicts one Health Level of non-aggravated damage.

Assamite *Antitribu*

Note: Assamite *antitribu* are not subject to the normal clan weakness and can drink other Kindred's blood with impunity.

Disciplines: Celerity, Obfuscate, Quietus

Advantage: Assamite *antitribu* are not bound in any way to their former clan. The Black Hand is growing stronger, and since most Sabbat Assamites are created to go into Hand service, they are privy to many secrets that even Sabbat clergy may not know.

Disadvantage: Assamite *antitribu* can easily become addicted to the blood of other vampires. Each time they engage in the Vaulderie, the character must engage in a Static Challenge to determine if she gains an addiction to the blood. If she loses the challenge, she gains the addiction and must attempt to drink that same blood mixture at least twice more during the night. One Willpower Trait may be spent to prevent the addiction.

Preferred Paths: Path of Caine (most follow this path), Path of Honorable Accord.

Brujah

The Brujah are the most factious and antisocial of all clans. Rebels, its members forever search for the ultimate expression of their individuality. They tend to be stubborn, aggressive, ruthless, sensitive to slights and extremely vengeful. Brujah appear in a myriad of guises: punks, socialists, skinheads, beat poets, bikers, philosophers, rockers, goths, freaks and anarchists.

Disciplines: Celerity, Potence, Presence

Advantage: Centuries of rebellion, sometimes in the face of insurmountable odds, have forged a powerful "us against them" attitude among Brujah clan members. Brujah are quick to side with their own, even at the risk of personal danger. Prestation is neither requested nor offered for this aid. They frown upon refusing a brother aid, resulting in the offender's loss of a Status Trait and possibly even ostracism. Those who overuse or abuse this advantage will find themselves losing Status. A Brujah who has lost all her Status Traits can no longer expect the aid of her former allies, who may ignore her at no risk.

The exception to this are the anarch Brujah, who have their own informal sort of status outside the Camarilla's social structure. These Brujah, although they have no recognized or official status, still willingly answer the call when help is needed.

Disadvantage: As a whole, the Brujah bloodline is cursed with an internalized, hair-trigger rage. While many members spend their existence trying to come to grips with the destructive force within themselves, few have ever conquered it. Whenever a Brujah slips into a frenzy, she gives herself over to it entirely. All Brujah therefore begin with the Negative Mental Trait: Violent. The character receives no compensation for this Negative Trait, nor may it be bought off or lost by any means short of Golconda.

Brujah *Antitribu*

Disciplines: Celerity, Potence, Presence

Advantage: Brujah *antitribu* blend in well with other non-Sabbat Brujah and are very persuasive. They can be extremely subtle recruiters, their genuine natures leading others to believe they are correct in opinion and philosophy.

Disadvantage: Brujah *antitribu* frenzy extremely easily, and they enjoy it. Generally very nice people until you make them angry, Brujah *antitribu* gain Path Traits at almost twice the rate of other vampires. Individual vampires, of course, can control this gain.

Preferred Paths: Path of Power and the Inner Voice, Path of Cathari or Path of Harmony.

Followers of Set

The Followers of Set, or Setites as they often call themselves, constitute one of the most widely loathed clans in the world. The Camarilla decision to ask the Setites to join came only after weeks of divisive debate, and the fact that few Setites responded to the call was met with a wave of relief from the young sect.

The explanation for this reaction lies with the very nature of the Setites. Masters of moral and spiritual corruption, they seem to have an uncanny ability to find the weakness in any organization or individual, as well as an irresistible urge to exploit it. Drugs, sex, money and power are their weapons of corruption, and they take great delight in using them against Kindred and kine alike. Fierce, cunning and amoral manipulators, the Setites believe that the power of decay and corruption is absolute.

Clan Disciplines: Obfuscate (Obfuscate, Mask of 1000 Faces), Presence (Awe, Entrancement), Serpentis

Advantage: The Followers of Set are all extremely well connected in the criminal underworld. Consequently, they automatically start with one additional Influence in Politics, Street, or Underworld (at the player's discretion).

Disadvantage: Setites are extremely susceptible to sunlight. Double the Health Levels inflicted from any exposure to it. They are also susceptible to bright lights and are one bid down on all challenges while in bright light (i.e., spotlights, nightclub strobe lights, searchlights, magnesium flares, etc.).

Serpents of the Light

Disciplines: Obfuscate, Presence, Serpentis

Advantage: Exceedingly subtle and cunning, these vampires enjoy a certain amount of Status within their packs because they are unusually effective.

Disadvantage: Serpents of the Light are extremely sensitive to light. They are down one Physical Trait when in the presence of light any brighter than a three-quarters moon or a 100-watt lightbulb.

Preferred Paths: Path of Caine, Path of Cathari, Path of Death and the Soul

Gangrel

The Gangrel are wanderers, rarely remaining in one place for any significant period of time. In this, they differ drastically from most Kindred, who usually find a haven and jealously guard it. There is no record of who the eldest of the Gangrel line might be, and the clan has no established leaders. On the whole, Gangrel seem unconcerned with such things. They are known for being withdrawn, quiet and solemn.

Disciplines: Animalism, Fortitude, Protean

Clan Advantage: Gangrel rarely allow themselves to be tied down to one place for long, except when they feel there is some task or goal they must accomplish before moving on. As a result, few princes enforce the laws of Presentation upon the nomadic Gangrel. This is not to say that a prince cannot tell them to leave, but they rarely worry about seeking out the prince of every domain in which they wander.

Furthermore, when Gangrel deal with werewolves, they do not show a taint of the Wyrm. Only Gangrel who have three or more Beast Traits will bear the scent of the Wyrm (see **The Apocalypse**). This is obviously of great advantage when dealing with the already unpredictable Garou.

Clan Disadvantages: Each time the Beast (in the form of a Beast Trait-provoked frenzy) washes over a Gangrel, it leaves a mark of its passing in its wake. These marks take the form of animalistic features, like a hairy mane, pointed ears or slitted pupils. The player should record these on her character sheet and include them in her description. For every three of these features she possesses, the character must take either Bestial or Repugnant as a Negative Social Trait. These Traits can and probably will be taken multiple times as the Kindred becomes more and more animalistic.

Gangrel *Antitribu*

Disciplines: City Gangrel — Celerity, Obfuscate, Protean; Country Gangrel — Animalism, Fortitude, Protean

Advantage: Gangrel *antitribu* are trustworthy and enjoy many privileges within the sect because of their devotion and sound instincts. Most are quite fearless, but they are rarely reckless. When missions of necessity are planned, Gangrel are often some of the first to volunteer, and the most likely to return.

Disadvantage: After a while, these Gangrel start to look like the animals they become. Each time they frenzy, their Beast Traits grow more pronounced. This makes it hard for Gangrel *antitribu* to pass as anything other than what they are.

Preferred Paths: The Path of Harmony and Path of Honorable Accord.

Giovanni

No other clan is more intent on maintaining a front of respectability than the Giovanni, and none is more repulsive at heart. Giovanni vampires are rich merchants, speculators and investors. They spend most of their nights manipulating their vast assets from skyscraper offices, and the rest in crypts and mausoleums performing necromantic rites. Every member of this clan is also a member of the Giovanni family. By long-standing tradition, Giovanni only Embrace those of their own mortal lineage, and most of their Retainers and ghouls are also of the family. As children, three members of each generation are chosen to be Embraced when they are ready and are carefully raised in order to prepare them for their destiny. Others in the family may be Embraced later in their lives, as a reward for extraordinary service. Because all Giovanni are related by blood (in both senses), they are extremely loyal to one another, and betrayal by one of them is unthinkable.

Clan Disciplines: Dominate (Command, Forgetful Mind), Necromancy, Potence

Advantage: The Giovanni hold considerable sway over mortal affairs, especially finances. As a result, Giovanni characters automatically gain one additional influence in Finance. Alternately, they can exchange this influence for an additional Health Influence (granting access to morgues and the like).

Disadvantage: Living creatures upon whom the Giovanni feed take twice as much damage as they otherwise should. Thus, if a Giovanni drank one Blood Point from a living human, her victim would take two Health Levels of damage. For this reason, Giovanni are among the most prominent blood bankers and, whenever possible, take vitæ from people who have died moments before.

Lasombra

Elegant and predatory, openly aggressive and competitive, the Lasombra are the leaders of the Sabbat. Almost all of the intrigue within the sect springs from the Lasombra, and they long ago earned the respect of the other clans during the Anarch Revolt, when they joined with a band of Assamites and destroyed their own Antediluvian. This act won them Status points which they still hold over the heads of the other clans in times of desperation and debate.

Disciplines: Dominate, Obtenebration, Potence

Advantage: The Lasombra are greatly respected and lead most groups within the sect, with the exception of the Black Hand.

Disadvantage: Lasombra are invisible in mirrors and on film of any kind. In mortal society, this flaw immediately identifies them as supernatural. It also makes them poor infiltrators into the Camarilla. (Although Camarilla vampires sometimes do not appear in mirrors, it is extremely rare, and it will draw attention).

Preferred Paths: Path of Power and the Inner Voice, Path of Honorable Accord

Malkavian

In each Kindred soul burns the corrupting breath of a ravenous Beast. The Beast scars each immortal differently, granting powers and weaknesses according to bloodline and ancestry. To those of Malkavian blood, the Beast has granted wisdom, insight and madness. While the "weak-minded" erect barriers to protect their "sanity," Malkavians revel in the chaos of their reality. Scoffing at the petty intrigues of other Kindred the way an adult scoffs at a child's infatuation with toys, Malkavians manipulate others to alleviate their boredom. They believe the insights they have distilled from madness prove that all other Kindred are insane.

Disciplines: Auspex, Dominate, Obfuscate

Clan Advantage: A large number of Malkav's children cavort through their vampiric existence as carefree, if not careless, buffoons. At least, this is how the majority of Kindred perceive them. As a result, once per evening, any Malkavian may choose to ignore one of the following: any use of Status Traits in a Social Challenge, the loss of Status, or any of the other uses of Status. This benefit may only be evoked in a single situation and can only benefit the Malkavian personally. Any Status Traits risked in a challenge are neither lost, nor are they bid — they simply do not exist to the Malkavian.

Clan Disadvantage: While any Kindred can become insane during the course of his existence, Malkavians begin that way. Upon character creation, one Derangement must be chosen to represent the madness their bloodline must bear (or enjoy, as the case may be). Furthermore, this Derangement is always active and should be continually played by the Malkavian. These Derangements can never be "bought off" or removed during the course of a chronicle.

Malkavian *Antitribu*

Disciplines: Auspex, Dementation, Obfuscate

Advantage: Malkavian *antitribu* are genuinely chaotic. They function primarily on the Traits dictated by their Derangements, and they are not bound by the stereotypes and quirks of other clans.

Disadvantage: Malkavian *antitribu* are genuinely chaotic. They begin the game with two Derangements and may continue to gain more as time goes by. They are by and large not well trusted because of their unstable natures and are always watched closely by their packs.

Preferred Paths: A Malkavian may follow any Path or her own medley of them all.

Nosferatu

Of all the clans, the Nosferatu appear the least human, resembling feral animals. Their smell and appearance are revolting — one might even say monstrous. Some have long bulbous ears, coarse-skinned skulls covered with tufts of hair or elongated faces covered with disgusting warts and lumps. Nosferatu only Embrace those mortals who are twisted in one way or another: emotionally, physically, spiritually or intellectually. They consider the Embrace too horrific to bestow on worthwhile human beings. By changing mortals into vampires, the sires hope to somehow redeem their childer. It's surprising how often this works. Underneath their grim exteriors, the Nosferatu are practical and mostly sane.

Disciplines: Animalism, Obfuscate, Potence

Clan Advantage: The Nosferatu are the undisputed masters of the undercity. In any city where the Nosferatu have had a chance to set up shop, they will be able to enjoy several advantages by using the city's sewer system. First of all, a portion of the city's sewers are the sole property of the Nosferatu clan; no others can access this area without a Nosferatu guide, the use of powerful Disciplines or Storyteller dispensation. Attempting to do so will result in the character either getting lost, alerting the Nosferatu or setting off any number of traps or precautions taken by the sewers' true masters. Furthermore, a Nosferatu standing near a sewer grate, manhole cover or the like may use it for the "Fair Escape" rule.

Clan Disadvantage: Because of their horrifying countenances, a Nosferatu may not initiate Social Challenges with others while her true visage is apparent. The exception to this is Social Challenges involving intimidation or threatening an opponent.

Nosferatu *Antitribu*

Disciplines: Animalism, Obfuscate, Potence

Advantage: The Nosferatu are potent information-gatherers, managing to gain access to just about everything. Their cordial ties with their Camarilla counterparts allows them more freedom than other Sabbat experience with regard to travel behind enemy lines.

Disadvantage: The Nosferatu are hideously ugly. They all have an Appearance rating of 0 and lose three Social Traits whenever they are in their natural form (i.e. not using Mask of the 1000 Faces).

Preferred Paths: Path of Caine, Path of Harmony, Path of Honorable Accord

Panders

The Panders are the Sabbat Caitiff. They were clanless until a man named Joseph Pander came along in 1952 and gathered the stray vampires under his wing. Pander himself now holds the rank of *priscus*, which is probably part of the reason those calling themselves Panders are able to function as a clan as well as a political faction within the sect.

Disciplines: Whatever their sire taught them. (Dementation, Obtenebration and Vicissitude are clan-specific and are not available to Panders except under the circumstances noted in "Disciplines" below.)

Advantage: Panders have very few guidelines and therefore possess certain freedoms other vampires within the Sabbat do not. Most of their advantages fall into play during character creation. Also, because they are a relatively new clan, each character has a significant say in what the future of the clan will be like.

Disadvantage: No Pander may begin the game with more than two Status Traits, and most begin with none, unless their pack has bestowed Status upon them.

Preferred Paths: Path of Cathari, Path of Honorable Accord.

Ravnos

The Ravnos share many characteristics with the Gangrel, but there is no other clan from which they differ more. Despite their shared Gypsy heritage, hatred of authority and nomadic lifestyle, Ravnos and Gangrel are often found in diametrical opposition. The Gangrel are loners; the Ravnos love companionship. The Gangrel are combative; the Ravnos try to avoid direct physical confrontations. The Gangrel are honest and forthright; the Ravnos are masters of lies and deceit. Theft and con games are the most prominent aspects of the Ravnos lifestyle. Constant traveling makes it harder for Ravnos to be caught engaging in their favorite pastimes and gives them an infinite number of marks and shills to exploit. Ravnos find no greater pleasure than taking advantage of other Kindred, and a vampire is advised to watch his wallet, gun and pants while these Licks are around.

Clan Disciplines: Animalism (Beast Within), Chimerstry, Fortitude

Advantage: This clan is often accepted into many cities, mostly because many princes prefer one Ravnos to the mass visitation that would occur should he try to bar his borders. Because of this, few princes will refuse a Ravnos entrance into their domain. Furthermore, as deception and trickery are the calling cards of the clan, Kindred rarely attempt retribution against clan members no matter how outrageous their stunts become. Instead, individual marks usually blame themselves for their own stupidity.

Disadvantage: Ravnos are infamous for their trickery. Each has a specific area of thievery and deception which she specializes in and practices every chance she gets. The player should decide during the creation process what type of "crime" attracts the character, and should indulge it at least once per session. Some common habits include con games, thievery, gambling, cheating and extortion. Players and Storytellers should feel free to create new ones.

Furthermore, because of the Ravnos' habit of dishonesty, they are thoroughly distrusted by the rest of the Kindred population.

Ravnos *Antitribu*

Disciplines: Animalism, Chimerstry, Fortitude

Advantage: Ravnos *antitribu* function well in teams, with some members working as distractions while their packmates commit crimes. They work hard to find ways to gain their freedom by seeming harmless.

Disadvantage: Unfortunately, most Kindred in positions of power know the truth: Ravnos *antitribu* are far from harmless. They are crafty and devious, and the Sabbat needs them that way. They are usually fairly low on Status and high on Derangements.

Preferred Paths: Path of Harmony, Path of Cathari

Toreador

The members of this clan are known for their hedonistic tendencies, although that description is a misinterpretation of their true nature. They are indeed proud and regal Kindred, highly excitable and possessed of expensive tastes, but the word "hedonistic" is sometimes a bit extreme. Known to be the most sophisticated of the clans, the Toreador are concerned with beauty in a way no mortal can fathom. They use the rarefied senses and tastes given to them by the Embrace to become as consumed and impassioned as possible. For a Toreador, nothing matters as much as beauty, though in many cases, the search for beauty becomes a simple search for pleasure.

Disciplines: Auspex, Celerity, Presence

Clan Advantage: In their worldliness and continued dalliance with mortals, members of Clan Toreador inevitably collect a herd of fans, followers and hangers-on that can form a convenient and relatively safe source of vitæ. The character may harvest one Blood Trait per evening per level of Performance Ability she possesses. No challenges need to be made, but the character must still take 15 minutes per Blood Trait and must have access to her Herd.

Clan Disadvantage: Toreador have a fine appreciation for artistic and natural beauty. This appreciation can reach epic proportions when it concerns truly captivating subjects. Any medium that the Storyteller decrees is sufficiently enthralling or the successful use of the Performance Ability at levels three or higher will entrance a Toreador for half an hour unless he spends a Willpower Trait. While in this state, the Toreador will ignore (but not be unaware of) her surroundings and avoid other responsibilities, even to the point of endangering himself. In this condition, any reasonably unobtrusive foe can surprise the distracted Toreador.

Toreador *Antitribu*

Disciplines: Auspex, Celerity, Presence

Advantage: This clan is widely liked within the Sabbat. No one really sees the Toreador as a threat, and they have proven themselves worthy over and over again.

Disadvantage: They are easily distracted. They are not as reliable as their leaders would wish, and they tend to wander off if not constantly brought back to the subject at hand.

In addition, Toreador *Antitribu* prefer forms of artistic expression that can be considered distasteful or even demented. Works of art produced by these vampires tend to dark excess.

Preferred Paths: Path of Cathari, Path of Death and the Soul

Tremere

The members of this clan are dedicated and extremely well-organized. Others, however, think of them as arcane and untrustworthy. They are aggressive, highly intellectual and manipulative and respect only those who struggle and persevere against all odds. The Tremere believe they must use the other clans in order to prosper. An odd lot indeed, they claim to have once been wizards who voluntarily gave up their "art" for the powers and eternal life of the vampire.

Disciplines: Auspex, Dominate, Thaumaturgy

Clan Advantage: Once they prove themselves to their superiors, lower ranking Tremere can expect training in both Disciplines and Rituals. Many elders are paranoid of younger, more aggressive Tremere and guard their knowledge jealously. However, most will reward loyal and effective clan members for their accomplishments. While they respect competent and powerful leaders, Tremere are highly competitive and will seize any opportunity to further their personal power as long as it does not jeopardize the clan as a whole.

Clan Disadvantage: The head of a chantry holds a Blood Trait of each member of that chantry. Furthermore, the Council of Seven in Vienna has access to another two Blood Traits, taken when the member was introduced as a childe. They use these Traits not only for punishment and control, but to help locate missing clan members, particularly those captured by any of Clan Tremere's many enemies. Upon his presentation, a childe is also fed a Blood Trait from each of the seven elders, bringing him one third of the way to being Bound to them.

Tremere *Antitribu*

Disciplines: Auspex, Dominate, Thaumaturgy

Advantage: This clan's advantage lies in the respect they receive as their price for not being leaders. Their advice is usually both sought and heeded.

Disadvantage: Their Camarilla counterparts can immediately recognize Tremere *antitribu* because of a magical curse that takes the form of a glowing brand on the Tremere's foreheads. All Camarilla Tremere can see this without any sort of test. It is suggested that the Storyteller give a small sealed envelope to the Camarilla Tremere at the beginning of the night and invite them to open it when they meet a certain (or a group of certain) individual(s). Inside will be the description of the glowing brand.

Also, because of the long-standing Tremere-Tzimisce rivalry, any Tremere *antitribu* caught manipulating others for her own purposes is put to death.

Preferred Paths: Path of Death and the Soul, Path of Honorable Accord, Path of Caine

Tzimisce

Clan Tzimisce is renowned for its twisted practices and unshakable cruelty. They are not notable for their sense of humor, and anyone within the clan who possesses such is surely a rare exception. Devoted to the cause of the Sabbat, they are scholars and warriors who prefer to hold themselves aloof from their Lasombra leaders. None shirk the duties of leadership, but they prefer to advise and exert their control by forcing the Lasombra to depend on them for information, guidance and whatever else is necessary. The Tzimisce clan is the second most numerous clan in the Sabbat. Next to the Lasombra, they also hold the most status and power within the sect.

Disciplines: Animalism, Auspex, Vicissitude

Advantage: The Tzimisce are among the oldest members of the Sabbat. Respected and sought-after mentors, they retain close relationships with their progeny.

Disadvantage: The Discipline of Vicissitude is actually a disease which somehow warps the mind of any vampire using it too often. Each time a Tzimisce uses the Discipline more than three times per night, he gains either a Path Trait or a Derangement (at the Storyteller's discretion).

Preferred Paths: Path of Death and the Soul, Path of Caine, Path of Honorable Accord

Ventrue

Culture, civilization, sophistication — the Ventrue are proudly dedicated to these tenets. After the Inquisition blazed across the world and scourged Kindred ancient and young, the Ventrue led the way in uniting the clans of the Camarilla. The Ventrue maintain the traditional structures that allow vampires to ignore the lesser concerns of safety and sustenance. Vampires are thus freed to attend to higher concerns and more sophisticated pursuits. Ventrue assume (or take) great authority and great power. They feel they are responsible for Kindred society and seek to impose order upon it — their own order, regardless of what others want. As part of this order, young Ventrue are taught to respect their elders. Even more respected than their superiors, however, are the laws and traditions of vampiric society; all new Ventrue are expected to uphold and defend the Camarilla's laws.

Disciplines: Dominate, Fortitude, Presence

Clan Advantage: Clan Ventrue has always been intimately associated with wealth and resources. Whether this is the result of their exacting choice in progeny or by virtue of their bloodline is debatable. In either case, each Ventrue receives a free Finance Influence Trait. While this Trait can be expended or temporarily neutralized, it cannot be destroyed, stripped from them or permanently traded away.

Clan Disadvantage: The Ventrue maintain that they are an uncommon, if not rarefied, breed among the Kindred. It is perhaps quite fitting that their taste for vitae is similarly demanding. Upon Embrace, Ventrue instinctively realize that only one type or source of blood will satisfy their hunger — sources such as "virgins," "children," "blond men" or "peasants."

Ventrue *Antitribu*

Disciplines: Auspex, Dominate, Fortitude

Advantage: Almost all Ventrue *antitribu* involve themselves with the Loyalist movement of the Sabbat, which preaches individual freedom over everything except sect loyalty. Of course, the best way to be loyal to the sect is to do whatever the hell you want. These vampires tend to disobey orders more than other clans and challenge ideas and tactics that other put forth.

Disadvantage: Sabbat Ventrue have the same weakness as their former clan. They are very picky eaters; only one kind of blood will do. Everything else is just, well...just not up to their individual needs. In addition, the rest of the Sabbat distrusts these renegade Ventrue, and as such Ventrue *antitribu* must constantly prove themselves to their peers.

Preferred Paths: Path of Honorable Accord, Path of Cathari

Bloodlines

The following are bloodlines that have been adapted for play in **Mind's Eye Theatre**. **The Vampire Players Guide Second Edition** offers a complete section governing rules for creating your own bloodlines. As always, get your Narrator's approval before you use any of these bloodlines, as they can dramatically change the scope of a chronicle.

Ahrimanes

This fierce and independent all-female bloodline sprouted from the Sabbat Gangrel. A vampire called Muricia, exhausted from the infighting between the country and city factions of Gangrel *antitribu*, abandoned her sire and ran south into the lands of the Native Americans. She studied the magic of the native shamans and found within it the ability to break her Blood Bond with her pack. The richness of the spiritual culture gave her many gifts, and she wanted to share them; thus she founded a bloodline of likeminded vampires. Today, only a handful of Ahrimanes exist. They all keep large estates in the Deep South as well as secret underground havens, and they keep out of Sabbat politics as much as possible. Though they live alone, they contact their pack sisters at least once a month.

Disciplines: Animalism, Presence, Spiritus

Advantage: The sect does not watch the Ahrimanes carefully, leaving its members essentially free to do what they want.

Disadvantage: Very few Ahrimanes exist because all are infertile. Their blood is weak, and they can neither pass on their gifts or Blood Bond anyone to them outside of the Vaulderie. They can, however, be Bound.

Preferred Paths: The Path of Harmony, the Path of Honorable Accord

Children of Osiris

The Children of Osiris are a group dedicated to practicing and spreading Osiris' art to the deserving. Working in the shadows of the vampiric world, the Children of Osiris continue to battle Set and his minions while preparing for the reawakening of their own lord. Osiris himself saw the Embrace of Caine as a violating corruption, as well as a gift of awesome powers. This understanding led him to fight his Beast, setting forth on an eternal quest to transcend the evil that consumed him. Osiris died a horrible, burning death at the hands of his brother Set, but taught his art to a select few of his childer. Unfortunately, all but one of them were destroyed in the great battle along with their sire. Khetamon, who now slumbers in a remote temple far from civilization, was the lone survivor whose awakening the Children anticipate.

Disciplines: All Children of Osiris originate within some other clan or the Caitiff because they cannot create progeny; they must adopt followers from among existing vampires. Consequently, newly created characters should take at least one other Discipline (from the clan they would have been a part of), then take at least one level of Bardo. The character does not receive Bardo in addition to her other Disciplines, but as a substitute for one. Pre-existing characters who convert and become Children of Osiris retain whatever Disciplines they possessed before joining and add Bardo to the list when their experience allows.

Advantages: Because the Children of Osiris have strong virtues, they can work to dissolve their Beast Traits by using their Discipline of Bardo. For every two years of service with the Children, each member adds a Willpower Trait to her original pool. Also, each member has at least one Background Trait in Mentor.

Disadvantage: The Children's blood is infertile, so they cannot create progeny. In addition, many are unfamiliar with the ways of technology since they live such ascetic unlives.

Daughters of Cacophony

The Daughters are distinctly modern phenomenon despite their Classical name. No Kindred claims to have heard of them before the 1700s, and had they existed, vampires feel sure they would have known. The Daughters are such masters of song that most Kindred believe them to be an offshoot of the Toreador, though those who have been on the receiving end of their powers think the Malkavians had more influence.

Bloodline Disciplines: Fortitude, Melpominee, Presence (Awe, Entrancement)

Advantage: Like the Toreador, the Daughters have a vast network of contacts in the mortal world which serve as a Herd. Every Daughter is allowed one free feeding each night, though the herd must be physically accessible in order for the character to use this Advantage.

Disadvantage: The Daughters of Cacophony are so caught up in their music that they hear it constantly. As a result of this distraction, they are one bid down on all Mental Challenges involving Perception. Additionally, a Daughter's Mental Traits dealing with Alertness and Perception can never exceed four.

Kiasyd

In an attempt to discover more about their Obtenebration Discipline, members of the Lasombra created the Kiasyd bloodline, which is a millennia older than the Sabbat itself, by infusing themselves with what was supposedly fae blood. Kiasyd are all extremely tall, growing from six inches to two feet upon their Embrace and taking on odd facial features. Their eyes are rounded and completely black, and their faces become thin and angular. The vampires must be locked up during the transformation period, which usually lasts two nights, because the madness that shakes them is extremely potent. The pain also drives them into constant frenzy until the change is complete.

Disciplines: Mytherceria, Necromancy, Obtenebration

Advantage: The Kiasyd bloodline is not part of the Sabbat, nor is it associated with the Camarilla. Outside esoteric circles, the Kiasyd are rare and virtually unknown, and thus their freedom is great. They possess strange knowledges such as Faerie and Wraith Lore, and it has been rumored they have been taught by ancient goblins to craft stone with their bare hands.

Disadvantage: Their unusual appearance keeps them from interacting with human society much. With a strong aversion to pure iron (steel and iron alloys do not qualify as such), Kiasyd tend to frenzy if in iron's presence for over half an hour, though a Blood Trait can be spent to prevent this (one per half hour over the original is needed). Touching cold iron causes them to frenzy immediately, and no Traits can be spent to prevent this. Kiasyd suffer aggravated damage when wounded with cold iron.

Salubri

This widely hated bloodline has far more enemies than it deserves. Only seven of these Cainites exist at a time, for after a Salubri attains Golconda, she ends her existence and passes her blood to the individual she has chosen to take her place. Few survive for more than a few hundred years, for the Salubri consider vampiric existence to be agony. These vampires can usually pass as humans until someone notices that they possess a third eye.

Other clans perceive Salubri as murderers and diabolists of the worst kind. Princes have been known to call a Blood Hunt at the merest suggestion that a Salubri might be in their domain; the Tremere are known to hate them with fervid intensity.

Clan Disciplines: Auspex (Heightened Senses, Aura Perception), Fortitude, Obeah

Advantage: Salubri can attain Golconda with more ease than any other Kindred, although the exact path to Golconda still very much depends upon the individual. Once they attain Golconda, they may purchase more advanced Disciplines with greater ease and any Discipline without penalty. However, if Salubri fall from Golconda, they lose all Disciplines gained while in this state.

Disadvantage: Whenever one of the Salubri takes blood from someone who resists, she loses one level of health for every Blood Point taken. This is not so much physical damage as psychosomatic, but it must be healed normally (with blood). To avoid taking damage, the vampire must know the target is not resisting and is at peace. Additionally, all Salubri must continually persevere towards Golconda; straying from this path leads to dire consequences (such as the inability to regain Willpower). When a Salubri finally reaches Golconda, she must immediately set out to find a successor and then end her existence.

Samedi

The Samedi bloodline may be an offshoot of the Nosferatu, or possibly a branch of the Giovanni, but neither clan will take the credit (or the blame?) for these Kindred. The Samedi bloodline has only been around for a few hundred years, and very few of these Kindred have come to the United States. Easily identified by the shreds of rotting flesh constantly falling from their bodies, the Samedi are often confused with zombies by those unfamiliar with them. This bloodline claims no allegiances, but is known to have members in both the Sabbat and the Camarilla. Those who have done battle with the Samedi seldom forget the experience, for the bloodline has the power to rob other Kindred of their immortality — at least temporarily.

Disciplines: Necromancy, Obfuscate (Obfuscate, Mask of 1000 Faces), Thanatosis

Advantage: None to speak of.

Disadvantage: Like the Nosferatu, the Samedi are hideous to look upon and suffer on all Social Challenges. Even in the lightest of winds, the stench of decay wafts from these Kindred, and the rotted texture of the Samedi's skin is enough to turn even the strongest stomachs. When their true visage is apparent, Samedi are unable to win any Social Challenges unrelated to Intimidation.

Disciplines

In addition to immortality and regenerative abilities, all Kindred have access to the special gifts known as Disciplines. These powers, while strange and often wonderful, only serve to further alienate the Kindred from their mortal ties. Indeed, many Kindred, especially those with Advanced Disciplines, become drunk with their power and may even consider themselves to be deities when compared to their lessers.

According to legend, the earliest Kindred had access to the full spectrum of the following Disciplines, perhaps even more. For evolutionary reasons, or perhaps because of a supernatural hiccup, after successive generations, their blood grew thinner and their powers became more specific. Whatever the case may be, the bloodlines or clans of today show a distinct definition in the Disciplines they possess. While any Kindred can learn and eventually master almost any Discipline, they will find their intrinsic or clan Disciplines the easiest to master.

To reflect this, characters may only begin the chronicle with Disciplines from their clan list (see "Clans," above, for details). To learn out-of-clan Disciplines, a character must first locate a willing mentor who possesses the desired Discipline. Furthermore, the character must pay an increased experience point cost for these Disciplines (see Chapter One, "Experience," for more details).

The clanless Caitiff pose an exception to this rule. Because of their mixed heritage, they may begin with any three Disciplines except Thaumaturgy. These Disciplines are considered their "clan" Disciplines from that point forward. Any other Disciplines are then considered out-of-clan and must be acquired and paid for as mentioned above.

When purchasing Disciplines, a character must first master the lower levels of a Discipline before moving on to more advanced levels: Before learning Rapidity, for instance, a character must possess Alacrity and Swiftness. Additionally, some Disciplines, such as Thaumaturgy, have special limitations that must also be observed. These are listed along with the Discipline in question.

Regardless of the nature of the Discipline, it is suggested that a character actually learn the Discipline between sessions. This prevents the character from instantly gaining the most efficient or effective Discipline during play, and it helps to realistically reflect the time it takes a Kindred to master her newly developing power.

Animalism

This collection of powers serves as a primal link between the Beast that lurks in the souls of all Kindred and the wild spirit of the natural order of things. While some might see the Kindred as unnatural, in truth, they occupy a very vital niche in the ecology of the World of Darkness. Especially to the Gangrel, this Discipline represents the Kindred's ability to remain in touch with and understand their role in nature's vast scheme.

Basic

Beast Within

Your affinity with the animalistic side of the Kindred gives you some power over it in others. In particular, you can draw upon a victim's bestial nature and force him to give in to this darker side.

This Discipline allows you to activate one of an opponent's Derangements (the victim chooses which one) if you can defeat him in a Social Challenge. You need not know any of your target's Derangements, but if you do, you need not risk one of your Social Traits when trying to activate that particular Derangement (knowing his Derangement takes the place of your Social Trait during your initial bid). If you should fail in the attempt to use Beast Within against a target, you may not try to use it again on her that evening. See Chapter One, "Derangements," for rules concerning active Derangements and recovering from them.

The Beckoning

You can issue a compelling siren's song to nearby animals. Almost any type of animal ordinarily found within your current locale may be called, but you must declare what you are calling when you activate the Discipline.

Generally, it costs one Social Trait to summon an animal, but a Narrator may issue a higher cost for larger, rarer or more unruly animals. As a rule, the summoned animal will arrive in 10 to 30 minutes. The animal can be represented by a card that should usually be displayed prominently. Use the animal stats listed in **The Masquerade 2nd Edition**, Chapter 10, as a guide.

Intermediate

Song of Serenity

By reaching deep within the soul of an individual, you can tame his bestial nature, or at least quiet it for a while. This is useful not only in calming your allies, but also for robbing a foe of her spirit and energy.

To use this power, you must make a Social Challenge. If you win the test, Song of Serenity brings a Kindred or Garou out of frenzy. Furthermore, if used against an individual who is not in frenzy, this Discipline quenches the fire in his soul, making him weak and malleable. In this state, he may not spend Willpower and gains the Negative Mental Traits: Submissive x 2. This use of the Discipline lasts for the remainder of evening or session. The Kindred may not use this Discipline on herself, and its effects are not cumulative.

Advanced

Embrace the Beast

This level of Animalism allows the user to tap the dark and brutal wellspring of power that lies in the souls of the Kindred, transforming her into a ferocious, unrestrained monster.

While under the influence of Embrace the Beast, the character is not affected by Dominate, Presence or Beast Within. Furthermore, for the duration of the power, the character gains the Physical Traits: Ferocious and Relentless. The Discipline is not without its drawbacks, however. The character may not initiate any Mental or Social Challenges (except for Intimidation). Additionally, the character temporarily gains the Derangement: Crimson Rage. If she already has this Derangement, it becomes very active for the duration of the Discipline's use. It costs one Mental Trait to activate this Discipline. The Discipline comes to an end either at the end of the evening or session or upon completion of the character's first physical confrontation.

Auspex

Auspex encompasses the vast array of expanded sensory powers that some Kindred experience and can develop upon the Embrace. Most Kindred fortunate enough to possess this power find it exceptionally useful not only in night-to-night survival, but also in appreciating the beauty of their surroundings. The Toreador, in particular, delight in this last aspect.

Basic

Heightened Senses

You can enhance one of your senses to access a world of sensory input most people will never enjoy. The character can use Heightened Senses to spy on conversations, see in inky (but not complete) darkness, read letters by touch, identify an individual's scent or pick up telltale tastes. The Discipline can intensify any sense, but only one sense can be magnified at any time.

A Storyteller may determine that a Mental Challenge is necessary for particularly difficult tasks. Additionally, if the character is bombarded by a large amount of sensory input while using this Discipline (i.e. loud music, bright light or an overpowering stench), she will totally lose the sense in question for 15 minutes.

Aura Perception

Halos of energy surround sentient beings and shift constantly to reflect their mental and emotional states. A Kindred with Aura Perception has honed her senses to such a degree that she can perceive and interpret these auras. By winning a Static Mental Challenge, with a difficulty equal to the target's number of Mental Traits, you may demand that the target answer one of the following sorts of questions honestly: "What is your Demeanor?", "Have you committed diablerie (within the last six months)?", "What is your current emotional state (brief summary)? ", "Was the last thing you said a lie?", or "What sort of creature are you?" (human, Kindred, Garou, mage, spirit, faerie, mummy, etc.). Additional uses of this Discipline will allow additional questions.

Intermediate

Spirit's Touch

This Discipline allows you to sense the residual energies and impressions remaining on an object after it has been handled or touched. Specific information, such as the identity of the individual, her emotional and/or mental state and her perceptions, may be acquired by using this Discipline.

Various factors, such as brief contact, multiple handlers and the unusual nature of the handler or object, can dramatically affect the use of this Discipline. In some strange cases, no impressions may be present at all (at the direction of a Storyteller). Curiously enough, Kindred using Obfuscation powers leave no impressions. If the possessor of the object is nearby, the character may question him and he must answer honestly. Often, however, Spirit's Touch will require a Storyteller's assistance to use.

Telepathy

You have honed your preternatural senses to such a degree that you can actually receive and transmit thoughts. Be forewarned, though — many of the things buried within the minds of others are best left untouched. With effort, you can even force your way into stubborn minds, but a voluntary subject makes the task less difficult and less unpleasant for both parties.

You can use this Discipline to communicate privately with a willing subject (or more than one). Roleplay this communication by passing notes or holding a quiet side conversation that cannot be "overheard" except by Telepathy or similar powers. (In order to accomplish this effect, other players are expected to ignore the note-passing or conversation. However, characters with Telepathy automatically notice something unusual going on and can attempt a Mental Challenge against either player to listen in on the conversation.)

You can also use Telepathy to spy on a subject, access surface thoughts or discern the truth. If you defeat your subject in a Mental Challenge, you can ask the victim one "yes or no" or short answer question about any subject or conversation in which the victim is currently engaged, and the subject must answer truthfully.

Individuals possessing active Derangements may bid them as Mental Traits when subjected to involuntary Telepathy. Each Derangement bid in this fashion requires the telepath to bid an additional Mental Trait, representing the difficulty of reading such a twisted mind. If the defender opts to bid one or more of her active Derangements against the telepath and wins the challenge, she infects the aggressor with her madness. The telepath must now either spend a Willpower Trait or actively play out one of the Derangements bid for 30 minutes. Unfortunately for the defender, the telepath is now acutely aware of the defender's Derangement and may use it against her in the future.

Advanced

Psychic Projection

With a conscious mental exertion, you can safely sever the bound between your spirit and your body. In this state, your invisible spirit may travel incorporally through the physical world. Mundane barriers cannot hold you, but supernatural ones, such as pentagrams and wards, are another matter entirely. Individuals with highly advanced sensory powers (such as Heightened Senses, Telepathy and the like) may realize something is amiss, but must still win a Mental Challenge to perceive you.

Exercising Psychic Projection is not without its dangers. Your body is left helpless and inert during your sojourn. Furthermore, your ability to interact with the physical world is greatly diminished. You cannot, for example, stop or interfere with physical actions occurring around you. A Kindred can only use sensory Disciplines, such as Aura Perception, Heightened Senses (sight and sound only) and Telepathy. The only powers that may be used against you are those that affect the spirit or mind, and even then, the attacker must first be able to perceive your presence. If you wish to become visible and communicate with a single individual in the physical world, you may do so at a cost of one Mental Trait for every 10 minutes.

Bardo

The Discipline of Bardo allows the Children of Osiris to protect themselves and others against the forces of evil without using the enemy's techniques. Bardo is a largely preventive Discipline, intended more to shore up defenses and to heal psychic wounds than to be wielded as an offensive weapon.

Basic

Restore Humanitas

This Discipline allows the Child of Osiris to purge herself or another of a Beast Trait. It is only possible to do this for others if it is a Trait they recently gained (within the last few weeks). The Child must spend one Willpower Trait and meditate or sit out of game for one half-hour. She must not contact or speak to any other players while out. To purge someone else's Beast Trait, the subject must spend one Willpower Trait and the Child must spend one Mental Trait.

Banishing Sign of Thoth

This Discipline allows the Child to defend herself from other vampiric Disciplines. To evoke this power, she must make the appropriate gesture where her opponent can see it. She may engage in a retest by spending one Trait that is appropriate to the challenge. The Discipline wards against Thaumaturgy, Dominate, Presence and Auspex.

Intermediate

Boon of Anubis

This Discipline allows the Child to protect a mortal from the Embrace, but not from becoming a ghoul. To effect the Boon of Anubis, the Child must spend a Willpower Trait; win or tie a Simple Test with a Narrator and meditate or sit out of game for one half-hour. Neither the mortal nor the vampire will be aware the mortal has not become a vampire until she wakes from her first sleep. This power must be used before or during the mortal's Embrace — it will not work after the Embrace has been given.

Pillar of Osiris

This allows the Child to establish her own temple where Bardo may be studied. For every month away from such a temple, the Child develops an incrementally higher risk of frenzy and may only decrease this tendency by meditating inside a temple. This Discipline requires one half-hour of meditation and the expenditure of one Status Trait.

Advanced

Mummification Ritual

This ritual allows the Child to cause torpor in a vampire for any given length of time. It is normally used to eliminate those who are evil and corrupt without causing Final Death. The Children have quite a collection of such vampires, some rumored to be Sabbat, whom they store for safekeeping.

To effect this ritual, the victim must first be incapacitated. Then the Child must retire to a private place with the victim for one hour to perform the ritual. Others may be present, but the Child must be left undisturbed. To successfully place the victim in torpor, the Child must win a Mental Challenge or spend two Willpower Traits to circumvent failure.

Ra's Blessing

The Child may engage in two hours of meditation or spend two Willpower Traits to evoke this blessing. Ra's Blessing enables the Child to withstand sunlight for as many hours as she is willing to spend Willpower Traits to do so. The first hour of immunity costs two hours of meditation or two Willpower Traits, while additional hours cost only one hour of meditation or one Willpower Trait per hour.

Celerity

After the Embrace, many vampires benefit from a variety of amazing physical improvements. One of these is the Discipline of Celerity. This power reflects the Kindred's mastery of her form in the areas of speed and quickness.

When employed against a foe with an equivalent degree of Celerity, many of the advantages of this Discipline are negated. For example, an attacker with Swiftness would still get her bonus attack against a foe who also possessed Swiftness (as would the foe), but neither suffers from the Trait penalties. In any case, each combatant using Celerity still gets his total number of attacks. Also, a character using her Celerity to evoke a "Fair Escape" can be intercepted by a foe with an equal or greater degree of Celerity.

Basic

Alacrity

You possess a supernatural degree of speed and coordination that outstrips both normal mortals and your fellow Kindred.

If you are aware of an upcoming physical threat, you may spend a Blood Trait to preempt the actions with a physical action of your own. Some examples of such threats include: melee attacks, falling objects, gunfire, oncoming cars or thrown objects. Examples of preemptive actions are: drawing a gun of your own, moving out of the path of a falling object, and so on. To preempt a foe using Alacrity, you must have a greater degree of Celerity.

Using Alacrity, you may also apply the "Fair Escape" rule against foes who do not have at least an equivalent degree of Celerity. This costs one Blood Trait to activate.

Swiftness

You can move with a shocking degree of speed. To a character using Swiftness, slower foes and bystanders often appear to be standing still.

Swiftness allows you to make a follow-up attack against a foe in physical combat. To do so, you must declare that you are activating Swiftness (an obvious breach of the Masquerade) before making a bid and expending a Blood Trait. The first challenge is then carried out as normal. Afterwards, if you are able, while using Swiftness, you may attempt an immediate followup challenge. Foes who do not have or have not activated Swiftness can only defend themselves in this challenge — they cannot harm the user of the Discipline in any way, nor in this followup challenge can they use any Traits that they had bid in the prior challenge(s), even if they did not lose them.

Using this Discipline, you may also expend a Blood Trait to cut in-game travel times in half.

Intermediate

Rapidity

With time and experience, you have outstripped the fledging power of Swiftness. What was once merely dazzling speed is now a mindnumbing blur of motion. In a moment's notice, you can burst into a whirlwind of destruction, crippling, if not slaying, a slower opponent.

The character may make two extra challenges when employing Rapidity. Otherwise, the power is the same as Swiftness, including cost. If used to cut travel time, the time is reduced to one-fourth.

Advanced

Fleetness

Your feats of speed defy ordinary logic. To the average observer, you almost disappear when your form explodes into motion. The roar of wind in your passing extinguishes small flames and causes loose clothing to whip about.

You may take three extra challenges when employing Fleetness. Otherwise, the power is the same as Swiftness, including cost. If used to cut travel time, the time is reduced to one-eighth.

Chimerstry

This is the Ravnos Discipline of deceit and trickery and represents their ability to create illusions and hallucinations. While using Chimerstry, keep this basic rule of thumb in mind: A vampire cannot create an illusion that she cannot sense. Thus, a blindfolded vampire cannot create a visual illusion, but could create a tactile one if she herself could touch it.

Basic

Minor Illusion

You can create a simple, static (i.e., immobile) illusion that affects only one sense. While this illusion is not real and cannot cause physical harm, with a successful Social Challenge, it can be used to trick or deceive others. The illusion lasts for as long as you want it to, until you leave the vicinity, or until your opponent succeeds in a Social Challenge.

This illusion only affects one person.

Intermediate

Complex Illusion

You can create a complex illusion that moves, looks and sounds like the real thing. However, because it is still not actually there, others can pass through it. As above, you must defeat your opponent in a successful Social Challenge and must also expend a Mental Trait to create the illusion.

This illusion only affects one person.

Advanced

Horrid Reality

You can now create illusions so realistic that you can even harm others with them. If your opponent believes the illusion to be real, she will treat it as real: an illusory fire will burn her, an artificial wall will stop her and a fake bullet will wound her. Again, you must defeat your opponent in a Social Challenge and expend both a Willpower and a Mental Trait.

This illusion only affects one person.

Dementation

The Discipline of Dementation allows Malkavian *antitribu* to induce their own mental state in others. Hallucinations, confusion, increased perception and Derangements — all these go a long way towards distracting, discrediting or otherwise befuddling mortals and other Kindred. Note that Malkavian *antitribu* keep this Discipline a closely guarded secret, not having been known to teach it to any outsiders.

Basic

Mind Tricks

You can induce minor hallucinations, but cannot control what your victim sees. To use Mind Tricks, find a Storyteller and engage in a Mental Challenge. If you win, your victim is affected in whatever way the Storyteller chooses (fear, disorientation and temporary Trait loss are common). This is an excellent distraction technique.

You cannot use this Discipline simultaneously with any physical action that would distract you from concentrating on the target. In other words, you could use this Discipline while walking slowly toward the victim, but not while running furiously away from, actively fighting or throwing an object at him.

As aforementioned, you must perform a Mental Challenge. If you wish to invoke this in a sneaky way (since it is difficult to tell who the source is), the Storyteller may perform the test with the victim and simply inform you of the result. This Discipline cannot be consciously resisted; either it works or it doesn't.

Intermediate

Confusion

Confusion allows you to completely befuddle anyone who is paying you direct attention. Victims have trouble remembering their names, where they are and what they are doing. If attacked while confused, they can still defend themselves.

By winning a Mental Challenge, you completely bewilder the victim for five minutes. If you win a second Mental Challenge against the victim, you may spend Mental Traits to increase the duration of the victim's confusion: This extension costs one Mental Trait per additional five minutes. Spending three Mental Traits would result in a total of 20 minutes of confusion for the victim.

Eyes of Chaos

This Discipline allows you to perceive an individual's true Nature and/or any patterns of insanity inherent in her personality. Patterns of insanity include Derangements, Beast or Path Traits and possibly Negative Traits if the character does not possess any of the aforementioned personality quirks or Traits.

This Discipline requires you to win one Mental Test for each item you wish to perceive. The first test might be for the victim's true Nature, the next for one Derangement or Beast Trait and so on.

Advanced

Total Insanity

Using Total Insanity, you can afflict your victim with five Storyteller-chosen Derangements for 10 minutes. Victims in this state cannot initiate Mental Challenges and should be encouraged to play out the Derangements within the context of the story.

To inflict Total Insanity, you must win a Mental Challenge against the victim and spend one Willpower Trait for every 10 minutes of complete insanity you wish your victim to experience.

Dominate

One of the legendary powers of vampires is their ability to control the thoughts and actions of others. This Discipline is partly responsible for this legend. Unlike its sister power, Presence, Dominate affects the conscious and sometimes unconscious mental facilities of a target.

To Dominate, you must first establish eye contact with the target. Even so much as a brief meeting of the eyes is enough to fulfill this requirement, about which players are expected to exercise a degree of honesty. Orders issued with Dominate must be verbal and clearly comprehensible to the target — or you may issue the commands using Telepathy.

Note that Dominate's one major limitation is that it is totally ineffective against Kindred of a lower generation than the user of the Discipline.

Basic

Command

This Discipline is a form of mind control focused through a piercing gaze and commanding voice. If you can catch the eyes of another player, you can attempt to exert your considerable mental control over her.

To employ this Discipline, you must first defeat your opponent in a Mental Challenge, then issue a single simple command to your subject, such as "sleep," "stop," "freeze," "sit" or "leave" ("Silence!" is also acceptable). The command cannot be blatantly suicidal or self-destructive, but it may drastically violate the subject's Nature or Demeanor. In any case, the effects of the command cannot last more than 10 minutes.

Forgetful Mind

You can use your mental powers to warp the conscious and unconscious memories of a victim. After defeating another character in a Mental Challenge, you may add, alter or eliminate memories concerning a single event. The extent of the information can be as limited as the color of someone's underwear or as encompassing as the entire experiences of a 15-minute period in the subject's life.

Intermediate

Mesmerism

By staring into someone's eyes, you can creep insidiously into her mind and plant subtle suggestions to direct and guide her behavior. These mental time bombs are hidden within the target's mind until a trigger event occurs.

Using this Discipline requires that you first defeat your subject in a Mental Challenge. Even if a suggestion is planted, your victim will ignore the order if it poses a clear threat to her life. You may only implant one suggestion in a given individual's mind at any one time. Furthermore, both the trigger and the suggestion must be concise and easily understandable. Some examples include:

Triggers:

- Upon seeing a particular person, item or place
- Upon hearing a certain word or sound
- At a precise time
- After performing a specific action

Suggestions:

- Behave in a bizarre or inappropriate manner
- Deliver a brief spoken message
- Experience a single emotion
- Suddenly "recall" planted information

The target subconsciously retains these details until the suggestion is triggered, but will not be able to explain why she performed the action. Once the suggestion is carried out, the Mesmerism is lifted.

Conditioning

Your powers of mental manipulation have reached such a level of prowess that you are now capable of completely reprogramming a target. The process involves a great deal of time and effort, but the results are astounding and practically irreversible. The end product is a fanatically loyal if somewhat dull servant. Your degree of control can even challenge the supposedly infallible power of the Blood Bond.

To begin the process, you must have complete access to the victim for the full duration of three consecutive evenings. During this time, you slowly erode the will of the subject, eventually replacing it with your own. To do so, you must defeat the subject in three consecutive Mental Challenges (one per night). Once accomplished, you must permanently expend a Mental Trait. If one of the challenges is unsuccessful, the entire process fails.

The resultant degree of control is intense. Foremost among the effects is a permanent and automatic command, wherein the subject carries out even the most self-destructive of orders. Furthermore, the conditioned victim gains three Willpower Traits for the sole purpose of resisting control and manipulation that would cause her to perform actions counterproductive to her master's wishes. If a previous Blood Bond exists, the Regnant and the Kindred who conditioned the subject must engage in a Mental Challenge (out of character) every time the two issue contradictory orders.

On the downside, the subject is little more than a pale automaton lacking free will, imagination and creativity. She is not without hope, however; this selfsame power can be used to restore the subject to normal, albeit at great risk.

Over the course of three nights, the reprogrammer must win three Mental Challenges. The Storyteller bases the difficulty of these challenges on such factors as the length of time and how intensely the subject was controlled. The subject's bonus Willpower Traits will come into play here to resist the would-be savior. If the reprogrammer fails just one of these tests, the subject's mind is permanently shattered, leaving her a vegetable. If successful, however, the reprogrammer only needs to expend a Willpower Trait to reaffirm the subject's identity and undo the effects of the Discipline.

Advanced

Possession

This Discipline allows you to forcibly inject your consciousness into another's body, suppressing his existing will and personality. In doing so, you gain complete physical control of your host's body, while leaving *your* body completely inert and vulnerable. Moreover, while in a foreign body, you will find yourself subject to its physical limitations; you may not use any of your Physical Disciplines or any of the host's Mental or Social Disciplines or faculties.

To Possess someone, you must first touch and then defeat your victim in a Mental Challenge. If successful, the original body falls over, apparently lifeless, and your consciousness immediately takes over the victim. You may remain in the host's body until sunrise, when you must return to your own form. If your body has been destroyed, you suffer Final Death. During the course of the Possession, the victim is totally unaware of her condition and surroundings.

Spiritually empty but physically viable bodies, such as the bodies of those Psychically Projecting or currently Possessing others, cannot resist Possession. However, when the Projecting spirit tries to return to its body, you must succeed in a Mental Challenge to retain control.

When you fail a Mental Challenge to possess a body, you become extremely disoriented. You cannot control your body or concentrate for a full minute, during which time you are very vulnerable to physical and mental attacks.

As a game effect, characters possessing the bodies of other characters should adopt the appropriate dress and trappings of the host body. Additionally, a name badge or label could be employed to signify the change.

Fortitude

All Kindred possess an amazing constitution, supplemented by gradual regeneration and an immunity to aging and most diseases. Kindred with Fortitude possess an even greater degree of toughness. Considering the numerous destructive forces a vampire can and probably will encounter in her long life, Fortitude can prove to be a tremendous asset.

Basic

Endurance

This level of Fortitude represents your ability to shrug off the effects of damage, including damage caused by fire or sunlight. With it, you can ignore the side effects of being Wounded or Incapacitated — you are not out of play until you reach Torpor or Final Death. This Discipline costs nothing to use and is automatically activated when needed.

Mettle

Because your form has been hardened against the dangers and threats of the world, you gain an additional wound level, which is recorded on your character sheet. You can temporarily lose and heal back this wound level just like any other, and you use it as a second "Healthy."

Intermediate

Resilience

You are highly resistant to harm and injury from all sources, including the traditional banes of your breed — fire and sunlight. While excessive or persistent forces can still bring an end to your immortal existence, this does not come about easily.

Whenever you suffer aggravated wounds, you may try to reduce them to ordinary wounds once per wound level taken. You must spend an appropriate Physical Trait (Stalwart, Resilient, etc.) and win a Simple Test for each wound resisted. Thus, if you suffered three aggravated wounds at once, you could attempt to reduce each of them separately to ordinary wounds by spending three appropriate Traits and winning three Simple Tests.

Advanced

Aegis

Your ability to survive the hostile forces of the world has surpassed mere physical resilience; it takes a truly monumental and unrelenting force to destroy you. In the face of annihilation, you can call upon deep reserves of tenacity, enabling you to shrug off fatal injuries.

When you suffer a result in a challenge that would destroy you, or if you encounter a lethal situation (such as direct exposure to sunlight), you may permanently expend either three Physical or one Willpower Trait to avoid destruction. If directly exposed to sunlight, you remain unharmed for five minutes. The damage is not inflicted — its results are ignored. Indeed, those witnessing this Discipline often find it hard to believe that any creature could survive. Many will assume the character is destroyed unless given cause to believe otherwise.

Melpominee

This Discipline allows the Daughters of Cacophony to use speech and song for a variety of supernatural effects.

Basic

Tourett's Voice

You can project your voice to any person with which you are familiar. In game terms, you pass a note or whisper in the target's ear. In addition to the target, only those with Heightened Senses standing nearby will be aware of and hear the exchange.

Intermediate

Toreador's Bane

With this Discipline, you can use your melodic voice to entrance others. If you win a Social Challenge, the target listens to your voice for as long as you can sing, up to 20 minutes. The target can break the trance if she expends two Mental Traits. Toreadors are especially susceptible to this Discipline and are automatically three bids down when attempting to resist it. Furthermore, a Toreador must expend four Mental Traits instead of two if she wishes to break the trance.

Advanced

Death of the Drum

You may now damage others using only your voice. If you win a Social Challenge and expend a Blood Trait, your target takes one aggravated wound. This Discipline is successful even if your target cannot hear you.

This can only be targeted at one victim at a time.

Mytherceria

Kindred of the Kiasyd bloodline are the only vampires who can possess this Discipline.

Basic

Fey Sight

This Discipline allows you to use your normal vision to see changelings and wraiths for what they truly are. You may then speak with any creature you see by winning or tying a Simple Test with that individual. For every test won or tied, you may speak with the wraith or changeling for five minutes. If you lose the test, you lose your vision of the other creature(s) for one minute.

Intermediate

Faerie Wards

Kiasyd can protect an area with faerie glyphs, more to prevent others from returning to the area than as a practical joke. By spending one Mental Trait per 10 feet protected, you can cause visitors to become extremely disoriented and remain that way for 10 minutes after they leave the area. The Discipline affects all worlds, including the Umbra.

You may spend as many Mental Traits as you wish to ward an area. By spending three or more Mental Traits to ward a 10-foot area (even though only one Trait is required to ward it successfully), you can boost the glyph's potence, raising the difficulty level for those wishing to avoid the ward's effects. To avoid these effects, the victim must engage in a Mental Challenge with you or the Storyteller and bid the same number of Mental Traits as you spent to establish the glyph.

Advanced

Stone Travel

Kiasyd have a natural affinity for earth and can identify all rocks and minerals without having to spend any Traits. Using this Discipline, you can burrow a tunnel into the earth by spending one Physical Trait for every 20 feet burrowed. While an enemy can follow you into this tunnel, it is probably not a good idea, since they tend to collapse. You may activate this Discipline on dirt or natural stone only. It may not be used with asphalt, concrete, brick walls or walkways, or stone tainted with synthetic substances such as non-clay or sand mortar.

Necromancy

This Discipline allows Kindred to summon and command the spirits of the dead.

Basic

Summon Spirit

You can summon a spirit providing you meet the following conditions:

• You must know the name of the spirit, although a strong psychic impression from Spirit's Touch will suffice.

• The spirit can be that of a dead mortal or of an extinguished vampire. Neither living spirits nor destroyed vampires who have reached Golconda can be summoned.

• A person or object with some connection to the spirit in its life must be present in the room during the summoning.

You must defeat an unwilling spirit in a Social Challenge in order to summon it. The spirit is not bound to remain any longer than one minute or one question, whichever comes first. However, if the spirit is willing, you can maintain contact for much longer.

Intermediate

Compel Spirit

You can now compel a summoned spirit to perform certain tasks. If you succeed in a Mental Challenge against a spirit who has already been summoned, you can force the spirit to perform one simple task or act on your behalf for one hour.

Advanced

Soul Stealing

You can now draw the spirit out of a living (or undead) body by spending one Willpower Trait and succeeding in a Social Challenge. Once withdrawn, the spirit is treated as a ghost. You can then use other Disciplines to bind this spirit or cast another spirit into the now vacant body. If the living spirit remains unbound, it can return to its body (providing that its body is still empty) at the cost of one Willpower Trait.

Obeah

The power to heal can be great indeed. However, Obeah is more than just a command of physical healing; it gives Salubri control of the body and soul and is said to be fundamentally connected to the power of their third eye. Indeed, other Kindred who learn this Discipline also develop the third eye.

Basic

Healing Touch

With but a touch and the expenditure of a Blood Trait, you can heal one Health Level of another's wounds, even aggravated ones. This touch requires no test, providing the subject is willing. However, you must succeed in a Physical Challenge if your subject chooses to resist.

Intermediate

Neutral Guard

By spending two Mental Traits, you can protect yourself and those under your care from harm. Once enacted, no one not already within 10 feet of you can approach unless you voluntarily drop your guard or they defeat you in a Mental Challenge. However, if you are successful at the challenge, they are paralyzed for five minutes. If you take any hostile action while using this Discipline, you automatically cancel the Neutral Guard.

Advanced

Healing the Mind

With this Discipline, you can diagnose and cure someone else's Derangements for an evening by winning a Mental Challenge. If you choose to expend three Mental Traits permanently, you may make your healing effects permanent. However, you are two bids down whenever you try to remove a Malkavian's Derangement, your effects will never be permanent, and you may never heal his last two Derangements.

Obfuscate

Kindred hide in the midst of teeming hordes of humanity. For those who are truly hideous, the gift of Obfuscation is priceless. Essentially, most of the powers of Obfuscate affect the minds of observers, preventing them from perceiving things as they truly are. As a result, surveillance devices, such as cameras, will still register the character normally. However, if a person employing such a device is relatively near the Obfuscating character, she will still be affected by the power and not be able to perceive the character. For example, a tourist with a video camera would not see a skulking Nosferatu at the base of the Washington monument through the camera's viewpiece. However, if he later watched the film at home, he would indeed notice the lurking figure that he somehow missed earlier.

Basic

Unseen Presence

This power allows you to remain obscured and unseen even in crowds. You can walk about without being seen or heard, lurk while listening to whispered conversations and escape from dangerous situations.

While this Discipline is activated, other players must pretend not to see you; if you choose to spy upon them, they must continue acting normally, as if you are not there. To engage this power, you must cross both your arms in front of you, demonstrating your actions to everyone around you. As soon as you touch objects around you (other than walking around), talk to others or otherwise interact with your environment, you instantly become visible to everyone (uncross your arms).

If you are moving, a Kindred with Heightened Senses will detect something is amiss, but must defeat you in a Mental Challenge to actually pinpoint your location and see you. In any case, you cannot surprise an individual with Heightened Senses by using Unseen Presence.

You may attempt to evoke the "Fair Escape" rule with Unseen Presence by winning a Mental Challenge. If you win, you have slipped away unnoticed (watch out for characters with Heightened Senses, however). You cannot use this method of escape if you are currently involved in a challenge.

Mask of 1000 Faces

This Discipline allows you to assume a completely different appearance. To adopt this convincing disguise, you may be required to assume new props and clothes, change badges or use the appropriate hand sign to indicate your change in appearance. This Discipline is extremely valuable to the hideous Nosferatu.

Characters with Heightened Senses can sense something is amiss about your looks, but they must defeat you in a Mental Challenge to pierce your projected veil. Because this power affects minds, it is useless against remote cameras and photographs (although a nearby witness will still discount proof if the Obfuscating individual is in sight).

You possess one "instinctive" illusory disguise that you can adopt automatically while conscious. You can assume other disguises temporarily, but each costs one Mental Trait. While asleep, when in Torpor or upon Final Death, you return to your true appearance.

Intermediate

Cloak the Gathering

Not only can you mystically mask your own passing, but others can also benefit from your power. You may place others (if they are willing) under your mantle of Obfuscation, thereby rendering them invisible. After you disappear, you must expend a Mental Trait for each individual you wish to Cloak. Each individual Cloaked in this manner must cross her arms to indicate the use of Unseen Presence.

Individuals under the effect of this power must always remain within three paces of you to remain hidden. While Cloaked, you and your allies can still see each other. Each individual hidden by this Discipline must abide by the limitation listed under Unseen Presence, or the Cloaked companion immediately forfeits the Discipline's effect. If one member of the group becomes visible in this manner, she can no longer see the rest, who remain unaffected. If the user of the Discipline violates the limitations of Unseen Presence, all participants become visible.

If a Kindred with Heightened Senses defeats one of the cloaked individuals in a Mental Challenge, she perceives only that individual. However, if a perceptive Kindred challenges and defeats the Kindred projecting the Cloak, all of the subjects are revealed to the challenger. Usually, it is not readily apparent which Kindred in the gathering is employing this power.

Advanced

Soul Mask

What Mask of 1000 Faces does to the body, Soul Mask accomplishes for the inner self. Kindred possessing Aura Perception and Telepathy often become smug in their ability to unearth others' deepest secrets and personalities. You, however, have the ability to render those powers impotent. Your true nature is inscrutable. This is not to say that your secrets cannot be fathomed, but it takes a very dedicated and decidedly nosy individual to do so.

A single Mental Trait must be expended for each piece of information about yourself you wish to alter. The types of information that can be masked are Nature, Demeanor, recent diablerie, emotional state, surface thoughts, type of creature and Derangements. Each of these "masks" must be recorded when the power is activated. The masks remain until sunrise or until you choose to change them (at additional cost).

Obtenebration

Vampires are creatures of shadow, none more so than practitioners of Obtenebration. This Discipline enables the Lasombra to shape shadows, the very essence of their twilight souls.

Basic

Shadow Play

You can blend in with shadows. If there is a real shadow, you may stand in it with arms crossed for Obfuscate and remain unseen. To see you, another Kindred must initiate a Mental Challenge which, even if successful, cannot distinguish between Obfuscate and Obtenebration. This Discipline may not be used unless real shadows are present; acceptable places include very dark rooms, closets, under tables (if it is dim) and so forth.

Intermediate

Shroud of Night

You can create an area of inky black matter that blinds everyone regardless of Heightened Senses or Gleam of the Red Eyes. This darkness extinguishes light and stifles, but does not eliminate, sound. Use of this Discipline looks unusual to those on the outside, appearing as a huge, black blob nothing like a natural shadow.

Shroud of Night costs you one Blood Trait for every 10 feet you wish the darkness to extend. A Storyteller should be present to explain the phenomenon to all involved. Unless others notice your high concentration level, they will be unable to trace the phenomenon back to you.

Arms of the Abyss

With this Discipline, you can force shadows within 15 feet of you to attack a specific target. Use of this Discipline requires a real shadow to be present and visible to the victim (although the victim does not actually have to be looking *at* it). If the character being attacked is blind, then a Storyteller may vouch for its existence. Furthermore, you cannot engage in any other physical action while causing the shadow to hold, knock over, trip, grasp, block or otherwise attack an opponent.

This Discipline costs one Blood Trait per shadow animated and requires a Physical Challenge (the shadow's Physical Traits, listed below, vs. the victim's Physical Traits). Once you have spent the Blood Trait, other characters see the shadow form into a tendril and move about, seemingly of its own volition. While the shadow tendrils cannot move around an area, they can whip, slash and grab from their initial point of origin. They both inflict and take normal damage.

Each shadow possesses three Physical Traits. Storytellers should feel free to allow characters with this Discipline to choose their own adjectives, as long as they suit the shadow. The Lasombra has the option of spending additional Blood Traits to add Physical Traits to her shadow tendrils at a one-for-one cost.

Advanced

Shadow Body

You can turn your body into an oozing form of shadow, making yourself impervious to physical harm except for sunlight or fire (which inflict one extra Health Level of damage in this form). You may not initiate any challenges or attack in any way. Shadow Body also allows you to slip through cracks in walls and slither at walking speed along any surface.

This Discipline costs two Blood Traits, one to assume the shadow form and one to return to normal form. It takes one full minute to change forms.

Potence

Another distinctly physical Discipline from which many Kindred benefit is a supernaturally heightened degree of strength known as Potence. Those employing this gift find themselves able to perform incredible feats and inflict brutal amounts of damage. Unfortunately, like so many of the physical Disciplines, Potence easily marks the user as something more than human. As a result, many consider exercising Vigor or Puissance a breach of the Masquerade.

Basic

Prowess

You possess a degree of supernatural strength beyond that of average Kindred. Even when your strength should be spent, you can call upon the might that is your bloodright.

You may expend a single Blood Trait to recover all Physical Traits related to brute strength that you have depleted or lost this session; you may not use Potence to restore any other type of Physical Traits. Thus, while Potence restores the Traits Brawny, Wiry, Ferocious, Stalwart and Tough, it can't restore Traits representing coordination, grace or speed.

Might

You can redouble your efforts in any test of strength, often overcoming obstacles that would daunt lesser Kindred. If you should lose a challenge involving strength, you may call for a single immediate retest. Any Traits you lost remain lost, although you need not bid another Trait. You do, however, stand to win the object of the challenge should you win the second test.

This Discipline can only be used once per challenge and cannot be recalled by an opponent's use of an Ability, but could be overcome by another Kindred using Might. Might may not be used in tests of coordination, grace or speed, only in tests that involve raw strength.

Intermediate

Vigor

Your physical strength has reached truly astonishing proportions, marking you as superhuman. Because many Kindred consider the use of Vigor in mortal company a breach of the Masquerade, they refrain from using this level of strength unless in dire straits.

When using Vigor, you should make the hand signal called the "Bomb," which is a clenched fist with thumb extended upward. You may apply the Bomb in combat and Physical Challenges that are strength-related, but not in challenges of coordination, speed, grace or the like. The Bomb interacts with other signals in a manner befitting its name: it defeats both Rock and Paper, but in turn is defeated by Scissors (the fuse is cut). You must declare that you are able to use the Bomb before you can use it to resolve a test.

Advanced

Puissance

You possess monumental strength. What you consider casual exertion is sufficient force to deform metal and fracture stone. Your full strength will shatter the bones of the toughest mortal, rend plate steel and grind marble blocks into gravel. Even your fellow Kindred cannot survive the type of punishment you can inflict for long.

In hand-to-hand combat, you inflict an additional Health Level against your foes. Furthermore, you win all ties in Physical Challenges involving strength, regardless of who possesses the most Traits. Of course, if your opponent also has Puissance, the winner is determined normally.

Presence

Presence can be seen as sort of a supernatural magnitude of charisma, personality and appeal. Particularly among mortals, Kindred possessing this Discipline are often seen as being magnetic or having an intangible quality that draws people to them. While Dominate controls the logical and conscious mind, Presence appeals to the emotions of the subject. Unlike Dominate, however, Presence can affect Kindred of lower generation.

Basic

Dread Gaze

You are able to inject others with feelings of terror and fear by looking into their eyes. By defeating your target in a Social Challenge, you can cause her to run from you in a panic. Unable to take any action against you or to initiate a challenge, the victim must flee the area without stopping until out of your presence. For the next hour, he actively avoids you and leaves immediately should you appear. If somehow forced to remain in your presence, the individual will be extremely uncomfortable and must bid an additional Trait in all challenges against you. If you attack the victim, he may defend himself as normal.

Entrancement

This Discipline describes your ability to attract, sway and control others. Your seductive glamour ensnares everyone you look upon — even those who despise you and wish you harm can be rendered civil, if not docile.

You may attempt to Entrance an individual by engaging him in a Social Challenge. If you are successful, the target must speak to you politely and in a civil manner. Furthermore, he may not attack you while Entranced. The Entrancement is broken if you initiate an act of aggression against the subject or behave in an obviously insulting or crude manner towards him — otherwise, the power lasts for one hour. If the user breaks the Entrancement by attacking the individual, she may not Entrance that individual again for the remainder of the night.

Intermediate

Summon

You can demand the immediate appearance of a person known to you, and he will come. Even across great distances, your mental summoning is not easy to resist.

The standard method of employing this power is to select an out-of-game envoy to carry your summons. This should be someone who doesn't mind or who can take the time out to perform the duty. You declare to the envoy the number of Social Traits you wish to devote to the power. Each Social Trait beyond the first allows a retest if the subject wins the Social Challenge or resists the power of the call. In the meantime, you must remain in the same place so that the subject can find you if he loses the challenge. Any Social Traits invested in the call are considered lost, even if the subject relents.

There will often be quite a time lag when using this power. This is easy to understand when one considers the amount of time it will take to find the subject, engage in a challenge and respond. Players are therefore advised not to use this power frivolously.

Advanced

Majesty

You exude an aura of power and insurmountable might. Those around you find it difficult to think about, let alone act out, offenses against your person. You can expect to be treated with great respect, if not awe.

The effect of this Discipline extends about 10 paces from you and immediately fades if you take offensive actions against anyone within range of your power. This effect is always active while you are conscious and takes no effort on your part. However, when in question, you should signify that you have Majesty by holding your arms out from your sides when you enter a room or other area.

Anyone attempting an offensive or aggressive action against you must first defeat you in a Social Challenge. If the attacker fails, she cannot continue with the planned action and cannot challenge your Majesty again that evening. Furthermore, unlike other powers, the subject may not spend a Willpower Trait to ignore Majesty's initial effects, although at a later time, she may spend one to challenge its effects. At least an hour must pass before the next attempt.

Protean

This Discipline allows a vampire to transform either her entire body or a part of her body into something nonhuman. The vampire can thus grow claws, turn into a bat or even become mist.

Basic

Wolf Claws

At will, you can instantly cause long, razor-sharp claws to grow from your fingertips. Because the claws are obvious and not easily hidden, using this Discipline among mortals constitutes a breach of the Masquerade. When used in combat, Wolf's Claws causes aggravated damage.

Earth Meld

Eerily and effortlessly, you can sink into the protective bosom of the earth. This is an ideal way to flee such threats as fire and the sun, provided you can find an open patch of earth. You can also use this Discipline as a "Fair Escape." However, a Kindred using Earth Meld during combat as a defensive action will have to relent if he is attacked; he will fade into the ground at the end of the turn. The power will not work on any substance other than soil. Earth Meld leaves no trace of its use and only a few powers may be able to detect the hidden Kindred (Storyteller's discretion). This Discipline costs one Blood Trait to use, but the character may return to the surface at no cost.

Intermediate

Shadow of the Beast

You are capable of transforming into a wolf or bat. The process requires a full 10 seconds and one Blood Trait. During this time, you may not engage in any other action, although you may make the transformation instantaneously with the expenditure of three Blood Traits.

The change only alters your body and normal clothes — weapons and other equipment do not change. Furthermore, certain Disciplines and Abilities may be impossible to use (for instance, bats cannot Drive). A Storyteller should be consulted in any questionable cases.

As a bat, you can navigate easily in darkness and use flight to escape most foes (as per the "Fair Escape" rules). You also gain the Trait: Quick x 3. However, you must avoid well-lit areas. Obviously, bats are difficult to attack in melee, so you are usually only vulnerable to ranged attacks.

As a wolf, you can pass as a normal animal to most individuals. You can communicate with other wolves (although this is different from understanding the Garou Tongue) and might be able to associate with Garou to a degree if they are not too hostile and you don't stink too much of the Wyrm. You gain the Traits: Ferocious, Tenacious and Cunning.

Advanced

Form of Mist

Through rigorous control of your physical form, you can slowly diffuse into a fine mist. This process requires intense concentration and one full minute. In this vaporous state, you can slip through any structure, provided it isn't airtight. You are also immune to physical injuries except for those caused by fire and sunlight. Movement in this form is slow, equivalent to walking, and strong winds will reduce this to a slow walk or even push you in an undesired direction.

It costs one Blood Trait to assume Mist Form and one to return to human form. While in Mist Form, you may not use Physical Abilities or Disciplines. Obviously, being in such a state also prevents you from using certain other non-physical powers, like Command, Thaumaturgy, Wolf's Claws, rituals and so on.

Quietus

A quiet death is the goal of this Discipline, ensuring the height of secrecy. Through their blood, the Assamites master this Discipline, often combining it with Obfuscate to form a most potent tool.

Basic

Silence of Death

At the cost of one Blood Trait, you can create a zone of silence. Everyone within 20 feet of you cannot speak or make any other noises. You gain the additional advantage of a one second surprise rule when employing this Discipline.

Intermediate

Poison Blade

With the expenditure of a Blood Trait, the Assamite can coat a blade with her own blood. Poisonous to other Kindred, the blood coating enables the weapon to inflict aggravated damage on an opponent. Poison Blade may be used one time per Blood Trait spent.

Advanced

Blood Sweat

You can make an opponent sweat blood by concentrating on him. You must announce how many Blood Traits you are trying to make your opponent lose, then initiate a Mental Challenge. If you are successful, your opponent must discard his Blood Traits. However, if you lose, your Willpower Trait(s) are still spent. Every three Blood Traits costs one Willpower Trait.

The victim of Blood Sweat does not automatically know who is affecting her.

Serpentis

This Discipline is entirely derived from the legendary powers of Set. As such, it is unique to the Followers of Set.

Basic

Eyes of the Serpent

You can paralyze others with your gaze. Like a serpent's, your eyes appear gold with large black irises, hypnotizing those with whom you establish eye contact. After

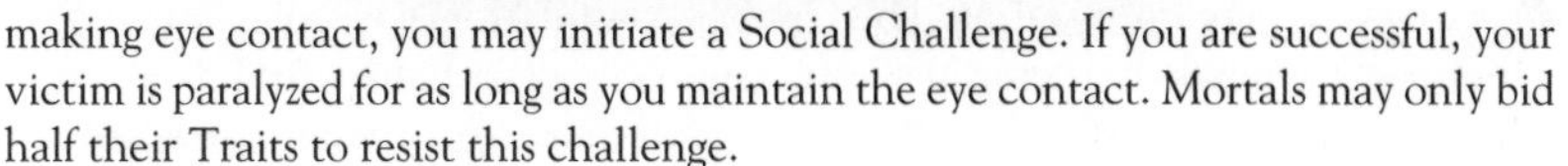

making eye contact, you may initiate a Social Challenge. If you are successful, your victim is paralyzed for as long as you maintain the eye contact. Mortals may only bid half their Traits to resist this challenge.

Intermediate

The Serpent's Tongue

You can now transform your tongue into that of a serpent's. Becoming 18-inches long, your tongue inflicts aggravated damage and drains a Blood Trait from your opponent on a successful attack.

Advanced

Form of the Serpent

You can now transform your entire body into the shape of a serpent, six inches in diameter and six-feet long. You gain all the obvious advantages of this form (slither through holes, rarefied sense of smell, poisonous bite — to mortals at least). To use this Discipline, you must expend one Physical Trait and one Blood Trait and may take no action for one full minute — you can't even speak.

Heart of Darkness

You can remove your heart from your body, thus rendering yourself immune to staking. However, if someone else finds your heart, you are completely at her mercy. With several hours of surgery, you can also perform this Discipline on other Kindred. Because Heart of Darkness takes several hours to perform, it is usually done between game sessions.

Prerequisites: Form of the Serpent

Spiritus

Native American shamans taught this Discipline to the Ahrimanes — no one else has ever been known to possess it.

Basic

Speak With Spirit

This Discipline allows you to speak to nearby wraiths without any Trait expenditure. Although you cannot see the spirits, you can smell them. A wraith must win a Simple Test to see if he can respond, and should also describe to you what animal he would most smell like. Note that because this communication is purely telepathic, it cannot be overheard by those with Heightened Senses.

Intermediate

Aspect of the Beast

By spending one Blood Trait, you can access Alacrity (Celerity), Vigor (Potence) or Wolf Claws (Protean). You may not use more than one of these Disciplines at a time, and any costs to activate the Discipline still apply. This Discipline is the direct result of your meditation and communication with animal spirits. Thus, in addition to the blood expenditure, you must concentrate for a full minute before you receive your requested Discipline — during this time, you ask the spirit of an appropriate animal to help you. The spirit's aid lasts for 20 minutes or one Physical Challenge, whichever passes first.

Advanced

The Wildebeest

Using this Discipline, you can attain a feral state in which you become slightly larger, more catlike in appearance and ready for vicious combat. You may not use any

Social Traits except Intimidating. This Discipline results from your communion with spirits of wild animals and being in close enough contact with them to allow them to lend their strengths to your body. It takes one full minute of uninterrupted concentration to evoke this state, in which you gain the following Physical Traits: Ferocious, Graceful, Lithe, Athletic, Dexterous and Tireless. You should be sure to describe your character's physical change in appearance to those around you.

Thanatosis

The practitioners of this Discipline are obsessed with the appearance of death and as such are shunned by all but the most twisted of Kindred.

Basic

Putrefaction

You can cause an opponent to decompose rapidly. After stating the number of Blood Traits you are going to spend, you initiate a Physical Challenge. If you are successful, every challenge or physical action (other than slowly walking) that your victim takes causes him to lose one Physical Trait until he is down to zero (this loss occurs after the challenge is over). Once at zero, he is so far gone that he is incapable of taking any physical action at all. This effect lasts for a full night. Additionally, the victim loses one Social Trait for every Blood Trait that you spend. If you lose the challenge, you do not recover your Blood Traits.

Intermediate

Ashes to Ashes

With this Discipline, you can transform yourself into a pile of heavy ashes, rendering you immune to fire and sunlight. While neither wind nor rain can separate you, force can: Your opponent initiates a Physical Challenge and, if successful, your ashes are separated. Reforming after being separated is painful at best — the Narrator must determine which parts are missing and how much aggravated damage you receive as a result. To assume this form requires the expenditure of one Physical Trait.

Advanced

Withering

You can now wither an opponent's limbs with a touch. By expending two Blood Traits and winning a Physical Challenge, you render an opponent's limb useless and cause him one level of aggravated damage. Even if your opponent heals this damage, the limb is withered and useless for the remainder of the evening. It should hang lifeless at his side.

Thaumaturgy

Perhaps the rarest of the Disciplines known to Camarilla vampires, Thaumaturgy is said to have been created by the Clan Tremere. Since it is almost exclusively found among Kindred of their bloodline, and because they are loath to teach it to others, there may be a degree of truth to this rumor.

While characters may only start with the Path of Blood, it is the fundamental key to learning the other Paths mentioned below. See the section on other Paths for further details.

The Path of Blood

Basic

Blood Mastery

In possessing power over a portion of a subject's blood, you can, in turn, exercise power over him. Used in such fashion, Blood Mastery often acts as a prerequisite to other Thaumaturgical rituals.

You can declare the use of Blood Mastery before or even during a challenge, as long as you do so before a test is performed. To use Blood Mastery, you must possess a Blood Trait from the subject which is destroyed when you activate the Discipline. By destroying the Blood Trait, you automatically win a single test, and the subject is not allowed any retests. If either you or the subject bid any Traits, those Traits are not lost.

Inquisition of Captive Vitæ

You are able to ascertain certain bits of information by carefully examining an individual's blood. Some types of information that you can glean are: clan, generation, creature type, diablerie (up to one year) and physical nature.

For each question asked, you must have at least one Blood Trait — which is destroyed in the process — and you must win or tie a Simple Test.

Intermediate

Theft of Vitæ

By concentrating, you can visibly coax blood from a container or target into your body. Because the source of the theft is obvious, you should expect an immediate attack if you use this ritual on another Kindred. This power works automatically against visible containers or receptacles, even those in somebody's possession. If the source of the blood is another creature or a hidden (but known) source, you must first win a Mental Challenge against the target. If you win, you may choose to expend a Mental Trait for each Blood Trait you want to siphon out of your target. You must spend all Blood Traits above your maximum immediately or they are lost.

Once in your body, this blood is considered yours and cannot be used against the original owner in any other use of Thaumaturgy.

Potency of the Blood

You can manipulate the blood within you, distilling it and making it more potent, effectively lowering your generation. The more dramatic the alteration, the greater the price.

Each step from 13th to 10th — One Blood Trait
Each step from 10th to 8th — Two Blood Traits
Each step from 8th to 6th — Three Blood Traits
Each step from 6th to 5th — Four Blood Traits
5th to 4th (maximum reduction) — Five Blood Traits

These costs are cumulative. For example, it would take the prodigious sum of 10 Blood Traits to lower a 10th generation vampire to 6th generation. While few Kindred can contain that much blood, vampires can store additional blood externally for the process. Kindred may only be under the effect of a single application of this Discipline at one time, and the effects fade at the next sunrise.

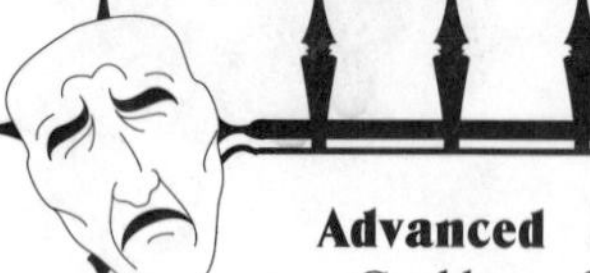

Advanced

Cauldron of Blood

With a touch, you can cause the very life-fluid inside a foe to boil and burn within her veins. Unless the victim cannot resist, you must first win a Physical Challenge to establish a firm grip on the victim. Once this has been achieved, you spend a Willpower Trait to activate the Cauldron of Blood. At this point, you may choose to expend a variable number of Mental Traits, each of which destroys a single Blood Trait and inflicts an ordinary wound. You may not inflict more wounds than the victim has Blood Traits. A human who loses two or more of her Blood Traits in this manner will die.

Other Paths

While the Path of Blood comes instinctively to the Tremere bloodline, other, more difficult Paths are available to Kindred who display arcane predispositions. Generally, you cannot take any of the following Paths upon character creation, although you can learn them through experience and the instruction of a tutor of arcane text.

The first Path that you learn — the Path of Blood — is your primary Path. You may not raise subsequent Paths above your mastery in this primary Path. Additionally, you or your chantry must seek out and uncover the knowledge required to study it. One method of doing so involves using the Occult Ability; other possibilities may form the basis for stories involving occultists or Clan Tremere in your chronicle.

Remember that you must first find knowledge before you can learn it. Learning new Paths after the first requires time, patience and experience, just as would any other Discipline.

Lure of Flame

This Path allows you to manipulate and create an unnatural fire that will not ignite objects until you release the flames.

Basic

Hand of Flame

You may instantly call forth a flaming wreath about your hands. If you defeat a foe in a Physical Challenge with the flaming appendage, you inflict an aggravated wound instead of a normal one. Flammable foes or objects hit with the Hand of Flame may ignite (Storyteller's discretion).

Flamebolt

By expending a Mental Trait, you can summon forth and hurl a fiery brand at range. This functions exactly like a ranged weapon, except that you use your Occult Ability instead of Firearms. Use Mental Traits for all challenges involved. Other trivial (no test needed) uses of this power include lighting cigarettes and candles at range or destroying light cloth and paper items. More resilient items require a Static Challenge.

Intermediate

Engulf

You can engulf a foe in a searing column of flames by initiating a Mental Challenge using the Occult Ability (to master the fiery energies and place the flames accurately), while the defender must employ Physical Traits (to avoid the flames).

To initiate the challenge, you must expend a Willpower Trait. If the casting is successful, the subject combusts, suffering two aggravated wounds. For each challenge or every full five seconds (whichever is greater) that passes, the victim may attempt to win or tie a Simple Test to extinguish the flames. Failing or engaging in alternative actions results in another aggravated wound and continued burning. Success indicates that the flames are out and no further damage is inflicted.

Advanced

Firestorm

By will alone, you can summon a firestorm that encompasses areas and can incinerate multiple foes. To activate this Discipline, you must expend a Willpower Trait and define the area you wish to affect. This area may be no more than 20 feet in diameter. Animated targets in this area must win a Static Physical Challenge (difficulty of six Traits) to leap to safety. If there is nowhere for a victim to escape (Narrator's discretion), he fails the test, or if he cannot or will not leave the area, he suffers one aggravated wound.

Movement of the Mind

This path allows you to move objects with the power of your mind.

Basic

Force Bolt

You can focus your will into a tangible, ranged bolt of mental force that can send a foe reeling. Casting this effect requires the expenditure of a Willpower Trait. If you defeat your opponent in a challenge (using your Mental Traits against the subject's Physical Traits), you knock down and stun the subject for 15 seconds (counted aloud). During this time, the victim cannot not initiate any physical actions, although she may use appropriate Stamina-related Traits to avoid damage from further challenges. Opponents with Swiftness are only stunned for 10 seconds. Rapidity reduces this to five seconds, and Kindred with Fleetness recover immediately. Treat this Discipline as ranged combat.

Manipulate

By concentrating intently, you can perform fine and delicate manipulation of items at range. However, because using Abilities in a challenge in this manner is somewhat difficult, you must risk two Traits instead of one. In general, you may only manipulate objects that an average human can lift in one hand. Furthermore, the speed of manipulated objects is equal to a casual walk. Range cannot exceed 100 feet.

Intermediate

Flight / Snare

You can lift and move large objects (no more than a few hundred pounds), but cannot exercise fine manipulation over them. If you use this power on yourself, you can "fly" for short distances and avoid falls. Used against an opponent, this Discipline holds foes at bay by lifting them off the ground. (This does not prevent the victim from firing a gun, calling for help or using her own Disciplines, however.)

To successfully snare an opponent, you must first defeat the subject in a challenge using your Mental Traits versus the subject's Physical Traits. This power is too awkward and clumsy to drop objects on foes accurately or to hurl projectiles at an opponent.

If used to fly, the power costs one Mental Trait per five minutes of use.

Advanced

Major Manipulation / Lifting / Control

With this power, you can lift great weights (up to an automobile) and immobilize or hurl foes away. To use this Discipline against an opponent, you must first defeat him in a challenge (Mental Traits against your foe's Physical Traits). If you choose to immobilize your foe, he must remain absolutely motionless for as long as you maintain complete concentration on him. While doing so, you can take no other action.

Alternatively, after winning the challenge, you can throw the opponent, who loses one Health Level and must move (as an out-of-game action) to an area within 100 feet as you direct. Finally, objects thrown at or dropped on targets cause one (for man-sized objects) or two (for larger objects) Health Levels of damage if they hit. Once again, a Mental vs. Physical Challenge (as aforementioned) is necessary to hit a foe.

You must spend a Mental Trait to activate this power.

Weather Control

This path allows you to manipulate, change and otherwise command the weather.

Basic

Cloak of Fog

You can call up an obscuring fog that blankets the area. The fog bank can only appear out of doors and can cover an area up to 100 feet across.

The Discipline costs one Mental Trait and takes 15 minutes to activate. Within the fog, visibility (and thus ranged actions) are cut to five feet. Furthermore, visual tests require you to risk two Traits instead of one, although Heightened Senses and the like eliminate these penalties. At the Storyteller's option, fog may reduce the damage a vampire takes from sunlight.

Downpour

You can cause the skies to darken and moisture-laden clouds to bring rain. The rain is very heavy, but only affects a small area (about 100 feet), while surrounding areas are overcast and sullen.

This power costs a Mental Trait and takes 15 minutes to activate. Everyone exposed to the torrential downpour risks two Traits for Physical Challenges, while ranged actions are reduced to 20 feet. At the Storyteller's option, darkened rainstorm skies may reduce the damage that sunlight causes vampires.

Intermediate

Tempest

You can alter the local weather patterns of large areas and call forth a variety of weather effects. By spending a Willpower Trait, you summon the chosen type of weather form, which lasts for one hour, plus an additional hour for each Mental Trait you expend. The Storyteller may assign a higher cost or require a Static Mental Challenge for very unusual or unseasonable weather. Weather you can create includes thunderstorms, hailstorms, blizzards or clear skies. The game effects are similar to that of Cloak of Fog and Downpour, but the Tempest's effects are citywide.

Advanced

Call Lightning

By will alone, you bring forth devastating bolts of lightning from the heavens to smite your foes. This power only works outdoors in overcast, stormy or rainy conditions and costs a Willpower Trait to activate. If your attack — using your Mental Traits and Survival Ability against your foe's Physical Traits — succeeds, your victim suffers three aggravated wounds.

Rituals

Rituals are arcane formulas and incantations that, properly and skillfully enacted, can bring about powerful magical effects. They are not, however, commonplace or easily mastered.

For each level (Basic, Intermediate or Advanced) of mastery in your primary Path, you can begin to study one of the following rituals of the same level, with Storyteller approval. You may learn additional rituals with experience and instruction from a mentor who has mastered the ritual in question. The guidelines for uncovering and learning Paths also apply to rituals.

Basic

Basic Rituals take 30 minutes to perform, unless an individual ritual description states otherwise.

Crimson Sentinel

This ritual allows you to inscribe a warding rune, making it difficult or impossible for a subject to enter an area. You must inscribe the rune with one of the subject's Blood Traits, which affects an area up to 15 paces across (a small room). The number of Mental Traits you expend when casting the ritual determines the difficulty: Once the ward is engaged, any time the subject attempts to enter the warded area, she must win a Static Challenge against this difficulty. If the rune is discovered and destroyed, the ritual is dispelled.

Defense of the Sacred Haven

You can use this handy ritual to protect your haven or chantry from one of the oldest banes of the Kindred — sunlight. The ritual costs one Blood Trait to cast, but lasts as long as the structure is intact and you remain within. After it is cast, no sunlight can enter the haven through a window or door (as long as they remain closed). The ritual affects structures up to the size of a small house, but a Storyteller may rule that it can also affect larger structures at a higher cost.

Deflection of the Wooden Doom

By performing this ritual within a circle of wood (of any sort), you can make yourself or someone else impervious to staking. The ritual costs one Mental Trait to enact, but lasts until you are staked — if this happens, the challenge is lost, the staking implement is destroyed and the enchantment ends. Neither party suffers wounds, and no Traits are lost. To represent the presence of this ritual, you should record it on your character sheet and carry a small wooden sliver (like a toothpick) on you. Only one of these enchantments may be present on a subject at a given time.

Devil's Touch

You can place a temporary magical curse upon a mortal, causing others to view him with revulsion and disgust. The subject must bid at least two Traits on all Social Challenges while under the effects of the ritual. Using either skillful roleplaying or the Streetwise or Security Ability, you should slip a penny or similar coin onto the victim. The ritual ends when the subject finds and discards the coin — or at sunrise, whichever comes first.

Purity of Flesh

This ritual mystically purges impurities (mundane pollutants, poisons and drugs, but not diseases or magical effects) from a target by concentrating these impurities into the subject's blood. To enact the ritual, you take one Blood Trait, which becomes thoroughly putrid and useless afterwards, from the subject. A Storyteller may require a Simple Test or challenge for particularly stubborn substances.

Engaging the Vessel of Transference

You can mystically prepare a vessel to act as a conduit, exchanging the blood it contains with the blood of anyone whom it contacts. While you need not initiate any tests to accomplish the transfer (causing a slight shivering sensation in the victim), the container only conveys one Blood Trait per use. Once you have transferred all of the original blood in this manner, the magic fades, but the collected blood remains. Often used to obtain blood samples or to Blood Bond a subject, this ritual costs a Mental Trait to perform.

Ward Versus Ghouls

You can create an arcane sigil that detrimentally affects creatures such as ghouls, who have both mortal and Kindred blood. Placed on an unbroken and immobile circle or loop, the ward produces discomfort in ghouls approaching the edge of this barrier (from within or without) and causes three aggravated wounds to ghouls crossing the barrier. Alternately, placing the ward on a melee weapon causes it to inflict an aggravated wound (in addition to normal damage) on ghouls.

To inscribe and enchant the warded area, you must destroy a Trait of mortal blood and permanently expend a Mental Trait. If the symbol is somehow discovered and destroyed, the ward's magic is destroyed. If you wish, you can exclude individual ghouls from either version of the ward if they are present at the casting and donate a Blood Trait to attune the ward to ignore them.

Intermediate

Intermediate Rituals take an hour to perform, unless the description of an individual ritual below states otherwise.

Bone of Lies

You can enchant a mortal bone to ascertain whether or not the holder is telling the truth. The bone must be at least 200 years old from a mortal who has never tasted of Kindred blood. This ritual takes one hour to perform, and the bone must be bathed in and absorb 10 Blood Traits. Thereafter, each time someone bearing the bone lies, it visibly darkens. The bone may be used 10 times before it is rendered useless.

Pavis of the Foul Presence

It is rumored that the Tremere created this ritual primarily to counter the Presence Discipline in which their chief rivals in the Camarilla, the Ventrue, specialize. Indeed, it is almost never found outside Clan Tremere. The ritual costs a Mental Trait to cast and lasts until you invoke its power or until sunrise, whichever comes first. When someone uses a Presence Discipline against you, a test is performed as normal, but if you win, the Presence Discipline instead affects your foe. If you lose, the Presence power has no effect. In either case, to use the ritual again, you must recast it. Only one of these enchantments may be present at a time.

To represent the presence of this Discipline, you should record it on your character sheet and wear (not necessarily visibly) a blue silken cord about your neck.

Ward Versus Lupines

You perform this ritual exactly like Ward Versus Ghouls except that you use silver dust, not blood, to cast it. The ritual affects Lupines in all their forms.

Advanced

Advanced Rituals require 90 minutes to perform unless stated otherwise.

Night of the Red Heart

You perform this ritual in two sessions of one hour each — the first just after sunset, and the other just before sunrise. If you enact the ritual successfully, its target dies horribly at sunrise: His heart boils and is consumed as if by the burning rays of the sun.

The ritual requires three of the victim's Blood Traits and a fellow Thaumaturgist (although only one of you need know the ritual). The subject immediately realizes that she is the target of a ritual after you have completed its first part, although she may not be aware of its origin. The target can only save her life by killing one of the Kindred performing the ritual or otherwise preventing the second ceremony. You must cast both parts of the ritual in the same place and within the same city as the target. To invoke the final effect, each caster must permanently expend a Mental Trait.

Nectar of the Bitter Rose

The mysteries of this ritual are held in strict secrecy by those able to cast it, for the ritual's very existence poses a threat few in the Camarilla would tolerate. During the course of this three-hour ritual, the participants drain and devour the life essence of a Kindred. The victim must be present and somehow restrained throughout the entire process. The end result is a draught that may be shared by up to five Diabolists. Each drinker may benefit from the generation of the victim, if applicable, though only once per victim and ritual.

There are risks, however. Each Diabolist must engage in a Simple Test (no Traits are risked) against the victim. If the Diabolist wins or ties, she lowers her generation. If she loses, the blood rejects her and she gains nothing from the ritual, nor may she ever benefit from the ritual in the future. At the very least, the victim of the ritual is utterly destroyed, his soul consumed in the process. See the Chapter Three, "Diablerie," in this book and Chapter Five of **The Masquerade 2nd Edition** for further information.

Abandon the Fetters of Blood

Through this powerful and taxing arcane ordeal, you can free a target from the legendary shackles of the Blood Bond. To perform the ritual, you must use all the blood from the subject and a single Blood Trait from her Regnant to fuel the ritual. At the ritual's climax, when the last of the target's blood leaves her body, she suffers the permanent loss of a Physical, Mental and Social Trait of her choosing as a result of the ordeal. The subject's blood is then returned and the Blood Bond is no more. You cannot use the Regnant's blood again, as it is destroyed during the course of the ritual.

Ward Versus Kindred

You perform this ritual exactly like Ward Versus Ghouls, except that you use Kindred blood to cast it and it affects vampires of all sorts.

Thaumaturgy Among the *Antitribu*

Antitribu vampires with this Discipline probably know some of the traditional rituals and Paths associated with their Camarilla cousins; paths and rituals belonging solely to the Sabbat follow.

Antitribu Paths

While other Tremere may have heard of the rituals and Paths that follow, it is unlikely that they possess them, since the Sabbat Tremere fiercely protect their secrets and advantages.

Gift of Morpheus

This path allows you to control others' sleep and dreams.

Basic

Cause Sleep

By winning a Mental Challenge with the victim, you can cause him to fall asleep. The victim will not fall over and snore on the floor, but he will, over a period of five minutes, gradually drift into a sleep from which loud noise or physical contact can

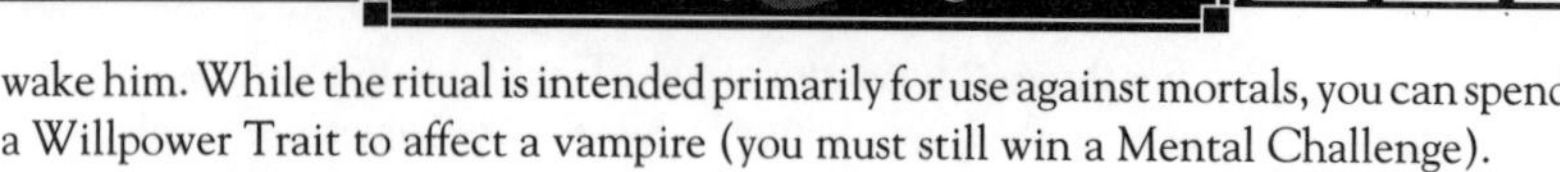

wake him. While the ritual is intended primarily for use against mortals, you can spend a Willpower Trait to affect a vampire (you must still win a Mental Challenge).

Mass Slumber

By spending a Willpower Trait, you can cause a group of mortals to fall asleep. To resist, mortals must spend a Willpower Trait and test against you in a Mental Challenge. If there are ghouls or Garou present in the "mortal" crowd, you must engage in individual Mental Challenges with each non-mortal. This ritual is best invoked in the presence of a Storyteller.

Intermediate

Enchanted Slumber

This ritual allows you to cause a person or creature to fall into a sleep from which she cannot be wakened until a specific event occurs (like a kiss from Prince Charming). This event should be achievable, though not necessarily easy. The target will rouse if her life is threatened, although she will be down two Traits in all areas. To invoke this sleep, you must spend a Willpower Trait and initiate a Mental Challenge.

This ritual is best used on a Narrator character. If used on a player character, you should remember that if the conditions are unachievable in-game, they could cause the player to be effectively cut out of the game for at least the duration of the evening. Storytellers may choose not to allow you to set impossible conditions such as, "She may not awaken until her body is physically transported to the planet Mars."

Advanced

Dream Mastery

You may enter the mind of a specific sleeper and induce nightmares or use Disciplines such as Presence, Dominate or Auspex if you yourself possess them. You effectively gain control over the sleeper's dreams and can do as you wish. Any Discipline used on the sleeper must incorporate the usual number of challenges and other Blood and Willpower expenditures. This requires you to win a Mental Challenge and spend one Mental Trait. The sleeper may take normal action in her dream.

Antitribu Rituals

Rituals are magical systems of action that require specific ingredients, incantations, blood and time. They are also very draining to the Thaumaturgist's will, neither easily mastered nor easily taught, and almost always guarded jealously.

While the Camarilla Tremere have many rituals, the Tremere *antitribu* have developed many of their own.

Basic

Blood Rush

Blood Rush allows you to trick yourself into feeling the sensation of drinking blood. With your eyes closed, you must spin three times to the left and chant the secret phrase three times in your mind. If you do not do so, you will not feel the ritual's effects. By creating a sensation of your consuming more than about two Blood Traits (although you gain no actual Blood Traits), this ritual proves most useful in preventing blood frenzies by making you feel as if you've just fed. You must spend one Physical Trait to enact this ritual.

Domino of Life

This ritual allows you to adopt one aspect of human life for the duration of the night. You may eat, drink, raise your body temperature, simulate a heartbeat or anything else you desire. Only one aspect may be invoked at a time and its presence will not change your aura in any way. To invoke life in this manner, you must consume two mortal Blood Traits, win a Static Physical Challenge with a two Trait difficulty, and expend one Physical Trait.

Rotten-wood

By speaking a ritual word aloud, you can crumble to dust any wood you touch — from an enormous antique table to a stake. The ritual, which you must perform upon waking, lasts one night. To enact it, you must chew through a one-inch-thick piece of wood without using your strength to break it. Thereafter, whenever you wish to disintegrate a wooden object during the course of that night, you must win a Static Mental Challenge against it and you can do so.

Intermediate

Fire In the Blood

This ritual causes your victim to suffer one aggravated wound every time she engages in a Physical Challenge. It requires physical contact between you and the victim (a Physical Challenge) and may be performed as a separate challenge during combat or in advance. You must also speak aloud a word of command, such as "burn" or "boil." In a noncombat situation, this word, though it must be audible, may be delivered quite subtly. When activated during combat, the ritual is an obvious attack, and the victim will be aware of what you are doing to her. In either case, you must win a second challenge against the victim in order for the ritual to be effective (your Mental Traits vs. the victim's Physical Traits). If you are successful, for the duration of the night, the victim experiences extreme pain from the heat of the blood in her body whenever she engages in a Physical Challenge.

If you perform the ritual in advance with the physical contact being, for example, a handshake, the Storyteller may wish to give the victim an envelope to open when she engages in her first Physical Challenge (not including the original challenge against you) which explains the effects of this ritual without directly revealing its source.

Iron Mind

Performed when you wake, this ritual renders you almost entirely invulnerable to Auspex for the duration of the night. By sitting in uninterrupted meditation for 15 minutes before joining play, wearing a piece of iron on your head, and spending one Willpower Trait, you engage the ritual.

If another character wishes to perform a Mental Challenge to use any of the powers of the Auspex Discipline, she must spend a Willpower Trait to perform the challenge. Having done so and won, the character can use Auspex as usual.

Recure of the Homeland

You can heal up to two of your own aggravated wounds. The ritual requires dirt from your homeland, which must be rubbed on the wound while you sit in meditation for 10 minutes. Although the meditation should be uninterrupted, it could feasibly happen in a communal haven with others present. Because one handful of dirt heals one aggravated wound, you can only hold (at most) two handfuls of dirt, and the ritual may only be enacted once per night, the maximum number of Health Levels you may heal is two. This ritual requires a Static Mental Challenge.

Advanced

Chill of the Windsaber

You can decapitate a victim with sheer telekinetic force. This very potent ritual costs two Willpower Traits and a Mental Challenge against the target. You must prepare it in one hour of solitary, uninterrupted ritual (the player must remain alone, out of game) by creating a voodoo doll of the intended victim using some piece of the victim's clothing, hair, flesh or blood (a card representing the item or a Blood Trait from the target character must be shown to a Storyteller before the challenge can occur). Next, you must chant over the doll and tuck it safely away with a small piece of glass. To activate the ritual, you must be within 50 feet of the individual, snap the piece of glass in half, point your finger at the target and engage in a Mental Challenge. If you win, the telekinetic force of your ritual chops off the victim's head. There is no warning for this very advanced and rare ritual, unless the targeted character manages to find out what is going on and put a stop to it before you can enact the ritual. Storytellers should disallow this ritual if it unbalances their game.

Invisible Chains of Binding

You can render another creature immobile by summoning a supernatural force of invisible chains and shackles. You may chain up to four people with this ritual, but must spend one Willpower Trait for each. You must be able to see your victims while making bold hand gestures like tying, and you must be sure the victim(s) sees you. If the victim wishes, he may spend a Willpower Trait to resist, after which a challenge between your Mental Traits and the victim's Physical Traits occurs. You or the Storyteller should inform any victim of Invisible Chains of Binding of his option to spend a Willpower Trait to initiate a Physical Challenge, as most players are unaware of this option.

Thirst Unquenchable

Within another vampire, you can create the sensation of the Hunger for the remainder of the evening. No matter how much the victim feeds, he will remain starving. To do so, you must stand in the victim's presence for five minutes and sprinkle salt around her in a circle. The prolonged effects of this ritual almost always induce frenzy.

Vicissitude

This Discipline allows the Tzimisce to alter appearances and physiological structures — whether her own or someone else's — sometimes in painful ways. Not just a Discipline, Vicissitude is often considered a disease (and some say more than just a disease). Using this Discipline can be a tremendous strain on a vampire's mind: If a vampire uses this Discipline more than three times per night, he permanently gains one new Derangement or one Path Trait at the discretion of the Storyteller.

Basic

Changeling

You can alter your own appearance as much as your natural bone structure allows. That is, you may not go from being a 5' 1" overweight, bald man to a six-foot-tall skinny person. You may look completely different, but your basic size and shape remain the same.

This Discipline costs one Blood Trait per use and takes five minutes. Unlike Obfuscate, you cannot just pop in and out of disguise: it requires time and concentration on your part.

When using Changeling, try to bring a few extra costume pieces with you so that people in your pack will know not to recognize you when you are wearing the brown jacket or the fuzzy green hat. Also, if your group is using numbers, you must change yours to identify you as someone different.

The effects of Changeling last until you change yourself (or are changed back) to your natural form.

Fleshcraft

Fleshcraft allows you to alter another creature's flesh. Often used as a combat technique in inter-Sabbat arguments or to terrify and intimidate other opponents, the Discipline requires you to engage in a Physical Challenge with an unwilling victim and win, or to tie a Simple Test with a willing one. The challenge's outcome determines whether or not you can lay your hands on the victim while invoking the Discipline. In any case, this Discipline does not function without physical contact.

If you use this Discipline to improve another's appearance (requiring a Simple Test), the victim gains one appropriate Social Trait for the duration of the physical alteration. Failure on the Simple Test means that the victim loses one Social Trait.

This Discipline costs one Blood Trait each time you use it and takes at least 10 uninterrupted minutes to perform (if altering an entire face).

Intermediate

Bonecraft

Bonecraft allows you to alter the bone structure of your victim. Since its effects are particularly painful, the Sabbat find this technique most useful in torture situations. With Bonecraft, you can increase or decrease the size of a bone, insert objects into bone (as long as the bone itself can be touched), carve bone with bare hands or engage in similar practices. You cannot use this Discipline to break bones in combat (that would involve your Physical Traits and Brawl Ability). However, you can bend bones while touching the victim (a Physical Challenge with strength-related Traits). The effects of this Discipline are permanent unless someone else alters them using the same Discipline.

Bonecraft costs one Blood Trait to use and requires a Physical Challenge (unwilling victim) or Simple Test (willing victim). If you wish to use Bonecraft on yourself to enhance the effects of Changeling, you run the risk of a pain frenzy. The alteration of an entire skeleton takes at least 20 minutes to perform, and the victim must either spend one Willpower Trait to avoid frenzying from pain or engage in a Static Physical Challenge.

Note that Storytellers may feel free not to allow the use of this Discipline in their games.

Advanced

Horrid Form

With this Discipline, you can assume the form of an enormous, disgusting monster. Your body is transformed into a seven to eight foot tall creature with blackish, oily skin and other enchanting features like bony knobs protruding from the spine, a hideously deformed head and huge, clawlike, seven-fingered hands. You also must find a way to alert other nearby players to this change. Raising your hands from your sides, fingers splayed and clawlike, can be appropriate.

You must spend two Blood Traits to activate Horrid Form and, while in it, cannot use any Social Traits except Intimidation. Moreover, you gain the following Physical Traits: Brawny, Ferocious, Dexterous, Quick, Enduring and Stalwart. All damage inflicted while in this form is aggravated.

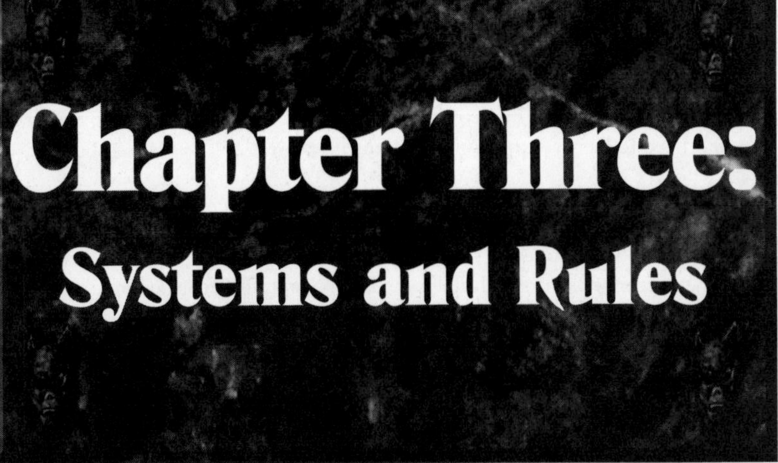

Chapter Three: Systems and Rules

This chapter covers the remainder of the basic rules for **The Masquerade** and presents a brief primer on the Sabbat.

Included is information on: **Time — Challenges — Testing — Complications — Overbidding — Health — Healing — Aggravated Wounds — Combat — Weapons — Ranged Combat — Cover — Frenzy — Diablerie — Golconda — Blood Bond — Status — Camarilla Stations — Sabbat Status — Prestation & Boons — Fair Escape — Sabbat Basics — The Black Hand — Packs — Rites & Rituals — Creation Rites & Conversion — Vaulderie & Vinculum**

Time

Time in **Mind's Eye Theatre** works as it does in real life, moving forward inexorably, relentlessly. For the most part, everything is played out in real time, and players are expected to stay in character unless they have a rules question.

During the course of a story, it is assumed that a player is always "in character." Because dropping out of character ruins the atmosphere for everyone involved, players should only do so under certain circumstances. If they wish to talk through challenges or need to take a break, players should inform a Narrator and should not interact with any of the other players while out of character.

The only other exception occurs when a Narrator calls for a "time out." This may be necessary to resolve a dispute or to change the scene if the story requires it. When "Time Out!" is called, all players within hearing distance must stop whatever they are doing until the Narrator calls out the word "Resume." Timeouts should be kept to a minimum, since they interrupt the flow of the story.

Challenges

During the course of most stories, there will come a time when two or more players will come into a conflict that cannot be resolved through roleplaying alone. This system allows for conflicts to be resolved simply and quickly, whether they're firefights or tests of will. This faceoff is called a challenge. In most cases, a Narrator does not need to be present when a challenge is played.

Using Traits

Before you can begin to learn how challenges work, you must first understand what defines a character's abilities. You create a character by choosing a number of adjectives that describe and define that person as an individual. These adjectives are called Traits and are fully described in Chapter Three of **The Masquerade 2nd Edition**. These Traits are used to declare a challenge against another character or against a static force represented by a Narrator.

Initial Bid

A challenge begins when a player "bids" one of her Traits against an opponent. At the same time, she declares what the conditions of the challenge are, e.g. firing a gun or attacking with a stake. The defender then decides how to respond — either by relenting immediately or by bidding one of her own Traits.

During bidding, players should only employ Traits that seem sensible within the context of the situation — that is, bidding players usually should use Traits from the same category as the opponent's, whether Physical, Social or Mental. Experienced players may offer each other more creative leeway, but that is strictly by mutual agreement.

If the defender relents, she automatically loses the challenge (for example, if she were being attacked, she would suffer a wound). If she matches the challenger's bid, the two immediately go to a test (described below). Those Traits bid are put at risk, as the loser of the test not only loses the challenge, but the Trait she bid as well.

Testing

Once both parties involved in a challenge have bid a Trait, they immediately go to a test. The test itself is not what you may think — the outcome is random, but no cards or dice are used. The two players face off against one another by playing Rock-Paper-Scissors (see below). It may sound a little silly, but it works.

If you lose the test, you lose the Trait you bid for the duration of the story (this usually means the rest of the evening). Essentially, you've lost some of your self-confidence in your own capabilities. You can no longer use that Trait effectively, at least until you regain confidence in your Traits.

The test works like the moment in poker when the cards are turned over and the winner is declared. From the test, there may be one of two outcomes: Either one player is the victor or the result is a tie.

In a tie, the players reveal the number of Traits they possess in the bid category (Physical, Social or Mental). The player with the least number of Traits loses the test and thus the challenge. Note that the number of Traits you've lost in previous challenges or for any other reasons counts towards this total. The trick to the declaration is that you may lie about the number of Traits you possess, but only by declaring fewer Traits than you actually have — you may never say that you have more Traits than you actually do. This allows you to keep the actual number of Traits you possess a secret, although doing so may be risky.

The challenger is always the first to declare his number of Traits. If both players declare the same number of Traits, they draw and both lose the Trait(s) they bid.

Incidentally, certain advanced powers allow some characters to use gestures other than Rock, Paper and Scissors. Before players can use these gestures in a test, they must explain what they are and how they are used.

Rock-Paper-Scissors

If you don't happen to know (or remember) what we mean by Rock-Paper-Scissors, here's the concept: you and another person face off and, on the count of three, show one of three hand gestures. "Rock" is a basic fist. "Paper" is a flat hand. "Scissors" is represented by sticking out two fingers. You then compare the two gestures to determine the winner. Rock crushes Scissors. Scissors cuts Paper. Paper covers Rock. Identical signs indicate a tie.

Adjudication

If you have question or argument about the rules or the conditions of a challenge, you need to find a Narrator to make a judgment. Try to remain in character while looking for a Narrator. Any interruption in the progress of the story should be avoided, so work problems out with other players if at all possible. If you don't know the exact correct application of a certain rule, try to wing it rather than interrupt the flow of the story — cooperation is the key to telling a good story.

Complications

There are a number of ways in which a challenge can be complicated. The above rules are enough to resolve most disputes, but the following rules help to add a few bells and whistles.

Negative Traits

Many characters have Negative Traits. These are Traits that an opponent can use against a character. After you have each bid one Trait during the initial bid of any challenge, you can call out a Negative Trait that you believe your opponent possesses. If he does indeed possess the Negative Trait, your opponent is forced to bid an additional Trait, although you must still risk your one Trait as usual. If he does not possess that Negative Trait, *you* must risk an additional Trait. (Blood Traits cannot be used to substitute for Physical Traits in this instance.) You may integrate as many Negative Traits as you wish one by one during the initial bid phase of a challenge, as long as you can pay the price if you're wrong.

If your opponent does not have additional Traits to bid, then your Trait is not at risk during the challenge. Additionally, if you guess more than one Negative Trait that your opponent cannot match, you gain that many additional Traits in the case of a tie or an overbid. The same works in reverse, favoring your opponent if you do not have additional Traits remaining to match incorrect Negative Trait guesses.

Overbidding

Overbidding is the system by which elder vampires (who often have considerably more Traits than younger opponents) may prevail in a challenge, even if they lose the initial test. An elder vampire with 18 Social Traits should be able to crush a neonate with five. This system is designed to make that possible.

Once the players have made the test, the loser has the option of calling for an "overbid." In order to do so, you must also risk a new Trait; the original one has already been lost. At this point, the two players reveal the number of Traits they possess, starting with the player who called for an overbid. If you have double your opponent's number of Traits in the appropriate category, you may attempt another test. As with

a tie, you may state a number of Traits less than the actual number you have and keep your true power secret. This can be dangerous, though, unless you are completely confident in your estimation of your opponent's abilities.

Static Challenges

Sometimes you may have to undergo a challenge against a Narrator rather than against another player, such as when you are trying to pick a lock or summon an animal. Under such circumstances, the Narrator chooses a difficulty appropriate to the task you are attempting and you bid the appropriate Trait, then immediately perform a test against the Narrator. The test proceeds exactly as it would if you were testing against another character. Of course, you may overbid in a Static Challenge, but beware, because the Narrator can overbid as well.

Sometimes Narrators may leave notes on objects, such as books and doors. These notes indicate the type of challenge that must be won for something to occur (such as understanding a book, opening a door or identifying an artifact). With experience, you may learn how difficult it is to open a locked door. However, difficulty ratings can be as different as lock types.

Simple Tests

Simple Tests are used to determine if you can succeed at something when there is no real opposition. Often used when determining the extent of a Discipline's effect, most Simple Tests do not require you to risk or bid Traits, although some may.

When a Simple Test is called, players use the Rock-Paper-Scissors test against the Narrator. In most cases, the player succeeds on a win or a tie, although at Narrator discretion, it may be necessary for him to win.

Health

A character in **The Masquerade** has five Health Levels that represent the amount of injury the character has suffered: Healthy, Bruised, Wounded, Incapacitated and Torpor. If a Healthy character loses a combat challenge, she becomes Bruised. If she loses two, she becomes Wounded, and so on.

• **Bruised** — When a character is Bruised, she is only slightly injured, having perhaps suffered a few scrapes and bruises, but little more until she is healed. In order to enter a new challenge, she must risk an additional Trait. Thus, to even have a chance in a challenge, a Bruised character must bid at least two Traits.

• **Wounded** — When a character is Wounded, she is badly hurt. She might be bleeding freely from open wounds and may even have broken bones. She must bid two Traits to have a chance in a challenge. In addition, she will always lose when she ties during a test, even if she has more Traits than her opponent. If she has fewer Traits, her opponent gets a free additional test.

• **Incapacitated** — When a character is Incapacitated, she is completely out of play for at least 10 minutes. After 10 minutes has passed, the character is still immobile and may not enter into challenges until she has healed at least one Health Level. At the mercy of other characters, she is only capable of whispering and is barely aware of her surroundings while incapacitated.

• **Torpor** — When a character is in Torpor, she is in a deathlike state. Effectively out of play until another character revives her, she is completely at the mercy of other characters and the environment around her. Only the blood of another vampire at least three generations lower than the Kindred in Torpor can revive her. The Storyteller may, of course, allow other exceptional circumstances to rouse a vampire from this state.

Healing

Vampires require blood in order to heal wounds. Blood Traits must be expended to restore Health Levels on a one-for-one basis. More information on Blood Traits can be found in Chapter Three of **The Masquerade 2nd Edition**.

Aggravated Wounds

Vampires cannot heal aggravated wounds with blood alone. Exposure to sunlight, fire and the claws or teeth of a vampire or werewolf cause aggravated wounds and require the expenditure of three Blood Traits and a Willpower Trait to heal. Additionally, only one such wound may be healed per night, representing the gradual regenerative properties a vampire possesses. Kindred can completely heal extreme injuries, such as broken or severed limbs, but they require blood and time to do so.

The Mob Scene

During the course of many stories, you are inevitably going to be drawn into a challenge in which several people want to be involved. Multiparty challenges can be confusing, but if you follow these simple guidelines, you shouldn't have much difficulty. These rules are most useful in combat challenges, but they can be used with nearly any sort of group challenge.

The first thing you need to do is to decide who is challenging whom. This is usually obvious, but when it's not, you need a quick way to work things out. Simply have everyone involved count to three at the same time. On three, each player points at the individual he is challenging.

The first challenge that must be resolved involves the person who has the most people pointing at him. Determine which category of Traits would be most appropriate — Physical, Social or Mental. Each player pointing at the defender bids one appropriate Trait, and the group chooses a leader. The attacking group cannot exceed five people — there is a limit to the number of individuals who can attack a single person at one time.

The defender then bids as many Traits as there are people opposing him. If he does not have enough Traits to do so, he automatically loses the challenge. If he does have enough Traits, he performs a test against the chosen leader of the attackers. The rest of the challenge continues as normal, although only the group leader can compare and overbid Traits.

If the defender wins the test, he remains unharmed, but he can choose to affect only one member of the attacking group — usually by inflicting one wound (as during combat). Additionally, the attackers lose all Traits they bid. If the attackers win, they may inflict one wound, and the defender loses all the Traits he risked.

After the first challenge is concluded, go on to the next one. Continue the process until each character who has declared an action has been the target of a challenge or has donated Traits.

Order of Challenges

Some players wonder exactly how to respond when challenged. Typically, if someone initiates a Physical Challenge, the defender can only respond with Physical Traits, unless he possesses a Discipline or some other ability that is considered to be always active. He cannot respond by using a Discipline or another ability until after the first challenge has been completed. Some Disciplines, which specify this contingency in their description, pose an exception to this rule. Social and Mental Challenges work the same way.

Combat

The basic challenge system used in **The Masquerade** has already been presented. This section contains a few basic modifications to the combat system and elaboration on it.

Combat is the usual intent behind Physical Challenges. Essentially, combat involves two characters in physical conflict. The players agree what the outcome of the challenge will be, each player bids an appropriate Trait, and a test is resolved, determining the victor. The following rules allow for variances to those basic rules, such as situations using surprise or weapons.

The agreed outcome of a Physical Challenge usually involves the loser being injured. This is not, however, the only result possible. For instance, you could say that you want to wrest a weapon from your opponent's hands or that you're trying to trip him. The result can be nearly anything the two parties agree upon, whether that's simply raking someone with claws or dramatically throwing someone through a window. The results of a combat challenge may also be different for both participants. (For example, a frenzied Brujah may wish to attack a Toreador who affronted her, while the Toreador may simply want to escape).

Surprise

If a player does not respond within three seconds of the declaration of a Physical Challenge, the player is considered surprised: He is not fully prepared for what's coming. Sometimes a player is busy with another activity, doesn't hear a challenge or is playing a character who just isn't prepared for the attack (such as when the character is led into an ambush). It is considered highly improper to sneak around whispering challenges to try to get an element of surprise. Surprise is only in effect for the first challenge of a conflict; all further challenges are resolved normally, as explained below.

Weapons

No real weapons are ever allowed in Mind's Eye Theatre games.

Even nonfunctional props are forbidden if they can be mistaken for weapons. This system does not use props of any kind, nor are players required (or allowed) to strike one another. Weapons are purely an abstraction in this game. Weapon cards, which display the facts and statistics of a particular weapon, can be used instead. The damage a weapon inflicts is limited only by mutual agreement, although it is generally assumed that an injury incurred from a blow reduces the target by a Health Level.

While some weapons have special abilities, most weapons give their wielders extra Traits, although sometimes a Negative Trait disadvantage offsets this advantage. Each weapon has one to three extra Traits; you can use these in any challenge in which you employ the weapon, but you *cannot* use them in place of your Traits when placing your initial bid. Instead, they add to your total when comparing Traits during a tie or an overbid (for instance).

Opponents may use a weapon's disadvantages, or weaknesses inherent in the weapon, in precisely the same way they do Negative Traits. The weapon's Negative Traits can only be used against its wielder and only when appropriate to the situation. For instance, if you're firing a gun and your opponent wants to apply the gun's Negative Trait: Loud against you, you can ignore that Negative Trait if you've taken the time to find a silencer.

If your opponent names your weapon's Negative Trait and it is appropriate to the situation, you suffer a one Trait penalty (i.e., you are required to risk an additional Trait). If your opponent calls out a Negative Trait that doesn't apply to the situation, your opponent suffers a one Trait penalty in the challenge.

Along with your character card, you carry cards listing the statistics for your weapons. Weapon cards specify the capacities of each weapon and allow other players to see that you actually possess a weapon — when you have a weapon card in your hand, you are considered to be holding the weapon.

Each weapon also has a concealability rating. If you cannot conceal a weapon, you must display that card at all times — you cannot, for example, pull a rifle out of your pocket. Optionally, you can pin weapon cards to your shirt, indicating that, for instance, you have an unconcealable weapon slung over your shoulder.

Bidding Traits with Weapons

During a normal hand-to-hand fight, you bid your Physical Traits against your opponent's Physical Traits. However, if you're using the Firearms Ability, you can use Mental Traits instead. If your opponent is also using a firearm, he too bids Mental Traits. If your opponent is not using a firearm and is merely trying to dodge, the attacker uses Mental Traits to fire, while the defender uses Physical Traits to dodge. This is one of the few instances when Traits from different attributes are used against one another.

Weapon Examples

• **Knife** — This easily concealed weapon is very common.

Bonus Traits: 2

Negative Traits: Short

Concealability: Pocket

• **Club** — This can be anything from a chair leg to a tree limb.

Bonus Traits: 2

Negative Traits: Clumsy

Concealability: Jacket

• **Wooden Stake** — If it transfixes a vampire's heart, the victim is immobilized.

Bonus Traits: 2

Negative Traits: Clumsy

Concealability: Jacket

• **Broken Bottle** — A good example of a weapon made from scratch.

Bonus Traits: 1

Negative Traits: Fragile

Concealability: Pocket

• **Sword** — This long-edged blade is nearly impossible to conceal.

Bonus Traits: 3

Negative Traits: Heavy

Concealability: Trench Coat

• **Pistol** — This covers nearly any sort of handgun.

Bonus Traits: 2

Negative Traits: Loud

Concealability: Pocket

• **Rifle** — Impossible to conceal

Bonus Traits: 3

Negative Traits: Loud

Concealability: None

• **Shotgun** — This powerful weapon fires a spray of pellets, making targets easy to hit and ballistics checks nearly impossible.

Bonus Traits: 3

Negative Traits: Loud

Concealability: Trench Coat

Special Ability: A shotgun may affect up to three targets if they are standing immediately next to each other and are further than 10 feet from the person firing the shotgun. Resolve this with a single challenge against a group in which the attacker risks a Trait against the entire group. The gunman performs up to three separate tests (one test for each target). In this fashion, it is possible to simultaneously wound up to three opponents in a single challenge. If any of the three opponents win, the attacker loses the Trait he risked. However, that Trait still applies to all three tests within that group challenge. Thus, a character can challenge up to three opponents while only risking one Trait with this weapon. Also, a shotgun can inflict two Health Levels of damage on a single target standing within five feet.

• **Submachine Gun** — Though difficult to conceal, this weapon is very powerful.

Bonus Traits: 3

Negative Traits: Loud

Concealability: Jacket

Special Ability: A submachine gun affects up to five targets if they're standing immediately next to each other and are further than 10 feet from the person firing it. Resolve this with a single challenge against a group (as described under the section on shotguns above).

Stake through the Heart

The bane of all vampires is the dreaded wooden stake. Although all Kindred must live in fear of this threat, placing a stake into the heart of a conscious opponent is a difficult task at best.

Staking a vampire's heart completely immobilizes him. However, in order to do so, a character must first win a Physical Challenge against the vampire, then two Simple Tests in which he impales the vampire's heart. If one or both of the Simple Tests fail, the vampire only suffers a wound from the stake, but is not immobilized.

Ranged Combat

Many weapons allow you to stand at a distance from a target and engage him in combat. In such situations, you still go over to the target (after shouting "Bang!") and engage in a challenge.

If you have surprised your opponent, even if you lose the first test, you have the option of calling for a second test. Once you call the second challenge, play continues as normal. Your target is considered surprised for the first attack, and if he has no ranged weapon with which to return fire, he is considered "surprised" for as long as you can attack him without facing resistance (that is, if he wins on a challenge, you don't take damage).

If your target is aware of you before you make your initial ranged attack and has a ranged weapon of his own, he is not considered surprised for your first attack. He may shoot back right away, and your challenges are resolved as stated below.

After your first shot is fired (the first challenge is resolved), your target may attempt to return fire, assuming he is armed. The loser of a firefight challenge loses a Health Level.

If the defender is unarmed, he may declare his victory condition as escape, providing he is not cornered. If the defender wins the challenge, the attacker remains unharmed, but his target, the defender, has escaped from view and must be searched out if the attacker decides to press the attack. In instances such as this, a new challenge cannot be made for at least five minutes.

Cover

Fighting with hand-to-hand weapons — clubs, knives or swords — requires that combatants be within reach of each other. Fighting with ranged weapons allows combatants to stand apart; participants can therefore "dive for cover." When you resolve each ranged combat challenge, you can present one Trait of cover to add to your total number of Traits. These cover Traits can't be used for bidding, but they do add to your total when comparing Traits. You can find cover behind nearby obstacles as long as they are within your reach (you *don't* actually dive for them). A Narrator might be required to tell you what cover is around, but if combatants know the area, they can agree upon what cover is available. In some instances, there may be no cover, leaving a combatant in the open with only his own defensive Traits.

If cover is extensive — a brick wall, perhaps — it may be worth more than one Trait for one challenger. The number of Traits available for cover is left for challengers to agree upon, or for a Narrator to decree. Hiding behind a car, for example, might be worth two cover Traits, while hiding behind a thin wall might only count as one. If one combatant goes completely under cover — he cannot be seen at all and is thoroughly protected — he is considered impossible to hit. The attacker must change his position to get a clear shot.

Frenzy

Vampires are creatures of instinct — the instincts of a hunter. They stand at the apex of the food chain, the harbingers of death.

Kindred call their own predatory vampiric natures "the Beast." Even the most sedate and civilized vampire can turn into a ravaging, mindless animal with enough provocation. While in this frenzy of emotion, a vampire often cannot tell friend from foe, control his desire for blood or preserve the Masquerade.

Most Kindred struggle against the Beast — some eventually yielding to its seduction and breaking the rules of vampiric society. If their crimes are not heinous, these vampires merely become outcasts; otherwise, they are hunted down and destroyed. Once a vampire has given herself to the Beast, it becomes incrementally easier to be lured into a frenzy, at which point the almost inevitable downward spiral towards constantly raging bestiality begins.

The Masquerade quantifies frenzy via Beast Traits: Each Beast Trait lists a situation(s) that causes a vampire to enter a frenzy. The rule is simple: When that situation occurs, the character frenzies. The only way to avoid entering frenzy is by spending a Willpower Trait, which staves off the frenzy for about 10 minutes. During that time, the character should try to get away from whatever is calling out to the Beast within her.

While in a frenzy, a vampire is capable of nearly anything, although the type of Beast Trait that caused it generally dictates the vampire's behavior during this time. There are three types of frenzies:

• **Rage Frenzy** — Such a frenzy causes the vampire to go berserk. The Kindred will often try to destroy everything nearby. He will start with whatever sent him into the frenzy, followed by everything else in the immediate vicinity. His anger is swift and impossible to control.

• **Control Frenzy** — These types of frenzies are usually associated with feeding. The Kindred will often begin to drink blood in huge quantities, going from victim to victim with no subtlety or attempt to maintain the Masquerade. The Kindred will tear through walls and even her friends to get at more blood until completely sated. Even then, she may still try to drink.

• **Terror Frenzy** — The few things that vampires fear — fire or sunlight, for instance — cause these frenzies, during which the vampire frantically flees the fear-invoking stimulus. The Kindred is dangerous to approach until she has fled the flame or sunlight and had a few minutes to calm down. Many well-intentioned Kindred have met their demise while trying to stop a vampire in a frenzy.

While in this state of blind emotion, Kindred can ignore all damage until reduced to Torpor or Final Death. Unfortunately, they can't heal themselves with or attempt Social Challenges. Also, a vampire need not risk any Social Traits if someone tries to initiate a Social Challenge against him during a frenzy, as reasoning with someone who is screaming for blood can be awkward.

When roleplaying a frenzy, players should remember not to do anything dangerous: don't actually run during a Terror Frenzy or physically attack someone during a Rage Frenzy. This may sound like a silly warning, but it's one of those times in which you are most likely to forget the prime rule of live roleplaying.

Ending a Frenzy

Before entering a frenzy, a vampire can stave it off for 10 minutes by spending a Willpower Trait. If already in frenzy, shecan try to end it at any time by spending a Willpower Trait and winning a Static Mental Challenge against a difficulty of four Traits. The vampire loses the Willpower Trait even if she fails the test. If the frenzy is about to cause a Kindred to do something completely against your Nature, she may try to end the frenzy *once* without needing to spend a Willpower Trait. She must still win the Static Challenge, however.

A vampire also get a free Static Challenge after whatever has caused the frenzy goes away. Otherwise, the frenzy will burn itself out five to 10 minutes after its source disappears. If undergoing a Rage or Terror Frenzy, a vampire must escape the cause of the frenzy in order for the frenzy to fade. For a Control Frenzy, she must either feed fully from a target or sate herself.

Kindred can also try to talk someone out of a frenzy by winning a Social Challenge against him. This is considered to be a Static Challenge with a difficulty equal to twice the number of Beast Traits the frenzied character possesses. (For instance, a character must risk four Social Traits to calm someone with two Beast Traits.) Remember that a frenzied vampire, when challenged socially, does not need to risk a Trait. The same rule applies here. Failing the Social Challenge often draws the frenzied vampire's attention to the one who attempted to calm him.

Rules Summary for Frenzy

Action	Rule
Starting a Frenzy	None. Event in a Beast Trait happens.
Stopping a Frenzy	Spend a Willpower Trait before the frenzy OR Spend Willpower Trait and win a Static Mental Challenge against four Traits OR go against Nature and win Static Mental Challenge against four Traits OR burn out 10 minutes after the problem goes away OR have someone talk you down by winning a Social Challenge against twice the number of Beast Traits you possess.
Special	While in a frenzy, you are not affected by Social Challenges You may ignore all damage until torpor.

Diablerie

Some vampires seek to become more powerful by draining the very essence of their elders. Particularly voracious Kindred can quickly come to rival the power of Methuselahs if they can pursue this dangerous course of diablerie for very long. Their goal, however, is made exceedingly difficult by the elders, who have made the drinking of another Kindred's essence the most heinous crime one of the Damned can commit.

Diablerie is very easy to follow. In **The Masquerade**, a diabolist's aura is tainted by black threads that remain for three months after the diablerie was committed. Any vampire who uses the Discipline of Aura Perception will recognize these bands and know the transgression of the diabolist. Someone who kills his elders is almost sure to end his existence as the target of a Blood Hunt. If the prince declares a Blood Hunt on a criminal, any recognized Kindred may hunt the criminal down and destroy him. Doing so immediately gains the prince's favor.

The advantages of committing diablerie, however, are enough to tempt many Kindred into preying upon their own kind. Upon successfully draining a Kindred of lower generation, the Kindred gains some of the power of that extinguished vampire. The diabolist lowers her generation by one, bringing her closer to Caine, increasing her resistance to control from more powerful Kindred, and increasing her Blood Pool. The diabolist also gains two experience points (on top of any which would normally be gained) if she can survive to the end of the evening. On the other hand, the diabolist also immediately receives a Beast Trait for the callous act.

For players choosing to risk diablerie, additional rules follow. First, the target must somehow be incapacitated via combat or Disciplines. He must then be drained of Blood Traits at a rate of one Trait per action. Once the target of diablerie is drained of Blood Traits, a lone vampire must drain her of Health Levels until the victim is in Torpor. Each Health Level drained in this way requires a separate Physical Test. The victim of diablerie may bid any remaining appropriate stamina-related Physical Traits to defend herself. However, if she wins a test, the diabolist is not harmed, but merely delayed another round. Once the Kindred has begun to drain Health Levels, he is incapable of any other physical action. If another Kindred attacks him or tries to pull him away from his feeding, the diabolist may not bid any Physical Traits to the challenge. His attention is fully consumed by the act of diablerie. Thus, he will lose automatically unless some if his friends are standing nearby to aid him.

When the second part of diablerie begins, both the diabolist and the target collapse and are completely unaware of the world outside them. No Mental or Social Challenges may be directed against either of them.

The final part of diablerie requires one last test for the diabolist to free his target's essence from her body. This is a Physical Challenge. The target begins the challenge three Traits up on the diabolist, so there will always be a test. The diabolist may keep trying to finish the Amaranth until he can no longer match the three Physical Traits. If he can no longer challenge, he loses a Health Level (from exhaustion) and drops away from the target.

No vampire may assist the diabolist. However, one Kindred may drain away someone's Blood and Health Levels to allow another to complete the final stage of diablerie. The seduction of the last feeding, however, is very strong. To stop before fully extinguishing a vampire, a Kindred must spend a Willpower Trait and win a Mental Static Challenge against a difficulty of three Traits.

Rules Summary for Diablerie

Action	Challenge
Stage 1: Drain Blood	Automatic one Trait/action
Stage 2: Drain Health	Physical Challenge against victim; diabolist cannot defend physically
Stage 3: Drinking Soul	Physical Challenge against victim (who has three additional Traits)
Stop drinking after Stage 2	Mental Static Challenge against difficulty of threeTraits

Golconda

Golconda is a state of being wherein the character has managed to control her frenzies and can restrain the Beast. This blessed state is not easy to attain, but for many vampires, it is the only goal worth having. It must not be misunderstood, for it is not a reconnection to one's mortality — quite the opposite. Golconda is an acceptance and mastery of one's Bestial nature. It is the final acceptance of one's curse and the subsequent gaining of power over it.

Benefits

A vampire who reaches Golconda makes peace with himself. He no longer exists in a life filled with horror and self-pity. He has finally mastered the Beast Within by accepting that the Beast is a part of him.

There is only one major benefit to attaining Golconda in **The Masquerade**: A vampire who reaches Golconda no longer frenzies. He is no longer at the mercy of the Beast.

A lesser benefit of this is the fact that the character does not need to drink blood as often. The character only loses one Blood Trait per week, rather than one Blood Trait per day. Even if the vampire has reached the age where the need for even more potent blood arises, the desire is more subdued.

Blood Bond

The exchange of blood between two vampires creates a Blood Bond. The Thrall must drink the Regnant's blood three different times on three different occasions (on different nights). It can be any amount of blood — a sip, or even a taste if the Regnant is of ancient blood. Unlike the limitations of the many Disciplines, it is possible for weaker blood to hold Regnancy over more potent blood. Thus, a 10th-generation vampire can hold Regnancy over a ninth-generation vampire.

As more blood is consumed, the Bond is reinforced. Most Regnants have their Thralls drink of their blood several times a year just to make sure the Bond remains potent. Many Regnants are fearful that if the Bond is broken, the Thrall will seek vengeance. This is perhaps why so many Thralls are treated fairly well by their Regnant — after all, any Bond can fail. Hate can weaken the power of the Bond.

Once a vampire has been Blood Bound, he cannot be Bound again by another. He is thus "safe" from other Blood Bonds if he is already Bound. However, he can be

Bound to a number of different vampires if he drinks their blood at the same time (eg., blood mixed in a chalice before consumption). In fact, one of the most severe punishments of the Camarilla is to be forced to drink the blood of all the Kindred attending a Conclave. Usually the feelings produced by such widespread Bonding are more diffuse than normal, but they are no less powerful: the vampire becomes attached to the group and not to any one individual. The Tremere desire this diffusion of attachment of their neonates, and thus often Bond them to the seven elders.

All characters are already on their way to being Blood Bound, for their sires have already given them at least one taste of blood. Thus, if a character partakes of her sire's blood two more times, she is held in Regnancy.

Power of the Bond

Blood Bond is primarily an emotional power. Thralls view the vampires to whom they are Bound as central figures in their unlives. They are invariably obsessed with them. Though a Thrall may despise his Regnant, he will do nearly anything to aid him. The Thrall will do nothing to harm his Regnant and will even attempt to protect him against enemies. Although the Thrall usually understands on an intellectual level what is happening to him, he is unable to do anything about it.

Blood Bonds sometimes (but not always) give the Regnant insight into the moods and feelings of the Thrall. A Regnant may even know his Thrall's location from moment to moment if the bond has been maintained long enough. Sometimes the Regnant can intuitively find the Thrall simply by following his hunches.

Just because the Thrall is under the Regnant's influence does not mean the Thrall is helpless; he may expend Willpower Traits to resist the power of the Blood Bond. Depending on circumstances, a single Willpower Trait eliminates the effects of the Bond for a single scene or conversation. However, if the Thrall wants to actively attack his Regnant, he must spend one Willpower Trait per challenge.

If a character's Regnant asks him to do a "favor," he does so if it is at all possible. However, if it requires him to risk his life, he need not do it. Thralls almost always fulfill requests in line with their Natures and Demeanors and at least consider others. If there is an emergency and the Regnant is attacked, the Thrall's first instinct is aid her. Self-sacrifice is not unknown, especially if the Bond has been reinforced over the years. If the Thrall is treated well, the Bond is reinforced and grows stronger. If the Thrall is humiliated and degraded, the hate that develops diminishes the Bond's influence.

It is possible to break a Blood Bond, but it can be difficult, as it requires not only a massive expenditure of Willpower over a long period time, but also that the character completely avoid his Regnant. Also, if a Thrall does not see his Regnant for some time, the Bond may eventually die (after many decades or centuries). Some types of Natures, such as Child and Fanatic, may never escape the Blood Bond, while others, such as Conniver and Loner, may do so more easily. Characters cannot escape the Blood Bond through experience points or successful challenges — the breaking must be roleplayed.

Status

Status is the central focus of many Kindred's existence. It represents the amount of power and social prestige a character has within vampire society. Those of lower status are expected to show respect to those of higher status. As one's status increases, one is granted more rights and powers within the hierarchy of the Camarilla. Within a city, the prince typically (though not always) has the most status. Neonates generally have little status, while anarchs and most Caitiff have no status. In-between are the powerhungry ancillæ and elders who continually jockey for position in hopes of increasing their status.

Common Status Traits include: Admired, Adored, Cherished, Esteemed, Exalted, Famous, Faultless, Feared, Honorable, Influential, Just, Praised, Respected, Revered, Trustworthy and Well-Known.

Several positions or stations exist which give their holders great sway over the status of other Kindred. These posts are greatly sought after and jealously guarded by those who hold them. Only powerful elders can attain many of these positions, but ancillæ and even a precocious neonate or two may hold a few.

Gaining and Losing Status

Once "accepted" by the prince, a neonate acquires a single Status Trait. This initial Trait is usually Acknowledged. During the course of a chronicle, the character may gain or lose Status. In small games, the Storyteller is generally responsible for awarding or taking away Status. However, larger games usually allow the Status system of Camarilla society to blossom fully, as other Kindred in the game govern Status gains and losses while the Storyteller only monitors (and occasionally arbitrates) them.

Characters may gain Status by helping to preserve the Masquerade, doing favors for the prince or an elder or saving an elder's unlife. They may also gain it by overthrowing the holder of a station and assuming her mantle, granting it in return for a boon, or defeating a Sabbat menace in the city. The possibilities are endless; the point is to get your fellow Kindred to view you as more than just another Lick.

Note that you may never gain more than one Trait of Status per story. There are only two exceptions to this rule: if the prince awards or sanctions an additional Trait, or if the Status Trait(s) are conferred when a Kindred assumes a station within Kindred society.

Status can be lost for a multitude of reasons, as well, such as making an enemy of an elder, ignoring a boon or refusing to recognize another Kindred's Status. You can also lose it as a result of breaking the Masquerade, committing diablerie or breaking any of the Six Traditions. Obviously, if you plan to commit such acts, it's best to ensure that no one is around to report your actions.

Using Status

Players usually begin with one Status Trait, representing the fact that they have been presented to the prince and accepted by the Kindred of the city.

There are two types of Status: permanent and temporary. Permanent Status is recorded on your character sheet. It is your actual standing in Kindred society — no matter how much Temporary Status is lost, it has no effect on Permanent Status. You can lose both Temporary and Permanent Status over the course of a story, although you'll probably lose Temporary Status more often. A Permanent Status loss or gain is permanently added or removed from your character sheet. Temporary Status losses or gains are added or removed for the duration of the story. Temporary Status Traits may be represented by Status Cards to keep track of them more easily.

You can use Status Traits in any applicable Social Challenge and can add them to your Social Traits during a Social Challenge (if Traits must be compared). You can choose to ignore another character's Status Traits, but by doing so, you risk losing one or more of your own Status Traits permanently if word of the offense spreads to the

Harpies. If you happen to offend less influential people, you may only lose Status temporarily or not at all.

It would seem that anarchs and Caitiff have an advantage in this case, seeing as they have no Status to lose. (Some anarch groups, however, have their own form of Status.) However, having no Status usually hurts more than it helps. Elders almost never grant favors to anarchs (they are untrustworthy and have no Status to back their deals), rarely give them the benefit of the doubt and are much more likely to vent their full wrath on them (it is much easier to pick on characters who have no political backing). Also, by not having Status, anarchs and Caitiff are considered outside the Camarilla's protection and are thus extremely vulnerable in times of crisis.

Although paying lip service to your elders has its price, the benefits are almost always worthwhile — receiving protection, gaining the benefit of the doubt and getting favors granted. Therefore, as a general rule, it is considered prudent to possess and preserve at least one Status Trait.

Examples of Status

The following are some examples of the uses of Status:

• Temporary Status may be used to add to your Social Traits during an applicable Social Challenge.

• Status is a measure of a character's credibility. In any situation where there is an open debate between Kindred (one Kindred's word against the other), Status is used as the determining factor. The same is true in the case of accusing another of a crime in which there is no concrete evidence. In all such cases, the character with the most Status is the one whose word is accepted.

• You may give Temporary Status to another to show your favor, though the individual to which you give the Status must return it immediately upon the asking. However, the bearer may spend this Trait as a Temporary Trait, after which it is gone for the duration of the story. (This is the only way a character's Temporary Status can rise above her Permanent Status rating.) You can use loaned Status exactly as you would use your own, but you can only give one Trait of Status to any one person in this fashion.

• You must posses at least one Trait of Status (your own or one borrowed from someone else) in order to petition the prince for any reason, such as when gaining feeding grounds or accusing someone of a crime.

• Anyone of higher Status may remove Permanent Status from those lower than themselves at a cost of one Permanent Status Trait per Trait removed. Temporary Status may be removed in the same fashion.

• You may grant Permanent Status to another of your own clan if he has less than half of your permanent Status. The cost for such a boon is one Temporary Status Trait, and the boon must be made publicly, such as during a meeting of the primogen or another such gathering.

• A clan may remove one Status Trait from its elder by expending a group total of Permanent Status Traits equal to the elder's Permanent Status. The primogen may also lower the prince's Permanent Status in the same fashion.

• Remember, you may only gain one Status Trait per story, but may lose more than one Trait. Again, there are two exceptions to this: Status granted or sanctioned by the prince, and Status received for assuming a station.

Stations

Kindred can hold seven stations, each of which grants Status within a city. Of course, there may be more than this, but these are some of the most common. Certain responsibilities and powers are inherent in each of these stations, and all powers that a station confers are lost if a character is removed from or relinquishes it.

The following is list of these seven stations:

The Prince

• The prince of a city automatically gains three additional Status Traits: Exalted, Well-Known and Famous. He can never lose these Traits permanently while remaining prince.

• The prince can remove one Permanent Status Trait from someone at a cost of one Temporary Status Trait per Trait removed.

• The prince can grant Permanent Status Traits to any Kindred at a cost of one Temporary Trait for each Trait awarded. The prince may also break the rule of only gaining one Status Trait per story, allowing a character to gain more than one Trait. If a prince wishes to confer more than three Permanent Status Traits upon another Kindred in a single session, the fourth and subsequent Status Traits will cost the prince Permanent Status instead of Temporary Traits. Note that it does not cost the prince Temporary Status to award a Kindred the first Status Trait when she is first Presented. The Trait: Acknowledged is automatically conferred as long as the prince chooses to recognize the neonate.

Seneschal

• The Seneschal gains the following two additional Status Traits: Cherished and Esteemed. The character cannot lose these Traits permanently while remaining Seneschal.

• The Seneschal can act in the prince's stead when the prince is out of the city. He is therefore entitled to all of the powers of the prince, although the prince may reverse or revoke them at any time.

Primogen

• Primogen members each receive the additional Social Trait: Revered when they join the primogen. As long as a character remains on the primogen, she cannot lose this Trait permanently.

• Primogen may grant or remove Permanent Status Traits to or from any member of their clan at a cost of one Temporary Status for each Trait granted or removed.

Harpies

• The leader of the Harpies receives the additional Social Trait: Influential upon attaining the position. As long as the character remains the leader, he cannot lose this Trait permanently.

• The Harpy automatically gets one Temporary Status Trait from each member of the primogen, who bestow these Status Traits to demonstrate their support of the Harpies. The Harpy, in turn, may use these Traits however she desires, even against the owner.

• The Harpy may remove one Permanent Status Trait from a Kindred who has backed out of a boon or is part of a major scandal. There is no cost for this, although there must be a grain of truth to the scandal. The Harpy must produce some sort of evidence at a gathering of Kindred, at which time the Status Trait is removed.

• The Harpy may restore Status he has removed at a cost of one Temporary Trait per Trait restored.

• The leader of the Harpies may sponsor lesser Harpies by giving another Kindred a Status Trait of his own. Lesser Harpies may remove Temporary Status just as the head Harpy removes Permanent Status, although their leader may choose to make such loss permanent.

Whips

• Whips have the same powers as the Primogen, although they do not gain an additional Status Trait.

Sheriff

• The Sheriff gains the additional Social Trait: Feared when he attains the position. While he remains Sheriff, he cannot permanently lose this Trait.

• The Sheriff may demand that any Kindred within the city accompany him for questioning or judgment. Failure to do so causes the offender to lose one Permanent Status Trait.

• The Sheriff is immune to the powers of the Keeper of Elysium.

Keeper of Elysium

• The Keeper of Elysium gains the additional Status Trait: Honorable upon attaining the office. As long as the character remains the Keeper, he cannot permanently lose this Trait.

• The Keeper may immediately remove one Permanent Status Trait from any Kindred he catches breaking the Masquerade. If he does not witness it himself, sufficient evidence must be brought forth. This removal costs the Keeper nothing.

Sabbat Status Traits

Status within the Sabbat is useful only within the sect, just as Camarilla Status is only useful within the Camarilla. Status has no function between sects because they despise each other so strongly that any Status the other would possess would have little or no effect on their antagonists.

The Traits themselves also differ, because what constitutes status within the Camarilla is quite different from what would describe status to a member of the Sabbat. Common Status Traits include: Battle-scarred, Blessed, Blooded, Confirmed, Devoted, Enlightened, Enriched, Feared, Hunted, Infamous, Initiated, Loyal, Ominous, Proven, Respected and Undefeated.

Battle-Scarred — A Sabbat who has participated in direct Jyhad and been wounded, but survived.

Blessed — A vampire who has been blessed by those of higher rank with the rank of bishop or higher.

Blooded — A Sabbat who has killed a member of the Camarilla. This Trait is not applicable to those recently converted who killed Camarilla members while members of that sect.

Confirmed — This Trait is possessed by all pack-priests.

Devoted — A vampire of pack-priest rank, leader rank or above.

Enlightened — A vampire holding the rank of archbishop or above only.

Enriched — A vampire who has committed diablerie.

Feared — A character may only acquire this Trait if someone has confessed he fears her, or if someone has witnessed more than one person getting out of the way when she approaches.

Hunted — A vampire who has survived at least one to four open Blood Hunts in which Final Death was the objective.

Infamous — A vampire who has survived four or more open Blood Hunts, diablerized or killed two or more Camarilla elders or completed two or more otherwise highly respectable tasks by Sabbat standards.

Initiated — A Sabbat who has been a member of the sect long enough to acquire a Path. You can gain this Trait during the Initiation Rites if the situation is applicable.

Loyal — A vampire who has Vinculum ratings of all five or more for her pack. This Trait does not disappear when the character engages in the Vaulderie with new or unfamiliar Sabbat.

Ominous — A vampire who has a reputation for being very Feared and Respected. Members the Black Hand often hold this Trait. You must have at least three other Status Traits (including Feared and Respected) in order to be Ominous.

Proven — A Sabbat who has been accepted as True Sabbat by her pack via some sort of trial.

Respected — A vampire who has won the respect of packmates and others through non-physical means.

Undefeated — A Sabbat who has not been defeated in three or more battles. Note: If the Sabbat loses any fight in which he has bid Physical Traits, regardless of how many contests he lost or won in the process, he loses this Trait. Those who have it are extremely respected.

Vampires under one year of age or who have not yet had the opportunity to choose a Path have no Status. Until a vampire has acquired the Status Trait *Initiated*, he may accrue no other Status.

Using Sabbat Status Traits

Status Traits within the Sabbat have several different uses:

• You may bid an applicable Status Trait in place of a Social Trait in any Social Challenge against a fellow Sabbat member.

• You may bid a Status Trait to prevent someone from attacking you or to force them to back down.

The Sabbat do not expend as much energy trying to impress each other as do members of the Camarilla. Thus, it is easier to acquire Status and easier to lose it. You may ignore Status Traits if they are bid against you, but by doing so, you forfeit any use of your own for the remainder of the night. If you possess Status Traits and you have used them all in challenges, you may not ignore someone else's Status Traits until you regain your own. If you have no Status to begin with, happy hunting, but beware the wrath of those you annoy.

Gaining and Losing Status

Status may be removed in several ways. One is a pack consensus. If a character reveals a pack secret, makes a big mistake that jeopardizes the pack, or fraternizes with the enemy, the pack can decide to punish him and remove one or more of his Status Traits. Because a Trait like Blooded is based on a physical accomplishment, you cannot remove it or any other past actions unless they occurred as a unit with the pack. You can remove a Status Trait like Proven without a thought because it is entirely based on pack respect and opinion.

Traits lost in this manner can only be regained through pack consensus. Sabbat packs are usually very close-knit groups, and any Status removed in this way is a source of humiliation for the vampire in question. This Trait, when the pack removes it, is completely gone. You cannot use it under any circumstances unless it is reawarded to you. Scratch it off your sheet.

Those with higher Status and rank can also remove Status Traits. A bishop may remove Status Traits from someone of lower rank whom they deem disloyal or ineffective. The ranking character must defeat the other in a Social Challenge in order to permanently remove the Trait. If the high-ranking challenger loses, she loses one extra Social Trait in addition to the one lost in the initial challenge. When the challenger initially loses, all parties only lose all the Traits they bid for the remainder of the night. Those of higher rank who remove Status from other leaders, pack leaders, priests and the like ought to be aware that the loyalty the pack has for the leader who lost the Trait could go two ways. It could cause the pack to realize that their leader is a loser, or it could cause them to mutiny against the individual of higher rank. The Sabbat respects proven over proclaimed power, and those who flaunt titles without being able to back them up should beware.

Characters can gain Status Traits in ways similar to that in which they are lost: through pack consensus for doing something of value and as a reward from a higher-up. Players should bring the addition or destruction of a Status Trait to the attention of a Storyteller as soon as possible without interrupting the flow of game play.

To award Status, the awarder must possess at least five Status Traits. If the reward is by pack consensus, the group must possess at least seven Status Traits. In order for rank to be issued during play, each member of the party responsible must permanently spend one Status Trait. For every two Traits spent, the newly elected character may gain one Status Trait totaling no more than three new Traits in addition to his current status.

Anyone with or without Status can endorse ranks such as pack leader or priest, but the honored party neither gains Status nor receives respect except from those who have sworn to obey him.

Status Traits for Special Occasions

The following are Status Traits especially suited to Narrator characters, among others:

Black Hand only — Enforced, Branded, Engaged

Inquisitors only — Supported, Protected, Sanctified

Prisci, Cardinals and others — Glorified, Gifted, Recognized (by the Regent), Fortified

Prestation

Prestation is the art of cutting a deal, an invaluable resource for those who know how to use it. Consequently, those ignorant of its applications should beware. Technically, Prestation is defined as the system through which one Kindred becomes officially indebted to another for services rendered. In actuality, it is something much more complicated — and deadly.

When striking a deal, players should make clear who's doing the favor and who's receiving it. Except in cases of mutual favors, there should always be a bestower and a receiver. The receiver owes a boon to her bestower which must be categorized as a trivial, minor, major, blood or life boon. The players either assign the boon an appropriate number of Status Traits which the receiver then gives the bestower, or they make other arrangements, such as giving Influence rather than Status. The agreement must be amenable to all Kindred involved in the deal.

The bestower may continue to use the Boon Traits just as he would any other loaned Status Traits. However, the bestower's loss of Boon Traits is only temporary — they are restored at the beginning of the next story, at which time he may use them again as usual. The primary difference between Boon Traits and other loaned Traits is that the original owner of the Traits may not request their return as is usual with such Traits. They may only be returned once the boon has been settled.

The only way for a receiver to rid herself permanently of a boon is to repay or ignore the favor. By ignoring a favor, the receiver not only certainly costs the Kindred Status, but also risks the bestower's ire. If the bestower is a minor Kindred, the receiver who ignores a boon may only temporarily lose a Status Trait (the Status Trait returns with the next story). However, if the bestower has considerable social influence, word may spread of the receiver's offense, causing the *permanent* loss of a Status Trait, especially if word gets to the Harpies. Furthermore, when the receiver disregards a major, blood or life boon (regardless of the bestower's standing), the receiver loses Status. Breaking boons is considered a major social *faux pas* among vampires.

When a deal is cut (a favor is arranged), both parties should agree on the nature of the favor, the number of Traits assigned to it and any other stipulations or additions. Kindred who bestow boons usually require only one thing: "You may not take any physical action against me for the duration of this boon." In terms of the story, the receiver may seek to eliminate the bestower rather than repay the favor, but the bestower can use the legal terms of their agreement as protection from harm. It is usually a good idea to clarify agreements in writing and to have both parties sign the document to assure its validity.

Paying the Piper

Paying back a favor — getting yourself out of debt — is usually an event arranged through roleplaying. Typically, players eliminate boons by returning equivalent favors. However, if a bestower is in sufficient trouble, you could pay off your debt by returning only a small favor; everything depends on your skill at bartering. To set some standard, a favor is as valuable as the Traits associated with it. Thus, a minor boon (two Traits) and a major boon (three Traits) are fair compensation for a life boon (five Traits).

Trivial boons are one-time favors, such as protecting someone for the evening, aiding someone using a Discipline or supporting another's political move.

Minor boons can last more than one evening and usually entail some sort of inconvenience, such as allowing safe passage through a hostile city, revealing crucial information or disposing of a threat.

Major boons usually entail a great expenditure of time or resources on the bestower's part. The effects of the favor usually last for many game sessions. An example of such a boon would be teaching the receiver a new Discipline or ritual or purchasing a nightclub to serve as the receiver's haven.

Blood boons occur when the bestower places herself in a potentially life-threatening situation in order to help the receiver. Thus the name "blood boon": The bestower is willing to shed her blood for the receiver.

Life boons involve the bestower actively risking her immortal life for the receiver so that the receiver may live.

Fair Escape

Fair Escape is a simple rule that allows players to escape from potentially deadly situations without actually vaulting over tables or charging headlong out of a room, possibly causing harm to themselves or others. This rule also allows players to avoid combat without going through cumbersome challenges to see if they can "get away."

When you use this rule, you can call "Fair Escape" anytime you see another player approaching with whom you do not wish to interact. Once you call "Fair Escape," you may leave the area without being pursued. There are several guidelines which must be followed when using this rule, however:

• You may not use the Fair Escape rule if the person approaching is nearby (within conversational distance). In such cases, you must initiate a challenge. Use common sense in places where there is a great deal of noise and conversational distance is reduced to a minimum (eg., a nightclub).

• If someone calls, "Fair Escape," you may counter by calling, "Celerity" (or "Rage") if you possess the appropriate Discipline. The person attempting to flee may then counter with Celerity. At this point, the players must determine who has the greatest amount of Celerity.

• Situations which involve an ambush (all exits are blocked or the target is surrounded) may negate the use of Fair Escape. Again, use common sense.

• A character with Obfuscate (Unseen Presence) may employ Fair Escape at any time before a challenge has been initiated, unless someone with Auspex (Heightened Senses) counters him.

These guidelines are intended to quicken play, not to obstruct it. Always try to use common sense when employing Fair Escape.

Sabbat Basics

The Sabbat is known as a terrifying sect of vampires whose primary goal is the destruction of the Camarilla. Their often heinous ways make them ideal antagonists in any setting. Sabbat vampires no longer possess any humanity, and the haunting tales of their torture chambers would turn even a butcher's stomach. The sect's hierarchy is run as a vicious parody of medieval Catholicism and considers anything mortal to be little more than food. It punishes those who violate its principles with horrid tasks, agonizing torture and, as a last resort, Final Death. Anyone with a desire to vanquish cruelty, violence, religious heretics or the forces of evil would find the Sabbat a most pleasing adversary, and anyone whom they challenge will certainly want revenge.

Sabbat Ideology

Sabbat ideology is based on the two main principles of freedom and loyalty. Each vampire is taught that she is part of a larger reality in which her life is dependent on those with whom she is Bonded. The Sabbat also teaches new vampires that it is their responsibility to become as strong as possible in order to be effective warriors when the Antediluvians wake. Before the time of Gehenna, they must hone their skills through contest and battle with the servants of the Antediluvians, the Camarilla infidels.

The Sabbat preach freedom from the ruling fist of elder vampires. The sect was founded on the principle that no vampire should be forced to die for the cowardice of those who created him. The idea behind the Vinculum is that this shared Blood Bond creates loyalty among all vampires of the sect and inspires them to unify in troubled times in order to destroy the enemy. Participation in the Vinculum also prevents one vampire from being secretly Bonded only to another. Like the Catholics they parody, the Sabbat see the ritual of Vaulderie, in which all participants spill some of their blood into a chalice and then drink from it, as a sort of vampiric communion with Caine.

Rank Issued	Number of Traits Spent	Number Gained
Pack Leader/Priest	2	1
Templar/Paladin	2	1
Bishop	4	2
Black Hand	4	2
Archbishop	6	3

The Paths of Enlightenment (detailed earlier) describe, to an extent, how each vampire views freedom, loyalty and his own vampiric nature. Sabbat have no humanity, so the Paths are essential to character formation, as they provide the moral code by which the vampire lives. Freedom and loyalty can be taken in many directions and usually are. Most packs have common ideas of how these two principles function, and many share similar Paths, clans and political factions.

Current Goals of the Sect

At present, the Sabbat continues to plan and raise sieges against Camarilla-held cities in hopes of spreading their dominion and word of the truth. It is a Sabbat belief that anyone who is not serving the Sabbat is serving the Antediluvians and must be converted or destroyed. The sect does not maintain strong ties in the mortal world, since they see kine as useful for only one thing: food. Although it has some control over mortal affairs in the cities it holds, the sect leaves such machinations up to its servants among the four revenant ghoul families. The Sabbat's primary goals include destruction of Camarilla elders, Methuselahs and Antediluvians.

The Black Hand

The Hand, as it is known, constitutes a tight militia within the Sabbat and serves as the sect's primary assassin pool. If someone needs to be taken out, the Black Hand are the ones to do it. Though Sabbat Assamites are responsible for the maintenance of the Black Hand, other clans are represented within their ranks. A secretive sect-within-a-sect, these elite warriors nevertheless do not exist in packs of their own apart from the rest of the Sabbat.

The Black Hand are all marked by a black crescent moon which is magically branded into the palm of their right hands.

Roleplaying the Sabbat

The Sabbat is not for beginners. Not only must Storytellers and players understand certain things about both the Sabbat and the Camarilla, but the mechanics of the game become more complex to suit the needs of this advanced style of play. Sabbat characters live by an ideology of survival infinitely more complex than that arranged for the Camarilla in terms of the Traditions. Not only is there a regulated set of laws within the sect, but the player must also be able to balance within herself the conflicting ideas of loyalty and freedom.

Running With the Pack

Almost all Sabbat vampires are members of a pack. Some packs are very small, with as few as three members; others are very large, with upwards of 20 vampires. There is an enormous difference in being a member of a coterie and being a member of a pack. A coterie is a group of vampires who profess allegiance to each other and agree to work toward similar goals. A pack is not a political group. It is not an agreed alliance. No child chooses her parents; no Sabbat member chooses his pack.

Every member of the Sabbat is a warrior of one kind or another and, consequently, despises weakness and cowardice because it does not fortify him for the coming battle. There is no doubt in the Sabbat consciousness that the supreme Jyhad will come to pass and that the sect's members are the saviors of the species. When the Ancients rise, the Sabbat will be there, swords drawn and AK 47s ready to destroy its blood enemies.

Pack Morale

Pack morale usually arises from roleplaying. If you need a system, try the following: When the pack is involved in a group combat of any kind and the rest of the pack notices one member losing a challenge, each pack member player must engage in a Simple Test with any nearby individual. If the majority of the pack wins the test, morale remains high, and the pack should engage in action to defend its brother or sister. If the majority of the pack loses, it will either run or get out of the situation as quickly as it can.

Sabbat Rituals

Using Rituals in a Game Setting

The Sabbat places great importance in its rituals, which serve both to bolster morale and to teach the sect's doctrine. Many packs possess more than one ritual freak who spends endless nights performing and creating more rituals.

Rituals within the Sabbat also serve as tests. Many, in fact, were created for the sole purpose of testing the strength and endurance of the warriors involved. It has also been the warrior's right throughout history to be blessed before battle and celebrated upon return. The Sabbat observes this custom and encourages it through use of various kinds of ritual.

Kinds of Rituals

The rituals of the Sabbat can be divided into three basic groups: the *Auctoritas Ritae*, the *Ignoblis Ritae* and the customs of each particular pack. All Sabbat practice the very traditional *Auctoritas Ritae*. Most packs, depending on their particular goals and makeup at the time, practice the *Ignoblis Ritae* in different ways. Each pack also develops its own customs, which often take ritual forms and change with the times.

Auctoritas Ritae

The following constitute some of the *Auctoritas Ritae* which are most useful in **Masquerade** games.

The Creation Rites

These are the series of rituals used to convert and Embrace new vampires into the sect.

The Vaulderie

During the Vaulderie, each vampire sheds some of her blood into a chalice. Once the blood has combined with the blood of all present, the pack passes the chalice around a second time for everyone to partake. This ritual initiates and maintains the Sabbat's collective Blood Bond, known as the Vinculum.

Monomacy

Monomacy is a ritual fight (usually to Final Death) that the Sabbat use to settle disputes. Either the winner or someone the winner chooses (if the blood is not useful to him personally) diablerize many vampires during this ritual. Unless rules are established at the beginning of the fight, the modus operandi is generally "no holds barred," as long as only the two involved actually fight.

Sermons of Caine

War Parties

This ritual occurs when two or more packs go on the warpath to acquire the blood of a Camarilla elder. The contest lies in seeing who can get him first. Most Sabbat go all-out during War Parties; war paint and rituals of blessing before and after are common.

Wild Hunt

The Wild Hunt is the Sabbat version of the Blood Hunt. Anyone who has committed a serious enough crime may be hunted. Archbishops usually call Wild Hunts, but packs have been known to spread the word on their own (although the members are usually severely beaten and otherwise punished later).

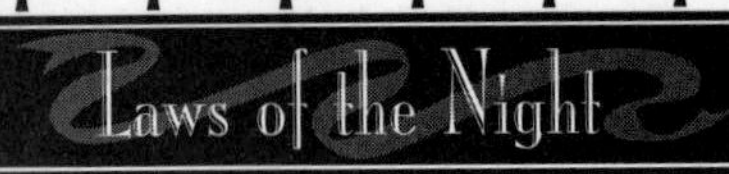

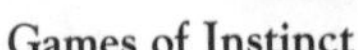

Games of Instinct

Ignoblis Ritae

These rituals change with each pack that performs them.

Acceptance Rites

Packs use this ritual to accept a new leader or priest, to welcome a recruit to her new standing as True Sabbat and to award Status Traits within the pack. If the vampire at the center of the ritual is becoming the pack leader, she should hunt for the pack before the ritual to show her willingness and ability to provide for them.

Initiation Rites

Welcome and Farewell Rites

Blessings

This ritual can be used at any time to bless the pack or an individual who has a specific quest. The pack usually receives a Blessing before fights, invading enemy territory or going after a desired object or individual. Blessings often occur during the Vaulderie since blood is required.

Call to Caine

Confession

Ghost Dance

Jyhad Rites

Oaths of Fealty

This rite is part of other Sabbat rites, most commonly the Vaulderie. After passing the chalice or while each member holds it in her hands, each individual pauses before drinking of the communal blood and promises loyalty to the pack. She then drinks and passes the chalice.

Sacrificial Rites

Pack Creed

Thanksgiving Ritual

Sunrise Service

Rituals of Justice

These are rituals the Sabbat isn't supposed to perform without Sabbat officials, but most packs do anyway. The Sabbat rarely metes out punishment without some ritual to help intimidate the accused. Often the pack gathers in two lines, the accused bound and laid horizontally between the lines of his packmates on the floor. The accused must then answer seven questions of the pack leader or whoever the pack leader allows to ask. At the end of the seven questions, the pack, still looking down on the accused, will either agree he is guilty and punish him however they see fit, or they will ask another series of 13 questions. If they determined that the accused is innocent, the accuser is normally punished in his place.

Using the *Ignoblis Ritae*

The *Ignoblis Ritae* can be used as often or as little as the players desire. Players should also feel free to make up their own rituals. The Storyteller may wish to allow Trait gain in the form of temporary Traits after the characters perform certain rituals. For example, the pack performs a sacrifice for strength in battle. Each member of the pack receives an additional Physical Trait for the duration of the anticipated contest. If the pack is blessed before going on a scouting mission into enemy territory, the Ritual may grant them each one additional Social Trait. If the pack performs a Rite of Loyalty and bonding other than the normal

Vaulderie, they may all go up one point in their Vinculum ratings for each member of the pack. All ritually gained Traits are temporary, lasting either until the end of the anticipated event or until they are used. A vampire who has six Physical Traits and who participates in a rite which adds one to her pool, may not, when spending her sole Willpower Trait at the end of the fight to regain her Traits, reacquire the gift Trait from the ritual. Moreover, if a character has any gift Traits left over from one night to the next, she must forfeit them.

Note that players in a pack can't just *say* they performed the ritual; they must either roleplay the rite in real time or sit out of game for half an hour. Gift Traits must *always* be Storyteller-approved.

Creation Rite Systems

Whichever ritual the pack performs, the pack must remain out of play (describing the physical and roleplaying the verbal aspect of the ritual is greatly encouraged) until its new whelp tests to see if he makes it out of the grave. This out-of-game period should last for one hour. If the game itself has been constructed to last only four to six hours, the Storyteller may feel free to shorten this time. The important thing is that the players receive a sense of having been through a ritual and/or an ordeal to create and initiate their progeny. Fifteen minutes is the shortest possible time this ritual should be allowed to take. The players must remain together (preferably somewhere isolated) and must not interact with other players at all. If they so choose, the roleplaying should continue through this time.

The new whelp must, at the end of the hour, engage in a Static Challenge with the Storyteller. The other players must not see the results out of character. Either they see the hand emerging from the dirt, or they sit there wondering why it's taking the fledgling so long to climb up. The potential Sabbat must win two out of three Static Tests to emerge successfully from the grave. If he wins only one out of the three, he only gets halfway. The player may, if he loses, proceed to engage in one retest for every Physical Trait he is willing to spend. He must still win at least two out of three Tests, although they are cumulative. In other words, if the player loses the original challenge by not winning two out of three Tests, he may proceed to call for retests until he is out of Physical Traits. Even if he spends four Traits, as long as he wins at least two of the tests, he may emerge from the grave successfully. The Storyteller may feel free to add five minutes extra onto his time in the grave for every additional retest he takes. It is possible for the other characters to dig up the tardy or unsuccessful progeny in times of great need, but, without his required time underground (for the retesting progeny) or being dug up at all for the unsuccessful candidate, he will be stark raving mad and completely uncontrollable for the remainder of the night.

The pack is advised to have some fresh blood on hand for the new arrivals, because when they emerge from the grave they are completely bloodless and mad. In frenzy, they must Physically Challenge the first person or blood source they see. They will not release the blood source until they have drained it completely. Freshly created fledglings have 10 Willpower Traits and no self-control until their Blood Traits have reached maximum, at which time their stats return to normal. The pack usually provides many previously captured mortal victims from whom the whelps may feed.

Sabbat vampires, thanks to the shock of the Creation Rites, emerge from the grave with one new Derangement resulting from an experience they had during their enforced burial. The Storyteller may wish to describe to the victim some of these events and select a Derangement for her. Because the new character wouldn't have had any control over what happened to her cracking, blistering mind during the creation, the player should not be allowed to choose this Derangement.

Note that the Derangement a character acquires during the Creation Rites is not permanent. Once the character has acquired two Path Traits, the Derangement from the Creation Rites dissolves.

After the Emergence

When a fledgling emerges from the grave and feeds, she may have no idea what has occurred. The grave has completely annihilated her morality, necessitating the Paths which simulate her old humanity. Converted vampires function on their former Beast Traits until they acquire the Path Traits to replace them.

The pack performs the Vaulderie once all fledglings who are going to survive emerge and feed. Fledglings should view this initial Vaulderie as a gift rather than as the right it becomes once they have been accepted as True Sabbat.

It is usually the responsibility of the sire to teach the new pack member Disciplines and instruct her in a Path. Instruction takes one half-hour of uninterrupted game time, during which the sire or teacher and the fledgling speak. Many packs consider this teaching part of the ritual and insist on all being in attendance. If the Path of the sire does not appeal to the progeny, she must petition the others of her pack to teach her instead. Most are willing to teach their Path because they believe their Path is the best and the one closest to truth.

In practical terms, the Creation Rites change the character permanently. Once a character becomes Sabbat, there is no going back; former Blood Bonds are broken, and a new, more powerful one has taken their place. The Vaulderie is such a rush, the best feeling of the Kindred's existence so far (either vampiric or mortal), that she has no desire to turn back to her former ways. The truth has been revealed! The Beast is not to be fought; it is to be nurtured until the new vampire and the Beast are one symbiotic organism, each feeding off the needs of the other.

Vaulderie and Vinculum

Of all the *Auctoritas Ritae*, the Vaulderie constitutes the most important ritual the Sabbat practices. In fact, it is essential to what the sect is, the foundation for Sabbat society and success. The Vaulderie (the ritual of shared blood) creates a Blood Bond among all participants and breaks any previous bonds for new members. The feeling the Vaulderie creates is one of fellowship, comfort and intense loyalty. It raises the morale of the participants and gives them a tremendous rush.

The loyalty created by this bond is far beyond any human emotion and therefore, much more profound. All vampires who share in the Vaulderie are Blood Bound to each other.

Vaulderie Rules

• Find a chalice, cup, bowl or some physical representation thereof (hats do nicely in a pinch) and dig around for those Blood Traits.

• Each character present should place between two and four Blood Traits into the chalice. It is the privilege of the pack leader or vampire of highest rank to put in the highest number of Traits, not exceeding the number of participants. The pack leader or priest then mixes the Traits around and passes the chalice back around the circle.

• Each character randomly draws the same number of Traits he or she contributed. The individuals (indicated by number) on your ritually acquired Blood Traits are those for whom you feel a heightened bond for the duration of the night or until the Vaulderie is performed again.

A Clarification of the Heightened Bond

Sometimes when you participate in the Vaulderie, you end up with a Blood Pool consisting of numerous Blood Traits from other characters. In such cases, the predominance of certain characters' Blood Traits over others' causes you to feel even more drawn to them than usual. This effectively increases your rating one notch: Once your Vinculum rating rises to a certain level, you must spend Willpower to even plot against the person. You may *not* intentionally harm, betray or fail to defend these individuals. An agreed Monomacy is the only exception.

Erase the numbers on your acquired Blood Traits and replace them with your own. Note that Blood Traits acquired during the Vaulderie are ingested into the other participants' blood streams and are *not* usable against the originator for any sort of blood magic or other rituals. All blood acquired during the Vaulderie becomes solely that of the vampire who ingested it.

In order to plot against someone for whom the character has a Vinculum rating of 3 or higher, the character must spend one Willpower Trait. In order to plot against someone for whom the character has a Vinculum rating of 6 or over, the character must spend two Willpower Traits.

To attempt the destruction of someone for whom the character has a Vinculum rating at all (i.e. has shared in the Vaulderie with and drawn their name even once, or begun the game with a Storyteller rating of 2 or over), the character must burn two Willpower in front of a Storyteller, or the attempt proves invalid. Without the burned Willpower, the character finds herself realizing that the person she hates is loyal to the sect and worthy of respect.

Monomacy and Vinculum

If you have a Vinculum rating of 6 or higher towards the person whom you want to fight, you must burn one Willpower to initiate the Monomacy contest. Whenever a challenger loses a fight within the rules of Monomacy, regardless of whether or not he burned Willpower initially, he must spend one more Willpower Trait to continue the contest. There is no cost to the defender, since she is obligated to accept regardless of Vinculum.

Punishment and Vinculum

If you are punishing someone in your pack for whom you have a Vinculum rating of 6 or higher and someone in your pack protests, you must engage in a Social Challenge. If you lose, you must burn a Willpower Trait to continue the punishment.

Storyteller pre-rating	Blood Traits Drawn	Willpower needed to burn
1-3	1-3	2
4-6	4-6	3
7-9	7-15	5
10	15+	Impossible

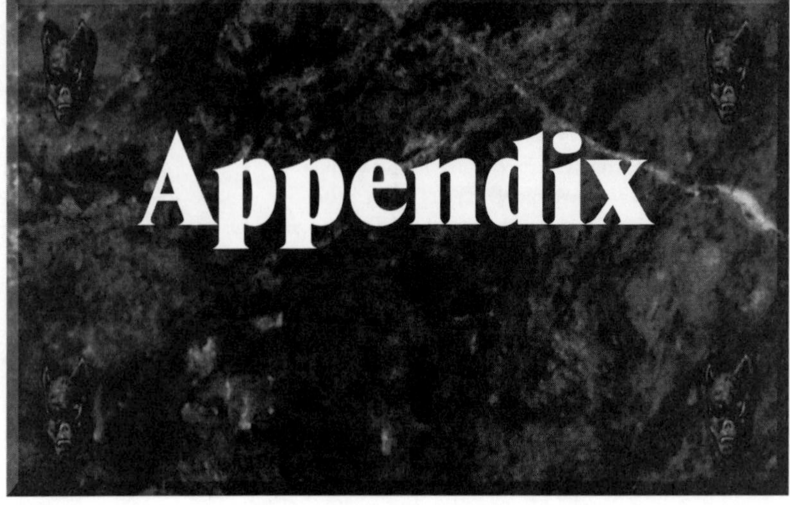

Appendix

The Basic Rules

These are the most important rules of **MET**, the only ones that absolutely must be obeyed. On one hand, there are a lot of people out there who either don't know or don't care that **The Masquerade** is just a game, and on the other hand, there are some people who take the game far too seriously. By following these rules, you provide yourself with ammunition against the former and protect yourself and your game against the latter. Both groups are equally dangerous to a solid **Mind's Eye Theatre** troupe, and these rules are designed to make certain that they're given as little opportunity as possible to interfere with your games.

#1 – No touching.

This means none whatsoever, even with consent. Things do have a way of getting out of hand. Better not to allow that opportunity. For that matter, running, jumping and swinging on chandeliers across hotel lobbies are also not allowed. Again, there's too much opportunity for someone to get hurt.

#2 – No weapons as props.

Props are a wonderful way to make a game real. However, real weapons or anything that even looks like a real weapon (and we're talking sword canes, peace-bonded claymores, rabid trained attack gerbils, matte-black painted waterguns and sword-shaped toothpicks from a dry martini) are a definite no-no. It's too easy for someone to get hurt with them. Even if you're responsible with your shiny new dagger, some idiot will choose the moment you take it out to come pelting around the corner full-tilt and impale himself on it. Regardless if the weapon looks amazing with your costume, leave it home.

#3 – No drugs or drinking.

This one is a real no-brainer. Drugs and alcohol are a way of distancing you from yourself. Roleplaying gives you the chance to be someone else. Why go to all the trouble of creating another persona to inhabit if you're just going to wander out of that persona in a haze?

On a more serious note, players who are impaired through drugs or alcohol represent a danger to other players and a threat to the flow and mood of the game. There's nothing wrong with *playing* a character who's drunk or stoned, but actually bringing drugs or alcohol into a game is going too far, not to mention the legal repercussions of the former.

#4 – Feel free to ignore or adjust any of the rules.

We at White Wolf call this "The Golden Rule." Obviously, it should be applied within limits, and rules changes should be consistent throughout a troupe. On the other hand, if your troupe finds a way to handle, say, Celerity, that works better for you than the one in this book does, by all means go for it.

#5 – It's only a game.

This is by far the most important rule. It is only a game. If a character dies, if a plot falls apart, if a rival wins the day — it's still only a game. Don't take things too seriously, as that will spoil not only your enjoyment but also the enjoyment of everyone around you.

Plus, remember to leave the game behind when it ends. Informal **Masquerade** is a lot of fun; spending time talking about the game is great. On the other hand, getting annoyed with your chantry regent because she wasn't up to plotting for Saturday's game at 3:32 A.M. on Wednesday signifies a need for a change in perspective.

#6 – Have fun.

Not "win." Not "Go out and kill everyone else." Just "Have fun," because in **Masquerade** it's not about how the game ends, it's about everything that happens to you along the way.

FAQ

Clans and Disciplines

Is Assamite blood normally toxic?

No, it must be made so through the use of Poison Blade (Intermediate Quietus). An Assamite cannot go around randomly bleeding on other vampires in order to cause them damage.

Can Necromancy be used to permanently place a spirit in a corpse and reanimate it?

No.

Does the target of Chimerstry know who is responsible for the illusion?

Not unless the Ravnos using Chimerstry wants him to know.

Does Fae Sight (Mytherceria) allow you to see Psychic Projections?

Yes.

If the target of Beast Within doesn't have any Derangements, what happens?

In this case, the target frenzies.

What happens when a Kindred under Embrace the Beast comes across someone with Majesty?

Majesty is a Presence power. Users of Embrace the Beast are immune to uses of Dominate, Presence and Beast Within. Ergo, characters under Embrace the Beast can ignore Presence.

Does Heightened Senses automatically allow me to detect when an Obfuscated character has entered the room, even if I wasn't using the power when he walked in?

No, you can't turn on Heightened Senses the second an Obfuscated character walks into the room, just so you can yell, "Gotcha!" It must already be activated when the Obfuscated character walks in, or there must be a valid in-game reason for it to be activated after the Obfuscated character has arrived.

Does Aura Perception automatically allow me to detect Kindred auras and Diablerie veins?

Nope.

Can I use Spirit's Touch to search through all of the impressions on an object until I find one that's useful?

No. Technically, this power only allows you to uncover details about the last time the object was handled. Additional information may be granted at Storyteller discretion.

Celerity is causing all sorts of problems in my game. What do I do?

An optional system for Celerity has just three powers: Alacrity (Basic), Rapidity (Intermediate) and Fleetness (Advanced). This tends to simplify things.

Can I ever remember what I've been told to forget under Forgetful Mind?

Only if Forgetful Mind is used on you to return your psyche to its original condition.

Would I know who Mesmerized me?

Only if Mesmerism were used on you again and the answer dragged forth from your subconscious.

Can I use Possession on someone in order to take his body and go use Possession on someone else?

No.

While using Possession, can I use the host body's Disciplines?

Yes.

What happens if I'm using Possession and the body I'm in is killed?

Your will immediately takes effect, and your heirs start divvying up your belongings. In other words, you die.

Can Shadow Body be detected with Auspex?

If Heightened Senses is already on when a character using Shadow Body comes into the room, yes. However, you can't see someone using Shadow Body wander in and then decide that you're at an appropriate juncture to turn Heightened Senses on.

Does Aegis protect against staking?

The only things that protect against staking are Heart of Stone and Misplaced Heart. Aegis will not quite work for an *immobilized* Kindred as a no-matter-what-defense; that was never its intent, anyway. What Aegis *can* allow in that situation (optional rule) is for a Kindred to spend Blood Traits, with each Trait protecting him for 10 minutes against injury.

Note: Immobilized and asleep are not the same thing.

Can Kindred under Cloak the Gathering interact with one another?

No. Cloak the Gathering works as if Unseen Presence has been projected over an entire group. The same rules apply.

How does Might work?

Might should be the last retest in any combat.

What happens when a Kindred with Majesty meets a Kindred with Majesty?

The effects cancel each other out.

Can I use Majesty to protect another character by stepping in front of her?

This is considered an aggressive action unless accompanied by a Social Challenge.

Can Majesty be turned off?

You can turn off Majesty for 10 minutes by expending a Willpower Trait. At the end of that time, it immediately turns itself back on.

Can a character using Earth Meld be dug up?

Assuming one can acquire a backhoe on short notice, yes. However, doing so is not easy...

Does a character notice when Theft of Vitae is used on him?

Yes. Any character who is the victim of Theft of Vitae immediately feels a sharp pain and probably gets very hungry as well.

Does Hand of Flame cause extra damage?

No, it simply turns normal damage into aggravated.

How fast can I fly when using Flight?

You can fly at normal walking speed. Celerity cannot be used in conjunction with Flight to make you fly faster.

Can I do anything else while using Major Manipulation?

No. It requires absolute concentration.

Other Rules Questions

Can Willpower allow you to regain any type of Attribute Traits?

Yes, even Physical.

Can I spend a Willpower Trait to ignore the result of a Mental or Social Challenge when Dominate or Presence is involved?

Only if you are from the same generation or lower as the vampire trying to use those Disciplines on you. Otherwise, spending a Willpower Trait merely allows a retest (i.e., it guarantees a success).

Is there a Military Influence?

For reasons of game balance, there is not. Tanks and aircraft carriers, even when legitimately obtained, tend to upset the power level of a chronicle a little bit.

World of Darkness Questions

Garou are supposed to be able to whump vampires, yet any vampire with Celerity can run rings around any Garou? How is this possible and what do I do about it?

Garou can spend Rage for multiple actions/attacks *up to* but *not exceeding* the number of actions a vampire using Celerity has. Of course, Garou tend to run out of Rage more quickly than vampires run out of blood, but this makes things more equitable. For more information, see the rules for Rage on pp. 112-113 of **The Apocalypse**.

How can a Garou regain Rage?

Examples of when a Garou can regain Rage include the following situations:

- When she first sees the moon at night.
- At the beginning of any conflict in which a challenge is involved.
- The first time she is wounded in an evening.

These situations restore one and only one Rage Trait.

- During a particularly humiliating situation.

The amount of Rage regained from this sort of situation is left entirely to Storyteller discretion.

Note: An alternate rule that some **Apocalypse** troupes have found useful is to allow a Garou who wins a challenge to recoup all Rage Traits used during that challenge. For more information on regaining Rage, see page 113 of **The Apocalypse**.

Can a Garou move from Incapacitated to Wounded by spending a Rage Trait?

Yes. Consider that rule reinserted into the system.

What's the deal with werewolf talons?

Garou talons don't maintain their ability to cause aggravated damage once they've been removed from the Garou in question. You can't take Garou toenail clippings, shove them into a shotgun barrel and expect to spread aggravated damage in a wide arc by pulling the trigger. Incidentally, the use of the Black Fury Gift, Wasp Talons is the one exception to this rule.

How do Wasp Talons work? Can I just shoot off one finger's worth at a time?

No, when using Wasp Talons both hands (paws?) unload their full ordnance at once. It's also extremely painful to do, incidentally.

How do I get my hands on a Garou fetish?

With great difficulty. These items are to be handed out only at Storyteller discretion, and discretion is the key word.

How strong is my Garou? Every time I go up against a vampire, even when I'm in Crinos form, I lose. Why?

Certain levels of Potence do give Kindred an unfair advantage over Garou. The suggested fix is to give Garou in Crinos form the equivalent of Fortitude and Potence for as long as they are dealing with Kindred.

Can Blur of the Milky Eye be detected by vampires with Auspex?

A vampire with Heightened Senses will be able to detect a Garou using Blur of the Milky Eye, but a Mental Challenge is required in order for the specific Garou to be identified.

Does Song of Rage cause a Beast Trait or a Derangement in vampires?

Whoops. It causes a Beast Trait.

How does Halo of the Sun work with Celerity?

Halo of the Sun allows the Garou to make a Simple Test to avoid the wounds for each level of Celerity.

The Scent of Running Water Gift under Red Talons refers to Galliard Gifts, but the information isn't there. Where do I look?

Whoops again. Check under Ragabash Gifts.

Why should Silver Claws cause an extra Aggravated wound to characters who don't normally take any extra damage from silver?

It doesn't.

I want to play a (mage, wraith, changeling, mummy, vampire hunter). Are there rules for that?

Many people have written unofficial rules for adapting other White Wolf games to the **Mind's Eye Theatre** system. However, there are no official rules for **Mage: The Ascension, Wraith: The Oblivion** and **Changeling: The Dreaming** yet. Expect **Oblivion** in fall of 1996. In the meantime, if you want to play a character for whom there isn't an official set of rules, take the matter up with your Storyteller. As for mummies and hunters, check out **Antagonists**.

Index

E